3

BLOODLINE

OTHER BOOKS AND AUDIOBOOKS
BY KATHI ORAM PETERSON

The Forgotten Warrior

An Angel on Main Street

The Stone Traveler

River Whispers

A Christmas to Remember

Cold Justice

Wanted

Deceived

Remembering the Joy of Christmas

Star Struck

Breach of Trust

A Familiar Fear

a suspense novel

BLOODLINE

KATHI ORAM
PETERSON

Covenant Communications, Inc.

For my mother

PROLOGUE

France, 4 March 1371

A CANDLE FLICKERED ON THE nightstand in the otherwise dimly lit room. Jeanne d'Évreux, the dowager queen, struggled for breath. Her linen sleeping tunic clung to her rail-thin, sweat-dampened body, and her long, stark-white hair splayed across the silk head sheet, covering her pillow.

Her secret, the one that would ensure survival of her beloved France and ally Scotland, was dying with her.

She wanted to tell someone—needed to tell someone—but she could not speak, could not make her lips form words. She had waited too long. Whatever curse had befallen her had left her mute and barely alive.

Her treasured, raven-haired daughter, Blanche, the Duchess of Orléans, sat on the edge of the feather bed, dampening a cloth in a small basin she used to wipe her mother's brow.

Tears leaked from Jeanne's eyes as she struggled to speak. She had neglected to tell Blanche so much.

The Almighty had not been kind to them. Before Blanche had even been born, her father, King Charles IV, had died. If Blanche had been a boy, France would have been her kingdom, and the Capetian dynasty would have lived on. However, that was not to be. The Salic Law France had adopted ruled against female succession to the throne. The crown had been stolen from Blanche at her birth.

With tired eyes, Jeanne watched her cherished daughter wring water from the cloth before placing it carefully on Jeanne's forehead.

"Your good health will return, Mother." Blanche smiled, but the corner of her bottom lip quivered, the way it had when she had faced another life-changing challenge—her wedding day.

She had said marrying a man eight years her junior did not concern her. Her marriage to Philip was something her father would have wanted. She believed Philip's youth would help give her a son.

Jeanne, too, had desperately wanted to give her husband a male heir. However, God had sent them only daughters. As difficult as that had been, she had at least given her husband children. Poor Blanche had not been blessed with offspring, male or female. This had been part of the curse.

Jeanne believed the Almighty had made her pay for marrying her first cousin. Charles had promised her the church had given them special permission to wed. He claimed he'd received a letter from the pope. But after Charles's death and so many other sorrows had plagued her, Jeanne had wondered if Charles had fabricated the letter.

Lying in this prison of a bed draped with royal-red silk curtains, her thoughts drifted to her other daughter, Marie, the one she had sacrificed for the betterment of her people, the one whose seed might one day rally two allied nations to fight for what was truly theirs.

She thought of the secret plan she had covertly devised with the clever Scotsman. His parting words to her had been, "All will be well. I promise."

Yes, he had promised that their actions would right the wrongs that had been done to both their people. So many years ago, they had fabricated the lie that Marie had died, and Jeanne had said goodbye to her little red-haired angel as the Scotsman had stolen her away in the dark of night.

Over the years, Jeanne had heard nothing. Had the secret marriage taken place? Had a new heir—the hope of two nations—been born?

"Mother, are you thirsty?" Blanche picked up the goblet of water resting on the table next to Jeanne's bed.

Jeanne managed to shake her head and, once again, tried to speak. She pursed her chapped lips, trying to form words, but only groans issued forth.

Blanche lovingly moved the cloth and ran her hand over the top of Jeanne's head. "Rest for a spell. On the morrow, you will be much improved."

With her arthritic hand, she grabbed Blanche's arm, desperate to share the secret. Again, only foreign sounds left her lips. Nothing discernible.

"Mother." Blanche lovingly stroked her cheek. "Do not struggle so. Rest. All will be well. I promise." Blanche smiled, and again, her lip quivered.

The Scotsman's deep voice echoed in Jeanne's mind with the exact same words. And she knew she would not see the sun rise. She slowly closed her eyes.

She would take the secret to her grave, but she had left evidence.

One day, the story would be discovered.
One day, the wrongs committed against her family would be avenged.

CHAPTER ONE

Present day

"*HELP HER.*" THE WISPY, GHOSTLY voice came from behind. I hadn't heard it since I was nine, on the night my parents had died. A chill swept over me. I thought of Aunt Marjorie, my only living relative. I whipped around, totally expecting to find her, and scanned the passengers seated in first class, all preoccupied with either TV screens or laptops or sleeping. No Auntie. Of course she wasn't on the Boeing 777 flying from London Heathrow to Salt Lake City.

Overly tired, I must have imagined the command in the quirky sounds of the jet engines or the air-circulating equipment. My weary brain had fabricated the voice. I smoothed my bangs away from my eyes and brushed a loose hair from my skirt, trying to act normal while, all along, the ominous feeling continued to grow.

Red-eye flights were always nerve-racking but not like this. Trying to keep it together, I started toward the galley, going over what could have triggered the voice and this feeling. As usual, I'd greeted every person who had boarded the plane. Although my assignment was in first class, I had helped wherever needed, so I knew Aunt Marjorie couldn't possibly be on board.

No. She was home in Salt Lake. I'd spoken with her yesterday. She had told me she'd planted pansies in the front-stoop flowerpot and herb seedlings in the windowsill planters in the dining room. Memories of that cheery conversation didn't stop the dark foreboding snaking down my spine.

"*Help her.*" The voice again. This time, I didn't look. I knew something was very wrong. Aunt Marjorie needed me.

"Skye, are you all right?" Elizabeth, my close friend and the purser for this flight to the States, stepped beside me. Impeccably dressed in her navy-blue uniform, with her long, brown hair twisted in a knot at the back of her head, she stared at me with her dark, copper-colored eyes.

Feeling foolish and not wanting to explain the unease that had lodged like a cannonball in the pit of my stomach, I said, "I think I have nostomania."

"Impressive five-syllable word." Elizabeth's jab reminded me of the never-ending count-the-syllable word game we liked to play. "Homesick, are you? Can't blame you for that." She motioned me toward the galley and away from the prying eyes of first-class passengers.

I followed her. "Twice I've heard a voice say, 'Help her,' and my aunt Marjorie has come to mind," I said in a hushed tone. "That same voice came to me on the night my parents died. Something is wrong."

"That's not good." She grabbed the cell phone we were allowed to use only for emergencies. "Here. I'm sure the captain wouldn't mind if you gave her a call. We have a long flight ahead of us, and I don't want you worried the entire time."

"Thanks. I know it's late in Salt Lake, but . . ."

"You're worried. Go up in the sleep cavern and call her." Elizabeth left to take earbuds to a passenger.

As much as I hated close, confined spaces, I climbed the hidden steps between the galley and the cockpit wall to the cavern lined with several sleeping bunks tucked above first class. Reaching the top, I flipped on an overhead light and sat on the edge of a bunk. I punched in our landline number, knowing Auntie sometimes didn't hear her cell phone. I let it ring several times.

"Yes." Her voice sounded heavy with sleep. She usually answered with *Hello dear*, her voice light, but it was late, and I'd probably awakened her.

"Auntie, I'm sorry to call at this time. I heard the voice, so I wanted to check on you." The plane bumped from turbulence. I clutched the phone to my ear.

Static stole her words.

"Auntie, I can't hear you."

More interference, but I caught the end. "Love you." And she was gone.

At least I knew she was all right. I clicked off the light and descended the steps.

"Well?" Elizabeth had returned.

"She answered, but the reception was awful." I placed the phone in its compartment.

"But you know she's okay. Is your aunt still dating that history professor?" Elizabeth stacked empty food trays on the dumbwaiter that would deliver them below deck.

"Yes, they're still an item, even though Auntie says she's too old for romance." My aunt would never be old to me. She barely sat still long enough to watch a movie and always had places to go, people to meet. She looked younger than her seventy-five years. And though her hair had turned a beautiful white, she kept it trimmed in a youthful chin-length bob.

"Too old for romance?" Elizabeth rolled her eyes. "I don't think love is dependent on age. What a bizarre notion. She comes up with some strange ideas, like being afraid of sending in a tube of spit to learn your ancestry because the government will use the findings against you in some way." She shook her head. "Did you tell her you've already sent in your saliva?"

"No." I felt guilty for going behind her back and doing it anyway. "I'm hoping the results are waiting for me so I can show her and she'll realize how fun it can be to learn where our people came from." I grew quiet, worried that instead she'd become more upset than ever.

Elizabeth patted my arm. "Maybe you heard the voice because you're feeling guilty for going against her wishes. Plus, you haven't been home for a while. You've racked up some impressive paid time off this spring. What are you going to do with all of it?"

"Let me see: sleep, sleep, and then sleep some more." An irritating blonde strand had broken ranks from the stylish bun I'd used to capture my hair at the nape of my neck. I tucked it in place.

"I hear you." Elizabeth sighed. "I might get home long enough to remind my husband who I am and get four hours of shut-eye before I have to return to work, deadhead the seven o'clock to Florida, and catch my assigned flight to Brazil." She gave a wistful sigh. "I'd give anything to have twelve uninterrupted hours of alone time with my pillow."

I caught a glimpse of Ian Murphy, a young, wet-behind-the-ears flight attendant Elizabeth had assigned to tend economy class. He flashed me a smile as he strolled the aisle collecting trash from passengers who were still awake.

Elizabeth nudged me with her elbow as she handed me a very full garbage bag to tie shut. "I think he's into you."

"What?" I quickly knotted the bag, storing it in the garbage collection bin.

She pulled her checkoff list from the counter and gave me the don't-pretend-you-haven't-noticed glare.

"I know. And he's a nice guy, but I'm thirty. He's got to be, what? Twenty-five, if he's a day?"

"So? That's not enough of an age gap to be a problem. You know, they say a woman in her thirties stands as much chance of getting married as she does of winning the Publisher's Clearinghouse sweepstakes." She tilted her head in that you'd-better-think-about-it slant.

"That's an old statistic, and it wasn't age thirty; it was forty, *and* the comparison wasn't about winning sweepstakes but getting killed by a terrorist." I sounded a little too sensitive about the subject.

"But the message is still the same. Women who put career ahead of everything else suffer in their personal life." Elizabeth was thirty-five but going on sixty in wisdom years, or so she liked to think.

We'd had this conversation a number of times, and it always ended with me pointing out the advantages of being single and her touting marriage. I decided I didn't have enough fight in me to make a big deal over her statement. About to tell her I didn't want to expound on my spinsterhood, I stopped as a tall, dark-haired passenger from first class interrupted.

"Excuse me." Jack Duncan, the passenger from seat 1B, stood next to us. He'd told me his name as I'd helped him store his carry-on. And I'd detected a slight Scottish brogue, which was more than a little intriguing. His lean yet muscular body seemed to have been chiseled from a mountain, like he had been the mold for a superhero. He even looked the part: ebony hair, blue eyes that could deliver laser rays, and a slight smile, as if he knew something he shouldn't. He walked past us and entered the lavatory. The Occupied sign slid into place.

Had he heard our conversation? How embarrassing. And if he'd overheard, how much had he caught? We'd been talking in hushed tones, and with engine noise, he couldn't have heard much, if anything.

Again, Elizabeth nudged me. "Now, *he's* not too young."

"Give me a break. He's a passenger and, I might add, a virtual stranger."

"Everyone is a stranger until you get to know them. You've given him more attention than any other passenger; you even made sure he had a pillow and a blanket before he asked." Elizabeth yawned. "You know you're attracted to him."

"Can we at least try to be professional? *And* I do that for everyone." I took my job seriously and always tried my best to know my passengers. "When that

English gentleman in the designer suit, who looks like Hugh Grant, declined the blanket I offered him, I politely asked if he wanted anything else, just like I do for everyone."

But Elizabeth shrugged. She must have noticed the difference in the way I'd conversed with Mr. Duncan. As I debated what to say next, I noticed my friend really did seem tired.

She nodded toward the steps that led to the sleep cavern. "I think I'll take a quick nap. Can you hold down the fort?"

I nodded, letting the argument dissipate. I always lost quarrels with Elizabeth anyway.

"Make sure Mr. Tall, Dark, and Handsome returns to his seat all right," she said as she climbed the stairs.

I so wanted to follow her and bring new life to our disagreement, but at that moment, the lavatory opened, and out he walked.

"Mr. Duncan," my voice squeaked, just as the irritating hair once again fell from my bun and tickled my neck. Swiping it aside and clearing my throat, I continued. "Can I get anything for you?"

His half-closed eyes and boyish smile gentled his manly face. "No, I'm fine. Thank you." He returned to his seat, leaving me alone with my wistful thoughts.

The foreboding over Auntie pounced again, shaking me out of my trance. Even though I'd spoken with her, I was anxious to get home. Something still seemed wrong. Why else would I have heard the voice? I'd had premonitions before, a gut feeling alerting me to danger. But the voice . . .

Although the plane cruised at a speed of over five hundred miles an hour, it would never be fast enough.

* * *

After we reached Salt Lake City and the passengers deplaned, Elizabeth shooed me away. "I know you're anxious about your aunt. Go ahead and leave. I can give the plane a final check by myself. Once I return from Brazil, you and I need to do something crazy, like . . ."

"Get a mani-pedi." I filled in the blank for her.

"That's not crazy. But it would be heaven." She headed down the aisle, checking for trash, blankets, and anything else that passengers might have left behind.

I quickly logged my report. Once I hit send, I touched up my lipstick to give me perfect landing lips. Flight attendants had to keep a fresh appearance, or so the handbook said. Grabbing my bag from the overhead bin, I clicked the button to extend the handle and wheeled it behind me as I left the plane. Walking through the jet bridge, I noticed Ian stood near the gate.

"You haven't been waiting for me, have you?" If he had been, why hadn't he stuck around to help Elizabeth clean up? Rookie. That sure wasn't a way to rack up points with his superiors.

"Thought maybe I'd buy you breakfast." He gave me that hometown-boy smile that suited him so well.

"Any other time, I would love to go with you, but I'll need a rain check. I haven't been home for a while, and I'm a little worried about my aunt."

"Your aunt? You live with your aunt?"

"Yes, I do."

"Is she disabled in some way?" He said it like that would be the only reason he could comprehend for living with a relative.

"If disabled means she's always on the go and hardly home herself, then yes." I smiled. I'd grown used to people reacting this way. "I'm never home very long, and Auntie takes care of the house and waters the plants." I'd only shared with Elizabeth the real reason I'd never bought a place of my own and why I wanted to keep living with the woman who'd raised me. I loved being with my aunt. Instead of coming home to an empty house, I came home to Auntie, happy to see me and wanting to know what exciting thing had happened on the flight. A selfish reason on my part, but I also wanted to keep an eye on her. We only had each other in this tough old world.

Ian shrugged. "Guess that makes sense. So, when is your next flight?"

"Not for a while. I'm off for a couple weeks." We'd reached the escalator that would take us down to the main concourse.

"Well, hopefully our paths will cross again." Ian stepped aside, letting me go first.

"I'm sure they will." We stood in awkward silence until we reached the bottom. "Take care." I waved at him as he headed in the opposite direction. Either he didn't hear me, or he felt embarrassed, because he didn't wave back. He looked above us and then took off. Almost ran, which seemed odd. I peered up at the balcony, wondering who he'd seen that had made him dash away like that, but I didn't recognize anyone in the crowd bustling to their flights.

I looked at my watch: 7:00 a.m. Aunt Marjorie would be up by now. Even though I'd spoken with her several hours ago, I pulled out my cell phone and called her. No answer. Then I remembered she usually tried to go to the gym by seven. If she was working out, she wouldn't stop to answer her cell. Maybe I could get home and have breakfast ready for her when she returned.

Storing my cell in my jacket pocket, I rolled my bag behind me as I left the terminal. A slight early spring breeze graced my face as I stepped out in the sunlight. Anxious drivers lined the curb.

Eager to catch the shuttle that would take me to employee parking, I started across the road. I'd taken only a couple steps when I thought I heard the wispy voice again.

I stopped dead in my tracks, with my flight bag beside me, and pulled out my cell to call Auntie again. Someone with strong hands grabbed hold of my arms and yanked me off my feet. My phone popped from my grasp. As we fell toward the ground, a rush of air and heat from an SUV hit me as the vehicle drove over my flight bag. My hip and shoulder slammed into the pavement, rattling my entire body. Turning to see my rescuer, I looked into the deep-blue eyes of Jack Duncan.

CHAPTER TWO

JACK ROSE AND PULLED ME to my feet. We stood on the sidewalk outside the airport terminal next to what I assumed was his black leather backpack, which he must have dropped to save me. Strangers gathered round, patting Jack on the back and calling him a hero.

"Why did you stop in the middle of the road?" someone asked.

I couldn't very well tell the truth, so I said nothing.

Another person shook his head like I was crazy.

At the moment, I agreed. Who in their right mind would stop in the middle of a street to make a call because they'd heard a voice? No one.

An airport policewoman came over. "Was anyone hurt?" Her eyes scanned Jack and me.

"I'm fine, but I'm worried about her." Jack pointed to me.

"I'm all right," I answered, wanting everyone to go away and leave me alone with my humiliation.

A horn blared down the way where a car had stalled, backing up traffic.

The officer glanced at me, the problem that needed to be solved. "You want to fill out a complaint?"

"Not necessary. It was my fault."

"If you change your mind, here's my card." She thrust it into my hand, then trotted off to take care of the tangle of cars and angry drivers.

Jack zeroed in on me. "Are you sure you're all right?"

"I think so." I tried to walk and wobbled a little.

He took hold of my arm, steadying me.

Someone handed me my damaged flight bag. The wheels were broken, as well as the handle, but by some miracle, the zipper held. Another person gave me my battered phone.

"Thanks." I set the bag on the ground and stared at my phone. The screen had fractured into a web of lines. I pushed the On button. Nothing. I slid it in my jacket pocket and looked up at Jack. His dark, hypnotic eyes reminded me of how lucky I had been. "You saved my life."

"Ms. Armstrong, I should take you tae the first-aid station. There must be one somewhere." He peered around as though to find one.

"I'm fine, really. And please, call me Skye." He only knew me by my name tag.

What was the proper way for a flight attendant to act when a handsome passenger saved her life? I'd never come across an incident like this in the handbook. I pried my gaze from him, brushed the loose dirt off my rumpled skirt, and straightened my jacket. "Thanks for rescuing me."

I reached to pick up my bag, but he stopped me. "I think I'd best walk you tae your motur. You're still a bit shaky."

I shouldn't let him, but he was right. My entire body trembled like it always did when I became nervous and upset. "That's awfully nice of you."

"That SUV came out of nowhere. I saw you standing right in its path." He slung his backpack over his shoulder and picked up my bag.

I hesitated a moment before resting my hand in the crook of his arm he held out for me. "I've been worried about my aunt and wasn't paying attention. Thanks again," I said as we walked.

"I was in the right place at the right time is all." He tilted his head to the side and flashed a dimpled grin my way.

"Lucky me." I wanted to keep him talking. "Do you live in Salt Lake?"

"I have a place in New York, but my home is in Scotland."

"You must spend a lot of time abroad."

"Aye, my business has me travel a lot."

We got on the bus that took us to employee parking. Getting off, it was only a short walk to my car, a cherry-red Nissan Altima.

"This is mine."

He handed me my bag. The handle slipped from my fingers, and I dropped it.

"You're still a bit upset and shouldn't drive. Is there someone you can call tae pick you up?" He studied me, taking note of my trembling hand.

I put it behind my back. "My aunt. I'll give her a call. Don't let me keep you." I pulled my cell from my jacket pocket, took one look at the screen, and remembered it was broken.

"That doesn't look right, does it?" He took it from me, checking it over. "Use mine." He returned my phone and pulled his out.

I dialed Auntie. It rang and rang. She must still be at the gym. I returned his cell to him. "No answer."

"Okay, well . . . how about I drive you home?" His eyebrows raised slightly like this was the best idea ever.

"That's too much. You've already saved my life. I couldn't ask you to do more." Though I was tempted. But I didn't *know* him. It would be foolish to get into a car with a stranger. However, he had heroically come to my aid earlier. And this was my car, not his. But I could see the headline: "Flight Attendant Found Dead in Own Car."

Again, the worry for Aunt Marjorie found me. I had to get home to check on her. "Could I use your phone to call Uber?"

Jack seemed to sense my urgency. "Of course, but why don't I order a ride we can share?"

Such a generous offer, yet I couldn't let him do that either. "I live at the other end of the valley."

"I'm in no hurry; besides, it gives me a good excuse tae get tae know you a little better." He tapped on his cell, ordering the ride. "The driver says he'll be here in less than five minutes." He turned his cell so I could see the app on his phone. A little red dot showed that our ride was very close.

Flattered that he wanted to get to know me, I thought of my conversation with Elizabeth and my need to date more. So why not let this guy take me home? We wouldn't be alone on the ride, and truth be told, he was darn good-looking.

However, he would know where I lived, and I didn't actually *know* him. Until I got to know a guy, I'd meet him at a restaurant a couple of times before I gave him my address.

He looked at my vehicle. "How will you get your car home?"

"My aunt can drive me out later, maybe even tomorrow." Once again, worry over Auntie found me. The voice had made me paranoid. I had no reason to be worried, yet I was. Wanting to be fair with Jack and his generous offer to see me home, I said, "At least let me pay for our ride."

"It's paid by my company."

"You probably have business you need to tend to." I wanted him to know he was under no obligation to see me home, especially if he had things he needed to do.

"Business will keep."

"What is it that you do?" I enjoyed this part of getting to know a person.

"I'm in security."

"What's the name of your company?"

"Providence Protection. You've probably heard of it. We're worldwide." A warm, friendly, I'm-not-the-boogeyman smile brightened his face.

"Sounds familiar. And I must say, you take your business seriously. You protected me from being run over." I gazed into eyes I could get lost in.

He tilted his head, and that lazy smile of his that made me feel safe tugged at the corners of his lips. He nodded toward the entrance of the parkway. "I think that's our ride."

The car pulled up, and the driver got out and opened the trunk. Jack took my bag from me, placing it and his leather pack inside. While the driver got back in, Jack ushered me to the passenger side.

"I can walk by myself."

"You've yet tae prove it." He opened the door.

"I guess you've got me there." I slid into my seat and gazed up at him.

"Let's just say I'm returning your kind service from the flight over the pond." He closed the door and quickly walked around the car, getting in.

The driver started the engine. "What address?"

"I'd like you tae drop off the lady first." Jack fastened his seat belt.

I gave the driver my address, and we were off.

As we merged onto the I-15 freeway heading south, Jack looked at me. "You said earlier that you were worried for your aunt and that's why you didn't see the SUV."

"Yes. My aunt and I are close. In fact, we live together." Would he have the same reaction as Ian?

"Is this the aunt the voice warned you about on the plane?" He looked at me briefly, long enough for me to know that, somehow, he'd overheard my conversation with Elizabeth.

"Yes." I cleared my throat. He'd probably heard her say I needed to find a man too. Was there no end to my humiliation?

"You heard the voice of your aunt who was at home?"

"Well, it wasn't exactly her voice. But I had a strong premonition that something was wrong with her." Darn. Why did I say that?

"Are you sure you don't want me tae take you tae the hospital? They can do a full physical—*mind* and body." His teasing smile set me at ease.

"I know you think I'm crazy, but here's the deal." I took a deep breath. "Aunt Marjorie is my only family, and she's seventy-five, *and* I'm worried about her." There. Maybe that would put an end to it.

His playful expression turned to empathy. "I understand wanting tae take care of family, and I don't think you're crazy. I once knew a man . . ." He stopped as though unsure he should tell me.

"And . . ." I couldn't contain my curiosity and hoped he didn't think me rude, but I was anxious to hear what had happened in case it would help calm my nervousness regarding Auntie.

"This happened back in the day when I had tae work construction tae make ends meet. That's where I met Fred. He and I were working this job, and he kept stopping what he was doing and going out tae the road tae look down it. Before too long, we heard sirens and knew there must have been a motur accident. He couldn't bear not knowing what had happened, and I knew we'd never get anything done unless he could concentrate, so we both got in my motur and went tae see. Sure enough, we came upon an accident." Jack shook his head as though he didn't want to finish.

"And . . ."

He huffed. "'Twas his daughter's car. She'd been killed."

Here I'd been thinking this would be something uplifting, something that would give me hope. Totally disappointed and a little irritated, I said, "I can't believe you told me such a horrible story. Are you saying my aunt might be dead?" If I'd known him better, I would have slugged him in the arm.

"Oh, no, lassie. Forgive me. I shared the story with you because I believe people are given second sight for a reason. Fred's premonition helped prepare him." He bit his lips together as if he realized what he'd said didn't make things better but worse.

Not wanting to dwell on his dreadful story a moment longer, I turned my attention out the window and saw my turnoff coming up. The driver took it, turned left at the light, and before I knew it, we were on the road that would take us up the hill to my house.

Jack and I sat in a pool of tentative silence. Was my premonition about Auntie conditioning me for something truly terrible? I thought about my parents and the other time I'd heard the voice. I shuddered.

We rode up the hill to the gated community where I lived, and fortunately, another resident had just entered the passcode to open the gate, and we were able to follow them through.

The driver pulled up to my home. The flowerpot on the front stoop had purple and yellow pansies in it. That's right. Auntie must have done that yesterday, like she'd told me on the phone she'd do. No windows had been smashed, no appearance of foul play. Auntie was probably in there right this minute making breakfast.

Jack got out, as well as the driver. I quickly trailed them to the trunk.

Jack handed me my travel bag. "I'm going tae wait while you check on your aunt, if that's all right?"

"That's so thoughtful of you. Thanks. I won't be long. And when Auntie hears how you came to my rescue, she'll want to meet you." I could hardly believe how considerate he seemed.

I inserted the key into the Brinks door lock and pushed open the door.

The house stood strangely quiet.

"Auntie," I called. No answer. Maybe she was in her bedroom. "Auntie," I called again. I looked down the staircase to the basement as I passed it in case she'd fallen this morning and hadn't been able to get up. Thankfully, she wasn't there. I made my way through the living room to her bedroom that overlooked the Salt Lake Valley. Her bed was made, nothing out of place. I checked her bathroom. Spit spot. Towels hung at attention, no water drops on the vanity.

Maybe instead of going to the gym, she had gone for a walk, so she might not have showered yet. I dashed to the door that opened to the double-car garage. Her Land Rover waited on the right side, near her gardening supplies. That confirmed that she must have gone for a small hike. But why wasn't she home yet? And why didn't she answer her cell phone? She must have it with her. I'd warned her many times to always take it wherever she went.

My watch said 9:00 a.m. She usually returned from walks by eight or eight thirty at the latest. Unless she'd run into a neighbor and started gabbing like she usually did and lost track of time.

I had to quit thinking the worst. There had to be a reasonable explanation for why she wasn't here, and I needed to quit jumping to sad conclusions. The stupid story Jack had told me had made me jumpy.

That and the voice.

Not knowing what to do, I decided to tell Jack to go ahead and leave. No sense making him wait until Auntie returned. When I got outside, the Uber car was gone.

Jack stood there with his leather pack. "Right after you went inside, he got another call and couldn't wait. It's okay; I'll just order another one. Where's your aunt?" He peered behind me as though expecting Auntie to appear.

"She must have gone for a walk." I tried to act as if I believed what I'd said. "You don't need to wait around for her to come home."

He shrugged and fussed with his phone. "Another driver should be here in . . ." He checked the app. "Ten tae fifteen minutes. They're not far."

"Why don't you come inside to wait?" I said, feeling awkward.

He followed me in.

"Do you mind if I check my laptop? Auntie may have sent me a message." I didn't wait to see if he said yes. My laptop waited for me at the minidesk in the kitchen. I logged on and checked my messages. Nothing. I closed the lid slightly, leaving it on, and looked up at Jack. His gaze met mine, and I knew he'd been watching me the entire time. I'd never had a poker face, so he had to know I was panicked, but I tried to act normal. "Would you like something to drink or eat while you wait?"

"I'm good." Jack's eyes scanned the area that blended the kitchen and living room seamlessly together. He walked to the picture window, which, like the one in Auntie's room, looked out on the valley below. "You have quite the view here."

"Yes, that was one of the selling points. Auntie insisted we needed to live in a gated community, said it made her feel safer. So when we found this place and it had such a magnificent view, we snatched it up."

"How long have you lived here?" His eyes roamed around, taking in everything from the landscape portrait hanging over the fireplace to the wooden rooster sitting on the granite countertop in the kitchen.

"We bought it when I first started with the airline ten years ago." Ten wonderful years.

"And where are your parents, if you don't mind my asking?" Jack's attention seemed drawn to the portrait of Auntie and me resting on the mantel.

"They died when I was nine." Even though they had died over twenty-one years ago, the pain of that day burned fresh.

Jack turned to me. Empathy heightened his deep-blue eyes. "I'm sorry. Were they in an accident?"

I tore my gaze from his, not wanting to tell him yet wanting to at the same time. I ordinarily didn't like to talk about their deaths. "Yes. My father was a pilot."

"Is that why your name is Skye?"

I nodded. "I always felt as though my name was a gift from him. My dad loved flying. In fact, he flew for the airline I work for. I think that's why they hired me. Anyway, Dad also had his own plane. He flew us on many family vacations. On the last trip, Auntie and I were supposed to go, but I got sick. Auntie volunteered to stay home with me, saying my parents needed some alone time. They'd only be gone over the weekend. And they weren't going far, just to Lake Tahoe." A flash of them giving me a hug before they left, of Dad kissing my cheek and whispering in my ear, "Watch over Auntie while we're gone," came back.

Where was she? My gaze fell on Jack again, standing there waiting for me to finish telling him the story. "An early snowstorm caught them, and his plane went down." I nervously rubbed my hands together. "The authorities didn't find the wreckage until spring. This time of year, actually."

"I'm sorry. Life can be tragic at times." Jack's voice brought me out of my own drama, and I wondered about his story.

"I've shared way too much of my personal life with you. I never do that. In fact, I've never told the men I've dated about my parents. Not that you and I are on a date. I mean, you saved my life and brought me home is all. Not a date." I needed to quit talking. Maybe my concern over Auntie had affected me more than I had thought.

A horn sounded in the distance.

"That might be my ride." He checked out the window toward the gate, then gave me that half smile I'd so admired on the plane. That, of course, made me think of everything he'd probably heard Elizabeth and me say, and I became even more embarrassed.

"Is there something you can do from here tae let him in?" He stood there waiting.

"Oh, yes." I grabbed the remote control off the kitchen counter that would open the gate, then went to the window and pressed the button.

"I guess this is goodbye." He started for the front door.

I followed, grateful he was leaving and yet not wanting him to go. Once he was gone, I'd have to look for Auntie. I'd have to face the fact that something could be seriously wrong. What if my premonition had been preparing me for the worst possible news, like it had Jack's friend?

Jack stopped at the door and turned as though to say goodbye, but he hesitated as he studied me. "I don't know anyone in Salt Lake, and I have all day. Why don't I stay with you until your aunt shows up? I know you're worried about her."

"I'm fine." Very gallant of him, but he had to go. "You've already saved my life. There could be other damsels in distress who need your attention." The Uber car pulled into my driveway. "Besides, your ride is here."

"I could pay him for his trouble and stay." Jack stared down at me, genuine caring in his eyes.

"No. That's okay. Really. Besides, I should pay him. You did me such a big favor, bringing me home; it's the least I can do." I couldn't impose on him further.

"No. I would have had tae call a driver at the airport, so it's no problem. And my company pays for it anyway." He tilted his head in that endearing way he had. "Okay, at least give me your phone number. You're the only person I know in Salt Lake except those working for me. I don't like tae mix business with pleasure. Besides, then maybe you can tell me more things you don't tell men you date."

I half chuckled and felt my face flush. "Sorry, I can't."

His brows knitted together as though he couldn't comprehend why not.

"My cell phone is broken, remember?"

A smile claimed his chiseled face. "I noticed a landline on your counter. Or maybe you'd rather give me your email address. That way you don't have tae answer if you don't want tae."

He certainly was persistent.

"Hang on a minute." I rushed back to the kitchen, found the small notepad on top of Auntie's phone directory we kept next to the landline, and jotted down my email. Elizabeth's teasing me about not dating echoed in my mind. I decided to give him the landline number too. I hurried back to him. Handing him the piece of paper, I said, "I gave you both, just in case."

He slipped it in his pocket, gave me a nod, and headed to the car waiting for him. He got in, and they drove off into the sunset, except it was morning and my world felt as though it was crumbling beneath my feet, because I didn't know where Auntie was. *Stop it!*

I closed the door and dashed to the phone. Rifling through Auntie's phone directory, I stopped on Professor Sumsion's name. He was the history professor she'd been dating. I dialed his number. As it rang, I thought of the savvy and debonair man and how he was always calling Auntie, taking her out, and filling her lonely days with his companionship. In fact, he'd asked her to marry him at least once, but she'd told him he was too young for her—she at seventy-five, he at only seventy. I thought of Ian and how he'd wanted to go out with me. Ironic.

Sumsion didn't answer. He was probably teaching a class. I dialed several of Auntie's other friends. No one had seen or heard from her since early yesterday morning, but Ethel Roundtree reminded me that Auntie owed her money, Lydia Thygerson told me the rummy card game Auntie played in had been moved, and the rest of the calls became a blur.

Hanging up the receiver, I paced. How long should I wait until I called the police? I'd heard that before they actually list someone as missing, the person had to be gone for at least twenty-four hours. If I told them I'd spoken with her last night, they'd think I was nuts bothering them. And if Auntie found out that I'd done such a thing and she was actually all right, she'd be upset and humiliated.

I needed to keep busy because staring at the front door was not going to make Auntie walk through it. Fatigue from my red-eye flight pressed upon me. If I showered, the water would revive me enough so I could go out and look for her myself. I scooped up my flight bag and headed downstairs.

As soon as I got out of the shower, I strained to hear if Auntie was upstairs humming that country song she loved while she cooked breakfast.

No song.

No sound.

No smell of bacon frying or coffee brewing.

I quickly dressed, putting on comfortable, boot-cut exercise pants, a tank top, and a crisscross long-sleeved T-shirt. I shoved my feet into socks and Skechers, then brushed my light-blonde hair into a ponytail. Still in flight-attendant mode, I slipped my travel wallet that held my credit cards and passport over my neck and secured it under my shirt. Then I grabbed my keys and fled up the stairs and out the door. I knew the trails Auntie liked the most.

Walking up the path, I felt a soreness in my hip. I must have bruised it when Jack tackled me to the ground. I made my way to the top of the hill. No sign of her. Disappointed, I returned to the house, hopeful once again that she would be there waiting.

She wasn't.

I dropped the keys on the countertop and checked the computer again for messages. None. Checked the landline messages. Nothing. A stack of mail with my name on the envelopes waited for my attention. I saw the return address on the one I'd sent my DNA swab to, but I couldn't look at it now. I hated to do it, but I needed to make a thorough search of Auntie's bedroom.

I checked the nightstand next to her queen-sized bed. Nothing unusual, though I was surprised to see a Harlequin romance novel. This proved she wasn't too old for romance. Once she was home, I planned to razz her about this.

Next, I checked her dresser drawers. She'd told me she always had a stash of cash hidden in a bra. If that turned up missing, I'd know something had happened. Rummaging through her unmentionables, as she liked to call them, I caught a whiff of violet, rose, apricot, and lily of the valley—her Charlie Red perfume. I found the bra with her stash in it. At least she hadn't taken that. As I turned to leave, my eyes were drawn to a key next to the lamp sitting on the table beneath her picture window. I didn't know why I'd missed it before.

I picked up the key. The number twenty-seven stared back at me. A strange key too. Not a house key or a car key.

My computer chimed, announcing a new email.

I raced to my laptop. A new message appeared in bold, but I didn't recognize the sender: bpuk666@gmail.com. I clicked on it.

I see you found the key.

I whirled around, looking for a camera, anything. Nothing seemed out of place or unusual. How did someone know I'd picked up the key? Fear wrapped its cruel, long fingers around me.

Another chime. I picked up my laptop. Another new message from the same sender.

Your aunt has fallen ill. But nothing will happen to her if you do what I ask. Take the safety deposit key to the First National Bank in downtown Salt Lake. Collect what is inside, then go to Liberty Park and wait on the bench near the aviary. We'll make contact with you there. If you go to the authorities or tell anyone, we'll know and kill her.

CHAPTER THREE

WHOEVER HAD AUNTIE MUST HAVE taken her after I'd called last night. I thought of the static and how the call had ended, with Auntie saying she loved me. What if the kidnapper had been with her? He must have done something to her if she'd become ill. She had always been healthy and strong.

The voice that had tried to warn me had been right. Auntie needed my help. An earthquake erupted within me while, at the same time, my entire body tingled. I dropped the laptop. It slammed hard against the tiled floor, bringing me out of my stupor.

With trembling hands, I picked it up, but the screen had turned blue, and the keyboard wouldn't work. I'd ruined my only other source to receive email.

Devastated, I scanned around, intensely aware that someone was probably watching me. Had they installed cameras in every room? I hoped they saw what had happened and knew my situation. My head throbbed as I struggled to breathe and comprehend.

Unbelievable. This can't be happening.

Auntie and I weren't rich, nor political. Why her? My body had a mind of its own as one hand grabbed my purse, the other my aunt's keys hanging on the peg by the garage door, and my legs carried me to Auntie's Land Rover.

Driving on I-15 to downtown Salt Lake City, I kept checking my rearview mirror, expecting a car to pull up close and trail me. But there were too many cars. All in a hurry. None stayed close to my bumper.

I took the downtown exit and parked in First National Bank's parking plaza, making a mental note that I was on the third level, parking section C. I glanced up at the concrete overhead and saw a security camera.

Good, I was being watched. But by good guys or bad? I couldn't let paranoia win. Banks had security cameras everywhere. And someone was always watching. But there was that TV show where different sources were able to hijack security cameras for their own illegal purposes.

Stop it! I stole a deep breath and got out of the Land Rover. As calmly as I could, I walked to the elevator, got in, and pressed the button that would take me to the main entrance of the bank. As the doors slid closed, I noticed yet another camera.

The doors opened, and I stepped out, making my way to the main entrance. My eyes scanned the room. Only two bank tellers were in their stalls; a male customer occupied one's attention, the other stood free. I looked for a security guard, and, of course, I couldn't see one. I stepped up to the waiting middle-aged woman teller. "Could I see Marjorie Armstrong's safety deposit box?" I held up the key.

She pressed well-manicured fingers on her keyboard, then looked at me. "I need to see your ID."

I pulled out my travel wallet that hung around my neck and showed her my driver's license.

"Skye." Her stern expression softened. "Yes, you have a signature card." As she walked around the counter and motioned for me to follow, I tried to remember when I'd signed a card for a safety deposit box and couldn't. But Auntie took care of business and had me signing papers all the time, so I could have easily signed it without even realizing it. I placed my license back in my travel wallet and slipped it under my shirt.

The woman dressed in a gray-green pinstriped suit kept looking back at me, a worried expression on her round-cheeked face. Could she be in on Auntie's kidnapping? What a stupid thought. But I couldn't afford to trust anyone.

Anyone . . . Jack came to mind. I'd given him my email address. He had been a stranger, a kind stranger, who had saved my life and taken me home. But why? Why would he do all that? Unless he wanted—needed— to get inside my home. And I'd fallen for it, thinking him handsome and my rescuer.

The teller stopped in front of the vault, entered a code, and turned the handle, opening the door. Before leaving me alone, she asked, "Are you all right, dear?" Worry puckered her forehead and created creases on the sides of her face. She seemed genuinely concerned. Could she really be involved?

Normally, I wouldn't have suspected her, but I'd watched too many true-crime shows and had seen how middle-aged women were indeed part of some pretty elaborate, heinous crimes. I'd best keep up my guard.

"I'm fine," I managed to utter.

"Is your aunt well? She's usually the one who comes in to check on her box."

The question could be a trick to see if I would tell about Auntie's abduction. I stared at the woman, not trusting her and wondering what I should say. Words came to me. "Auntie wanted me to do it this time."

The woman seemed satisfied and left, closing the door behind her. I turned to the room lined with safety deposit boxes. In the center rested a table and a step stool beneath. I checked the key in my hand. The number twenty-seven shone up at me. I scanned the boxes, searching for a match. Twenty-seven waited just above my head.

I set my purse on the table, returned, and inserted the key, opening the small metal door. There was a box inside. I eased it out, expecting it to be heavy, but to my surprise, it wasn't. I carried the box to the table and pushed open the lid. Inside waited an old manila envelope. Shouldn't there be some sort of treasure, something worth kidnapping a person for? I noticed Auntie had written my name on the envelope. She probably knew if something happened to her, I would be the one to get into her safety deposit box.

I turned it over. The back had two round tabs: one on the flap and one on the envelope's main portion. A red string crisscrossed between each one, keeping the flap closed. I untied the string, pulled up the flap, and emptied the contents onto the table.

Two eight-inch-by-ten-inch pieces of cardboard were taped together. I pulled away the tape and opened them. A plastic page protector shielded a small beige vellum of about two-and-a-half inches by three-and-a-half inches. The page appeared nearly transparent and looked ancient. This was some type of artifact, with miniature, painted characters, an intricate border, and ornate letters that seemed . . . illuminated.

"*In quod* . . ." I couldn't make out the rest of the handwritten Latin wording. I couldn't tell an *i* from an *l* or an *m* from an *n* or a *u* from a *w*. The text on the top line was in red ink, but the rest of the words were dark tan, except for the first letters of a few sentences. They were blue. Clever, intricate, three-dimensional drawings surrounded the text. In the top left corner, a small character appeared to lie on its belly, looking down on the words. Other characters hung from vines that crept down the right margin. Along the bottom, a woman with a crown peered up at the text, a curious yet noble expression on her face.

"Interesting, but this can't be all there is." I checked inside the box. Nothing. No notes, no explanation.

I stuck my hand into the envelope. Empty.

I couldn't stand here wasting time. I had to take this weird little page to Liberty Park like the kidnapper had ordered. If only I had my cell phone, I'd take a picture of it. I secured the little protected vellum between the two cardboard pieces once again and put it in the envelope, then reached to place it inside my purse but stopped. Maybe I shouldn't.

With Auntie's life hanging in the balance, I had to keep this page safe and with me at all times. The envelope wouldn't fit in the travel wallet around my neck. I pulled up my long-sleeved T-shirt and tank top, then carefully slipped the envelope beneath the waistband at the back of my workout pants so it was against my skin. The page wasn't going anywhere I wasn't. I put the safety deposit box in the slot and shut the door, locking it.

As I grabbed my purse and left the vault, I straightened my posture, feeling the envelope against my back. No one could tell I had the page on me. Still, I felt self-conscious. How long had Auntie stored this document? How long had she kept this secret? I had to know. It might help me discover why she had been abducted.

Scrutinizing the bank foyer and seeing no other customers, I hurried toward the woman who had shown me to the room; she had returned to her stall. "Could you check how long my aunt has had the safety-deposit box and if she's current on the rental fee?"

The lady's fingers flew over the keyboard, bringing up the information. "She's current. In fact, she's paid up for the next five years."

"Does it tell you when she first rented the box?"

She moved her mouse on the pad, then rolled the little ball. "From what I can tell, as far back as the bank has kept records on a computer."

"How long ago was that?"

"Nineteen eighty-five. If you want, I can request more information." She shifted her gaze to something behind me. A couple of people had lined up and were waiting their turn.

"No. That's okay. Thanks." I hurriedly left.

I entered the elevator with another couple. They were chatting about a loan, then seemed to notice me and quit talking. When the doors slid open on the third level, I stepped off. Glancing around, I saw a few shoppers putting bags in the trunk of a car and another couple walking to their vehicle. None of them seemed threatening, but what did I know? The sooner I got out of here, the better. I hurried toward Auntie's vehicle.

I thought about what the bank teller had told me regarding the safety-deposit box. Auntie had had it since before my parents had died, before I had even been born. Why? What was so important about this tiny piece of paper? Where did she get it?

All at once, a man—Caucasian, brown hair, pocked face and a crooked-teeth grin—stepped beside me. Before I could bolt away, he grabbed my arm, and something hard poked my side. The barrel of a gun? My heart hammered against my ribs.

"Do you hav ze page?" he said, still grinning like he'd known me for years, like he wasn't threatening to shoot me right here, right now.

Despite my fear, I needed some answers. "I thought I was supposed to meet you at the park. Where's my aunt?"

The barrel of the gun pressed harder against my ribs. He grabbed my purse out of my hand and started to run.

"Wait! It's not in there!" My voice echoed through the parking plaza.

He didn't stop, just kept running.

I tore after him, my Skechers slapping hard against the pavement. I even started gaining on him.

As the man reached the turn to the next level, a blue Ford Mustang screeched to a halt, blocking his path. The man's accomplice? If he got in that car and they didn't find the page in my purse, Auntie could die.

Instead of getting inside, he slid across the car's hood and kept running like a hundred-yard sprinter.

Jack Duncan leaped out of the car.

Jack?

What was he doing here?

"Did he hurt you?" he yelled, prepared to give chase.

"No!" I rushed by him. "You've got to catch him."

Jack took off, racing by me like an Olympian. I tried to keep up, but a sharp pain in my side nearly doubled me over.

Jack disappeared as he turned in the same direction as the thief. I kept going and reached the bend as Jack returned.

"He got in a waiting motur and took off," he said in between deep breaths. "I'm sorry. Your purse probably has your ID and credit cards in it."

I wanted to scream. Instead, I walked in circles, trying to cool down. "No. With all the traveling I do, I keep those in my travel wallet." I patted it beneath my shirt. And then suspicion took hold of me. "How do I know you didn't let him go?"

"What?" He reared back. "I was trying tae help you."

"Help me?" I stopped circling and stared at him. "For all I know, you're behind all this. How's Auntie? If you've hurt her . . ."

"I've no knowledge of how your aunt is. You need tae sit down and calm yourself." Jack took my arm, herding me toward his Mustang.

I pulled away. "Why are you here?"

"That's rather a strange question tae ask the man who, for the second time today—I might add—has come tae your rescue."

I glared at him. "Answer my question."

"Call me crazy, but I was worried about you, so I rented a motur, and when I got back tae your place, you pulled out, so I tailed you here."

I had thought the man dreamy before, but now his kindness seemed malevolent, sinister, diabolic. "Sure. What have you done with her? Where is she?" I shoved him away.

He grabbed my arm and dragged me toward his waiting car. "Look, I know something about this. I can help you and your aunt."

"Let go!" I struggled, trying to wrench free. His grip grew stronger.

He flung open the passenger door. "Get in."

"I will not!"

"We don't have time for this. Get in the motur!" His friendly manner had vanished. In its place, the real man behind the playful flirting appeared.

Though I wanted to protest more, going with Jack was my only option. He knew something about Auntie's kidnapping. I remembered a warning on those true-crime shows I'd watched. *Never go to a second location.*

If he was going to hurt me, he'd had plenty of opportunities. And I really had no choice. Not if I was ever going to see Auntie again.

CHAPTER FOUR

I watched as Jack shifted his Mustang down to first gear and pulled out of the parking plaza into the main flow of traffic heading south. "Are you taking me to the park?"

"What park?" He didn't look at me but kept his eyes on the road. "We're searching for the motur the thief got into."

"You know where he's going. He works for you." Did he think me an idiot because I hadn't connected the dots in this out-of-control nightmare?

Bewilderment furrowed his forehead as he concentrated on traffic.

"The park where you told me to meet you," I said it a little louder, answering his question. "I assume that's where the guy is going and where you're holding Auntie." I could not believe he was feigning innocence. For a second, I wondered about pulling out the artifact and handing it to him, but as I looked at him, I realized something seemed off. He appeared appalled by my accusations.

"I don't know what you're going on about." He came to a red light and braked.

Cars zoomed through the intersection, making it impossible for him to run the light. Could he be telling the truth? "You said you knew something about this and that you could help me."

"That's right. I'm here tae help you." He saw the light change to green and drove on.

The rage and fear I'd bottled up spilled out. "You conned your way into my house, set up cameras so you could spy on me, and I'm supposed to believe that you're here to help me?" Did he really think me so gullible? Of course he did. I'd been duped by his rescue at the airport and had even allowed him to take me home.

He shook his head. "Conned my way? Set up cameras? I still don't know what you're going on about. But I do know this: you're up tae your eyeballs in trouble, and you and your aunt need my help. I can help you hide and keep you safe. My job is security. You have tae believe me, Skye."

I shook my head. "This is some kind of sick, twisted game. Who did you pay to try to run me down at the airport?"

He didn't answer, just looked concerned and deep in thought.

I stared out the window. Even though anger pumped through me, I still registered where we were. If he kept going south on State Street, he'd miss the turn to Liberty Park. Of course, if he was the kidnapper, there was no need to go to the park. But then, why didn't he have Auntie with him, and why hadn't he asked for the page he'd sent me to get?

What if he didn't have anything to do with Auntie's abduction? But why was he here? I didn't have the focus to solve this riddle. If he missed the turn to the park, he probably didn't know I was supposed to go there.

"I would never pay someone tae try tae run over you . . . or anyone else." He drove past the turn.

"Why are you following me?"

"I'm here tae help you."

"Again with the helping me." Frustration triggered a headache, and I tried to calm down. "Why would you help me? I mean, you're a stranger. Sure, you might be friendly and good-looking, but so are serial killers. Ted Bundy comes to mind." I couldn't figure him out, and I didn't want to try.

"Who's Ted Bundy?" Perplexity creased his chiseled face.

I couldn't believe he hadn't heard of the man who had struck terror in the nation. But then again, he traveled a lot, and though he had a place in New York, his home was in Scotland. "He was a horrible man who murdered a lot of women." It dawned on me how absurd this conversation had become. "Bottom line, Jack. Do you know where my aunt is?"

He gave me an earnest please-listen-to-me look. "No, but I want tae help you find her." That slight smile he'd used to win me over at the airport tugged at his lips. He took a deep breath. "Okay, I'll tell you what I can. I work for the CIA. We believe that foreign agents want something your family may have kept hidden for hundreds of years."

I became keenly aware of the envelope pressed against my back.

"Skye, you and your aunt are in grave danger. If that man stole your purse with the folio in it, we need tae find it." He looked at me earnestly.

I wanted to give in but couldn't. First, he'd claimed to be here to help me, then he'd brought up the page. He'd said he was with the CIA, so if that was true, it would make him a good guy. Yet, he hadn't shown me a badge. Of course, he was driving. But still . . . with Auntie's life at stake, I had to be certain. And the kidnapper seemed to see all at the house. Could they possibly know I was with Jack, a CIA agent? And if they did, would they kill Auntie? I felt trapped and confused and jumbled all at once.

Everything tightened into a knot. I knew two things for certain: I didn't trust Jack, and I had to get to Liberty Park. And I had to do it alone. I couldn't risk bringing him with me.

He pulled up to the next stoplight. This was my chance. I unfastened my seat belt, unlocked the door, opened it, and ran.

"Skye!" he yelled. "Wait! You can't do this alone. You need me . . ."

His voice faded as I kept running.

I cut across streets and took alleyways. I wanted to make it impossible for him to find me. He didn't seem to know what park I'd been talking about, and with so many in the valley, there was a good chance he wouldn't.

I slowed to a fast walk as I drew near the park and the aviary. I scanned the area. A few mothers sat on benches near a playground while their little ones traversed the jungle gym. A couple of park maintenance workers were repairing lawn mowers near the work shed. I didn't see anyone else. I walked across the sprawling lawn, heading for the aviary. I couldn't remember a bench near it, but I had been here only a few times. A bench sat just beyond a stand of trees.

Once again, I took stock of my surroundings. The mothers seemed oblivious to everything. The maintenance workers were totally engrossed in their mowers.

A wad of nerves settled in my stomach like a swarm of bees as I timidly sat. What if I was too late? What if I'd wasted too much time with Jack and now I'd never see Auntie again?

Time seemed endless as I waited. The sun beat down through the trees. A squirrel chattered, making me jump. I'd turned into a bundle of raw nerves.

From beneath me, I heard ringing.

What the . . . ?

I got down on my knees. Taped to the bottom of the bench was a cell phone. I tore off the tape and answered. "Hello."

"Skye." The male voice sounded tinny, like he spoke into a can in an effort to disguise his identity.

Could it possibly be Jack? I couldn't tell.

"Yes. How's Auntie? Is she all right? I don't see her. I want to talk to her. I need to know she's okay." I studied my surroundings, hoping to find her walking toward me.

"My men were with her when you called her from the plane. After hanging up, she suffered a stroke. Unfortunately, she's taken a bad turn and can hardly speak."

Only Elizabeth and Auntie knew I'd called her last night. A frisson raced over my skin. A stroke. "Are you getting medical help for her?"

"She's being looked after and is safely out of your country."

Out of your country? "Where did you take her?"

He cleared his throat. "I've informed you of your aunt's grave condition. You'll learn where she is later. Did you do what I told you to and collect what was in the safety deposit box?"

A spark of fight ignited within me. "You know I did since your man stole my purse and found it wasn't there." I scanned the area again.

"Why would I send someone to steal your purse?" He didn't wait for an answer. "Do you still have the artifact?"

"Yes." Movement I caught out of the corner of my eye pulled my attention. The maintenance workers were riding their lawn mowers and seemed to be headed my way. They must be working for the kidnapper and were coming to collect the document.

"There are others besides myself most anxious to obtain the pages."

"Pages?" Plural. Did I hear him right?

"Yes. Two more exist besides the one in your possession. If you want to see your aunt alive, I suggest you find the other two and bring all three to me."

"How am I supposed to do that? I don't even know who you are or where you are, let alone where the other pages could be." Total panic swallowed me as I kept my eyes on the workers and their mowers.

"You're the one who hears the voice. Perhaps it will tell you. Keep the phone. But find the other pages. Remember I'm watching your every move." He hung up.

He knew I heard the voice. His men must have been listening when I called Auntie. And he was watching my every move. But then, why didn't he know my purse had been stolen? But wait. He didn't imply that he didn't know. He implied that he wouldn't have stolen it.

The phone pinged. I glanced at the screen. A text message. Tapping on the icon, I watched the screen open with a picture of Auntie strapped to a reclined seat. Her head lolled to one side; a reddish-purple bruise marred her forehead. I clung to the phone as if I could will myself to her.

The lawn mowers grew louder. The maintenance men had abandoned their work and were walking toward me. The kidnapper had tasked me to find the other pages, so why would he send these guys after me? Unless they didn't work for the kidnapper.

He'd said there were others who wanted the page as well. These men were about fifty feet away and closing. I couldn't stand here worried about Auntie. I had to do everything I could to help her. I shoved the phone in my pocket and ran for the mothers still sitting near the playground, hoping the men wouldn't follow.

The women saw me coming and stood.

"Are you all right?" the one with long dishwater-blonde hair said. She hefted a toddler on her hip as her gaze went to the men.

The other mother, a slim athletic type, must have noticed them as well and pulled out her cell phone, prepared to dial. "Are those lads bothering you?"

I turned around. The crew abruptly changed direction like they had been heading toward the work shed all along. Maybe they had been, and I was being paranoid. "No." I didn't want to elaborate, so I answered the first question. "I'm fine, really. But I'm in a bit of a bind. See, I lost track of time, and I'm supposed to meet a friend for lunch. There's no way I'm going to get to Foothill Drive by noon." My eyes were drawn to a bus sign near the road, but I had no money for it. I carried only credit cards, my driver's license, and my passport in my travel wallet around my neck, and buses wanted cash. "And . . ." What could I say? When all else failed, try the truth. That was what Auntie always said. "As I left the bank awhile ago, some guy stole my purse, so I have no money."

"Oh, that's horrible. Do you want to use my phone to call the police?" The lady with the toddler on her hip shook her head while wiping her child's runny nose.

"What can the police do? They'd only file a report and never catch the guy." I had to get the women away from that notion.

The athletic woman motioned to her little boy, who had been playing with the other mother's son. "I can give you a lift. I'm heading that way."

I couldn't hide behind this woman and her child. I couldn't put them at risk. And I didn't even know why I'd said Foothill Drive, except that Elizabeth lived a few blocks from there. She might be able to help me. Yes,

Elizabeth's home would be a good place to collect myself. Though I hated dragging her into this, I seriously needed help.

"If you could give me enough money for fare, I'll take the bus." I patted my pockets in a feeble attempt to emphasize that I didn't have money, all the while very aware of the artifact stuck in the back waistband of my pants.

"I can drop you. It's no bother. Cyndy, would you mind taking the kids to McDonald's alone?"

The other mother with the toddler on her hip grabbed her bag. "No problem at all." She motioned to the boys. They reluctantly climbed down from the jungle gym. "You guys ready to go to lunch?"

Both of the boys' sad faces brightened as they bounded over. The smaller one took hold of his mother's outstretched hand. "The lunch prize this week is Laser Bob."

With her toddler on her hip, Cyndy guided the two eager boys toward her car.

The athletic mother led the way to the parking lot. I checked behind us and caught a glimpse of the men near the work shed. They stood there watching us. A chill passed through me, and I quickly got in the car. I reasoned that I'd ride with her until we were out of sight, then I'd bail. If by chance the men chased her, they wouldn't bother her once they realized I was no longer with her.

At least that was what I told myself and prayed I was right.

She shut her car door, and as I turned to thank her, my gaze landed on the semiautomatic pistol aimed straight at me.

CHAPTER FIVE

I FROZE. THE WOMAN KEPT the gun on me as she started the car with the touch of a button, then pulled out, picking up speed. The seat belt warning dinged.

"Fasten your seat belt, or I stop the car and hand you over to the men at the park."

I fumbled with the belt until it fastened. "Who are you?"

"Doesn't matter who I am." Though only driving with one hand, the other one holding the weapon on me, she expertly passed slower cars. "What matters is who you are and whether you have the page."

She ran a red light. Horns honked; cars swerved, barely missing us. Buildings blurred in my periphery as the blocks flew by. My mind scrambled as I tried to make sense of what she'd said and what was happening.

I'd been in a free fall since returning home. *No, since hearing the voice.* I looked at the semiautomatic in her hand. Could I knock it away, unfasten my seat belt, and jump out of the moving car before she could shoot me? Probably not. And, we'd probably crash, which might not be a bad thing. First, I had to have some answers. "Who do you think I am? And why is the page so important?"

She looked straight at me, her calculating eyes studying me as though gauging my intelligence. She turned her attention back to the road. "Of course I know who you are, and you know very well who you are too and how important that page is."

She ran yet another red light. Where were the police? If I stayed in this car, I'd end up dead, and then what would happen to Auntie? I had to reason with this woman. Get her to slow down. "Look, I think this is some big misunderstanding. I'm nobody special. Really."

She glared at me. "But you have the page."

"Honestly. I'd never laid eyes on it until just a little while ago."

We'd reached Foothill Drive. I had to get away whether the car was moving or not, whether she shot me or not. Summoning courage I didn't know I had, I slid my hand down to the seat-belt clasp. Heavy traffic had forced her to slow down. In one desperate move, I released the seat belt, unlocked the door, wrenched it open, and jumped out.

I hit the asphalt with full force on my side. Pain ricocheted through me as I rolled to the curb. Brakes from other cars squealed. At the same time, the woman's sedan screeched to a stop.

I had to get out of there. Ignoring pain, I pulled myself to my feet and ran into traffic.

Horns blared.

Drivers slammed on their brakes and yelled.

I kept going, running across the street. I raced up the hill into a neighborhood, sprinted through yards and over hedges, and hid behind a stately evergreen, trying to catch my breath. The branches scraped my face. A dog barked.

My arm and knees throbbed from my landing. But I still felt the envelope against my back and the kidnapper's cell phone in my pocket. I peered down the street at the peaceful neighborhood, looking for the woman's sedan.

She hadn't followed yet. Could she track me here? Once again, I thought of the phone. I pulled it out and turned it off, just in case she could follow me using GPS. I had to keep going.

Gaining my bearings, I read the street sign: 2400 East on 1400 South. Elizabeth's house was five blocks up the hill. With any luck, she could help me figure out what I needed to do without getting too involved. Levelheaded Elizabeth was always reasonable and knew better than I did.

As I limped along, I kept a watchful eye on every car that came in my direction, always turning away so they couldn't see my face. It seemed to take forever, but finally, I turned on the right street where Elizabeth's Tudor-style house stood. A gas company van sat parked at her neighbor's house, but no one was in sight. I raced up her sidewalk to her front door and pressed the doorbell, listening to the chimes ring through her home.

No one answered.

I tried again and peered around, worried I'd be spotted at any second. I checked my watch: 1:50 p.m. Time was slipping away. Elizabeth had said she'd be in town only a few hours and then she was deadheading to Florida to work a flight to Brazil. I thought that was at seven.

But if she'd left already, where was her husband? It sounded like she expected him to be home. Why didn't Frank answer? Maybe he had taken her to the airport or shopping. A black SUV slowly drove by. Frantic, I remembered Elizabeth kept a spare key hidden under a loose brick on her steps. I found the key and let myself in. Closing the heavy oak door behind me and locking it, I leaned against it, exhaling a wary sigh of relief. At least I was safely indoors, where no one could see me.

The safe feeling didn't stay long as shades of intrusion overcame it. I'd never been alone in Elizabeth's house.

A sunken formal living room decorated with traditional furniture stood to the left, a sweeping staircase leading to the second floor to my right. Straight ahead was a hallway passing the dining room and ending in the kitchen. I'd visited Elizabeth many times, so I knew my way around, yet it seemed strangely different without her here.

"Elizabeth. It's Skye," I called out. Even though I knew she must be gone, someone else might be home.

No one answered.

My shoulder burned. I looked beneath my shirt at the raw skin. I limped down the hall to the immaculately cleaned kitchen with matching stainless-steel appliances. The sand-colored backsplash tucked between white shaker-style cabinets gave the room a modern feeling. Elizabeth's sleek-minimal taste. The back door's frilly Priscilla curtains drew my attention; they seemed out of place.

I'd teased her about those fancy curtains many times. She'd claimed they were her husband's choice. The thought made me feel normal, like, for a moment, the nightmare I'd been living wasn't real. But I knew it was. How I wished my friend were here right now.

I took the envelope with the precious page in it out of my waistband and set it on the counter. Then I set the cell phone and my travel wallet next to it and pulled off my T-shirt to expose my tank top and my wounded shoulder.

Opening several drawers, I found a dish towel. I dampened a corner and dabbed my raw skin. It burned. What I needed was antiseptic, which was probably upstairs in the bathroom.

Before going to get it, I grabbed a glass from the cupboard and poured myself a drink from the filtered faucet. I gulped down the entire thing. I hadn't realized how thirsty I'd become. My stomach growled. I grabbed an apple from the bowl of fruit on the granite countertop. But as soon as my gaze stopped on the manila envelope, my appetite disappeared again.

How in the world was I going to find the other two pages? I opened the packet and pulled out the cardboard. No way could Auntie have been the only one to have kept this hidden. It looked ancient. Who'd had it before her? And who before that? I mean, the thought that people had been hiding this for centuries was mind-boggling.

But here it was. Pulling the top cardboard away, I studied the quaint illustrations and text again. *In quod muros . . .* And then I was lost, except it looked like the last two words in the sentence were *Notre Dame.*

Desperation settled on my shoulders. What was I going to do? How could I find the other pages without knowing what this one said or what it even was? There had to be a clue somewhere. Did I know anyone who could read Latin? None of my friends did.

I thought of Professor Sumsion. Auntie had told me once that he spoke five languages. He also taught world history, with an emphasis on Rome. Maybe he understood Latin. I had to get to the University of Utah and track him down.

The chimes of the front doorbell rang throughout the house.

I froze.

No way would I answer the door.

But maybe I should see who it was. I grabbed my shirt and travel wallet and slid them both over my head as I quietly tiptoed down the hallway and peered through the peephole. Two guys from the gas company: one short, with a five o'clock shadow, and the other taller, with pock-marked cheeks. He looked like the man who had stolen my purse. This was bad. Very bad.

A knock banged on the door, and the bell rang madly again and again.

I held my breath. *Just go away.*

And then the doorknob jiggled.

I had to get out of here. I sprinted down the hall, past the dining room, just as the front door burst open. I dodged into the kitchen. A bullet whizzed by and thudded into the wall beside me. I sucked in long draughts of air, trying to focus and not freak out.

"Ms. Armstrong, you cannot hide from us. Bring us *le papier*, and we leave." Whoever spoke had a French accent.

Once they had their hands on the artifact, they'd kill me.

The vellum! Where was it?

I looked at the countertop where I'd left it only moments ago, and it still sat there, alongside the apple I hadn't eaten and the stupid cell phone the kidnapper had given me.

Footfalls thundered down the hall. At any second, they'd find me. I lunged for the counter, grabbing the page in the plastic sheet protector and the cell.

The whiskery man jerked my arm and wrenched the plastic sheeting with the page in it from me, along with the phone. "*Merci*, madame." He threw me to the floor, banging my sore hip against the tile. I rolled to the other side, ready to spring to my feet, but came up short as the Frenchman's companion aimed his weapon at my head. I froze with my hands clasped together, willing my nerves not to betray my fear. *Hang on.*

The Frenchman's eyes went to the countertop where the two cardboard pieces waited with the manila envelope. As if realizing what he held was priceless, he set the cell phone on the counter and carefully put the folio between the cardboard, then slid them safely inside the envelope. He hid it beneath his gray gasman shirt and picked up the phone. "*Se débarrasser d'elle.*"

I didn't know what he'd said, but by the evil smile spreading over his companion's pocked face, he meant to kill me. How could I fight back? I didn't have a weapon. But I might as well go out fighting. With a surge of terror-filled courage, I screamed and lunged at the man, knocking him to the floor.

The back door crashed open, breaking the glass behind the ruffled Priscilla curtains. Jack stormed in. The Frenchman made a beeline for the front door. The thug I'd attacked shimmied up the wall to his feet. Jack gave the guy an uppercut to the jaw, making him drop his weapon. I scooped it up as Jack threw the man down and punched him again, knocking him out.

"Excuse me, lass." Jack took the gun from me, aimed at the man down the hall who was about to escape through the front door, and shot.

The man fell hard to the entryway floor. The cell phone in his hand slid across the tiles, stopping inches from the front threshold.

Stunned beyond belief, I didn't know what to do, what to say. I'd never seen anyone die. And even though only a minute ago the Frenchman had ordered me killed, I tore off down the hall toward him, hoping he was still alive and that I could help him.

Falling to my knees, my gaze fixed on a blood-rimmed hole in the back of his shirt. I turned him over. His eyes were frozen open and lifeless. A larger hole cut through the left side of his chest. The bullet had gone completely through him. I looked at the wall. Blood splatters and a bullet hole marred the cream-colored wall. Suddenly, I remembered he'd stored the page beneath his shirt.

Panicked, I popped open his shirt buttons and found the envelope. A smattering of red stained it, but it appeared as though the small page within was still protected.

Blood puddled on the ceramic tile beneath the body.

The grinding wheels of the garage door opening echoed through the house. It had to be Elizabeth's husband.

I turned to see where Jack had gone. He stood directly behind me and, just then, grabbed my wrist, "Come on. Time tae leave."

"But . . ." I stared down at the dead man.

"You cannot bring him back. You have what's important; now, let's get on."

"How can we leave?" Again, I stored the page at the small of my back.

"We have tae." He pulled me toward the door.

I grabbed the cell phone off the floor and checked behind me. The man in the kitchen was still out cold. More than anything, I wanted to stay and explain what had happened. I hated leaving those two men in Elizabeth's house for her husband to find. But with so many different people trying to kill me and steal the page, I had no choice, not if I was going to save Auntie.

CHAPTER SIX

WE RACED DOWN THE TRADITIONAL neighborhood street with well-manicured lawns and stately trees, where crime rarely happened, leaving behind the grisly scene we'd just left. Somehow, some way, I would make it up to Elizabeth.

"How did you know where I was?" I said, trying to keep up with Jack. Though grateful that he'd suddenly appeared and helped me get away, I felt unnerved because he'd known where to find me.

"I'm CIA. I know all about you and your friends." He motioned to his blue Mustang parked at the curb. We hopped in, and he sped off.

"I can't believe you killed that man." With shaking hands, I buckled my seat belt while fighting the most intense onslaught of nerves I'd ever experienced.

"I had tae stop him. Have you forgotten that they tried tae kill you?"

A flash of the pock-faced man standing over me with a gun came to mind. "No, but you shot the Frenchman in the back. Just killed him."

"Couldn't be helped. Killing the enemy is the sad part of being a spy." Jack expertly sped around slower traffic, as if he'd driven like James Bond his entire life.

"I'm glad you brought up being a spy. You never showed me your badge or credentials. Besides, I thought you had to be a citizen of the United States to work for them."

"My billfold is in my hip pocket, which is a bit difficult tae mine out at the moment. And I have dual citizenship. Remember, I have a place in New York."

"It's just that I don't know who the real enemy is. And why should I believe you? You lied to me before, said you were in security."

"That part wasn't a lie. I *am* in security. I saved your life. In fact, this is the third time I've come tae your rescue *in one day*. That has tae count for something."

He was right. It did count for something, but at this moment, I didn't know what. "Are you going to tell me who those men were?"

"My main job is tae keep you safe."

"The CIA must have told you who is after me. I mean, they don't just out of the blue say, 'Go keep this person safe.' Besides, I'm nobody special. Neither is Auntie."

"That envelope says otherwise. As long as you have it, your life is in danger. Now, why don't you give it tae me?"

"You're kidding, right? Like I'm going to hand it over to you. This artifact is the only thing keeping my aunt alive." But I wanted to give it to him. I didn't want anything to do with the stupid little page pressed against my back.

"What does a man have tae do tae win your trust?" He studied me for a second.

I couldn't answer him.

He returned his attention to the road. "Has your aunt's kidnapper been in touch with you?"

"Yes. At the park. He called me on this." I pulled the phone from my pocket.

"Blimey." He grabbed the phone, rolled down the window, and tossed it out into the traffic.

I gasped. I couldn't believe he'd done that. I strained to see where it had landed and saw a car run over it. "That's just great!" I slammed my hand against the dashboard. "How is the kidnapper going to get in touch with me now?" I shook my head, feeling completely desolate and beaten. "He'll kill Auntie, and it's all your fault." I glared at him.

"That mobile had a GPS tracker on it. Doesn't matter if the phone is off or on, they could find you. At least now you're off the grid for the time being. Believe me, they will find you again. They have their ways. When the kidnapper makes contact with you, get as much information as you can from him. When he called before, did he say anything about me?"

"Your name never came up. Probably will now though. Jack, if you truly are CIA, what do you know about the people chasing me? What do you know about the artifact?"

He stared intently at me, then heaved a deep sigh. "A man who many in the spy-game call the Black Prince is trying tae use your aunt as leverage."

"Black Prince?" This sounded like something from *Mission Impossible*. Jack pushed the turn-signal lever.

"Where are you going?" I couldn't imagine him stopping.

He'd pulled into a convenience store parking lot and shut off the car. Turning in his seat, he pulled out his billfold and handed it to me.

I flipped it open. His CIA badge and credentials stared up. "Okay, you're CIA." I handed it back to him. "So we're on the same side. Tell me what's going on."

"It's a long story that I can't tell you. It's classified, and you don't have the clearance." His brows slanted, sympathy showing in his eyes. "I've got tae get you tae a safe place until we can think about what tae do next."

"What do you mean, I don't have clearance? What does it take? I was nearly roadkill at the airport; I've had my purse stolen; some guys at the park chased me; a woman at the park who offered me a ride pulled a gun on me; and then those Frenchmen at my friend's house tried to kill me, all because of this page. Add that to the fact that some crazy man kidnapped Auntie, causing her to have a stroke, and"—emotion threatened to overwhelm me, but I blinked it away—"she might already be dead."

"They told you your aunt had a stroke?" His brows knitted together.

"Yes. They even texted me a picture of her. She looked really bad, like she was unconscious." A shudder came over me. I folded my arms.

"She may have been drugged. Next time they get in touch with you, demand to speak with her." He rubbed his chin. "I can tell you this: the vellum they're after actually belonged tae your father. I believe your aunt was keeping it safe for your family." He stared at me, not blinking or saying another word.

"For me? And my father . . ." My mind swirled. I rubbed my throbbing head. "You stood there in my home, asking me about my father, and you already knew? Did you know my aunt had been kidnapped?" My entire world shifted beneath me. Nothing was as it seemed.

"I had a good idea but couldn't say." His eyes darted away.

I remembered how friendly he'd been on the plane. "You knew on the flight, didn't you?"

He didn't answer, which spoke volumes.

"Why now? What triggered this? Auntie's had the page for years."

He stared at me.

I became very conscious of the folio pressed against my back. "And Auntie kept it safe. Why would she do that? Clearance or not, I deserve to know the whole story."

"I'd like nothing better, but I can't tell you. In this case, ignorance may keep you alive. My job is tae keep you and the artifact safe."

It was obvious he wasn't going to go rogue for me. "Has the CIA always been watching me and my family? I mean, you say it was supposed to be my father's and now mine. That sounds like an ongoing thing." The creepy thought made me feel unsettled and yet, in a strange way, comforted.

"I can't answer that."

"Can't or won't?"

"Can't." Jack clenched his teeth, making his jaw muscles flex.

"Okay, I can play along," I said, feeling trapped and not knowing what else to do, "mainly because I have no one else to turn to, and Auntie and I need your help. The kidnapper told me there are two other pages, but I'm sure you already know that."

"Until recently, the pages were folklore. That you have one makes the legend fact, a part of history many would like tae erase, even kill whomever is linked tae them."

My mind spun as I tried to fit together the puzzle pieces of why this was happening. "I don't have a clue as to why my family had this page. And now, since you tossed the phone away, the kidnapper won't be able to reach me."

"Believe me, lass. They will find you. The mobile just made their job easier."

"I hope you're right because I have no other choice. The only clue I have to find the other two pages is the text on the first page itself. But it's in handwritten Latin and is very hard to read. Do you read Latin?"

Jack shook his head. "The agency has a secure app that might help us out, though handwritten text can be tricky. And there are various forms of Latin." He pulled out his cell and tapped it several times. "It's loading. Get the page out here. The app will want me tae take a picture."

With great reluctance, I leaned forward and drew the manila envelope from beneath my clothes. I pulled the cardboard out and opened it.

"Ah, let me see it." He reached out.

"This is not leaving my hands." I glared at him.

"Okay." He rolled his eyes. "Can you at least hold it up?"

I did as he directed, and he took the picture. I quickly returned the vellum to its packaging and put it back in my waistband. I couldn't take any chances.

Jack tapped his cell a few more times. "It's not reading." He drilled his fingers on the steering wheel. "Of course, that would have been too easy, wouldn't it?" He looked at me. "Know anyone who can read Latin?"

Even though I had thought Sumsion might help me, I wanted to keep him out of it if I could. "Doesn't the CIA have sources that could translate the text?"

"Of course; however, this case is top secret. My boss let me know that I'd be on my own." He stuffed his billfold back in his hip pocket.

Top secret. Something didn't seem right about that, but the CIA was very secretive. Not many people knew exactly what the CIA did.

"I think I may know someone who could help us. He's one of Auntie's friends and a professor at the University of Utah."

starting the car, Jack shifted into drive and pulled out onto the road. "Then we need tae find him. Think he's still at the university?"

"He is. He teaches world history. He and my aunt go out for the early-bird dinner specials after his last class on Friday afternoons. So he's still up there."

We rode in silence, with me checking the rear window to see if we were being followed. Every time we passed a car, I wondered if the people inside were involved, if they were sent here by the Black Prince, whoever he was.

Heavy traffic because of an accident slowed us down, but it was also Friday, and people were heading out of town for the weekend.

We reached the university, and I directed him to the humanities building. "Professor Sumsion should be in his office. It's in the basement."

Jack parked the Mustang in visitor parking.

"What does your professor look like?" he asked as we raced to the building.

"He reminds me of the guy who played Dumbledore in Harry Potter, only his hair is silver and short, not long and gray, but he has the same puffy eyes and long face. And the same impressive bushy eyebrows."

We entered the building, dashed through the hallway to the stairs, and flew down them. I spied Sumsion, dressed in his black leather sports jacket over his black turtleneck jersey shirt, locking his office door.

"Professor," I called to him.

He turned about. Once he saw me, a smile brightened his seventy-year-old face. "My dear Skye. What a pleasure to see you." He looked at Jack and paused a moment as though leery, then peered past him. He must have expected to see Auntie. "Are you and your friend joining Marjorie and me for an early dinner?"

"No." How was I going to tell him what had happened? I knew he had strong feelings for Auntie. He'd be heartbroken.

Worry claimed his confused face. "Something is wrong. I can tell by your expressions. Is Marjorie all right?"

I had to be truthful. "No. She desperately needs your help."

"Where is she? What's happened?" Again, he studied Jack as if questioning his very existence.

A group of students walked by.

"We can't talk here." I checked up and down the hallway.

"Come into my office." Sumsion graciously opened the door. His office was a cavern lined with overflowing bookcases, with more books stacked on the floor next to his desk.

I couldn't help but double-check behind us before closing the door. As I turned to face him, the warm, sugar-berry scent of the pipe he often smoked drifted to me, giving me comfort that I'd made the right decision. I pulled the envelope from beneath my waistband and handed it to him.

Confusion slanted his baggy eyes. "What's this?"

The gravity of the moment hit me head-on. If he couldn't help me, I didn't know what I'd do. I took a deep breath. "I'm hoping you can tell me. It's been stored for decades in Auntie's safety deposit box. Her very life depends on it now."

CHAPTER SEVEN

"WHAT DO YOU MEAN, HER life depends on it? What's wrong? Where is Marjorie?" Sumsion's face flushed.

"She's been kidnapped. And to find her, I need you to tell me what the page inside this envelope says." I hoped he wouldn't ask more questions I couldn't answer.

Disbelief and then grave concern crossed Sumsion's face as he opened the manila envelope and pulled the contents onto his desk. He carefully drew apart the cardboard and stared at the vellum beneath the transparent sheet protector for a second before looking up at me. Furrows formed on his age-spotted forehead. "Marjorie had this artifact?"

"Yes. I don't understand why or where she got it, for that matter." I shot a dagger stare at Jack. An irritating hair that haunted me at the worst possible times floated in front of my eyes. I reached a shaky hand to smooth it away.

"Are you quite all right, my dear?" Sumsion studied my face as if looking for the truth.

Suddenly, emotion fell upon me like a crumbling tower. I didn't know if it was because he was putting my welfare before the puzzle in front of him or if it was just being with this lovely man who cared almost as deeply for Auntie as I did or if it was just a reaction to all I'd been through. Trying not to cry, I bit my bottom lip and nodded that I'd be okay.

Sumsion grabbed a tissue from his desk, handed it to me, and then put a comforting arm around my shoulders. "There, there. I'm glad you came. Now, tell me everything that has transpired and who this young man is." He gave Jack another once-over.

Getting my emotions under control, I was about to reply when Jack reached out his hand and shook Sumsion's. "Special Agent Jack Duncan."

The professor's bushy brows rose on his long face. "Special agent, you say?"

Jack nodded.

"Good." Sumsion cleared his throat. "I'm glad the authorities have been notified. FBI, I presume."

"CIA, sir."

Sumsion stared at Jack as if the cogs in his mind were trying to keep up, but then realization set in. "So Marjorie's abduction is an international problem?"

"Yes, sir." Jack held his gaze.

"The kidnapper said Auntie had a stroke and isn't even in the country anymore." I wanted Sumsion to know as much as I did. Besides, he loved Auntie. He needed to know everything. I pointed to the folio lying on his desk. "Auntie's life depends on me finding two other pages like this one and giving all three to the kidnapper."

Sumsion's hand covered his heart. "Oh, my poor Marjorie. What is this world coming to?"

"She really needs your help, Professor." I knew what I'd told him had been a shock.

"Of course." He rubbed his chin. "The pages must be worth a fortune." His puffy eyes were drawn to the artifact. "Have you any idea where the others are?"

"No. But I think there must be a clue in the text. It's in Latin and very hard to read."

Sumsion nodded, still looking at the page. "So it is. Could be Vulgar or Medieval or Old Latin. We need to understand what body of work this page is from and go from there." Sumsion sat at his desk and picked up the vellum. He grabbed a magnifying glass from his drawer and continued to study the text.

He set the page down, jumped up, and went to one of his overburdened bookcases. He dragged out a large, hardbound book. The jacket cover had drawings similar to the ones on the small page itself.

Lugging the book to his desk, he rifled through it, stopping where a heading read: "The Hours of Jeanne d'Évreux, Queen of France." He read for a moment, then looked over the vellum, and then back at the book. He inhaled deeply. "Mind you, I could be wrong, but the style of this work is very similar to that of Jeanne d'Évreux's *Book of Hours*."

"What is that?" I'd never heard of it before.

Sumsion leaned back in his chair, making the springs squeak. "Queen Jeanne d'Évreux was married to King Charles IV of France back in 1322 or thereabouts. I'm not sure of the exact date. He loved her so much that he commissioned a prayer book to be made for her. I believe the author-artist was . . . oh, let me see." He scanned the open reference book. "Yes, here it is—Jean Pucelle. He excelled in *de blanc et de noir* style, which was what grisaille was called. Though I have heard that many critics don't believe the *Book of Hours* to be Pucelle's work, there are many who do." He picked up the sheet, studying it as he spoke. "See how thin this vellum is?"

Gazing at the page, I nodded. "It's almost transparent."

"Yes. Similar to other pages of the prayer book. If this is part of that work, it is priceless, my dear." Sumsion sucked air between his teeth. "Jeanne's *Book of Hours* has scenes of the passion of Christ, events of His life and death. It also has pages that give tribute to Saint Louis of France, who was Jeanne's great-grandfather.

"The book now resides in the Metropolitan Museum of Art in New York. It is rumored that not all the text of the little prayer book was included." He studied the page. "This may be proof that other pages do exist. See, after King Charles died and left no male heir, there was that nasty business of a disagreement with England as to who would be France's new king. Thus started the Hundred Years' war. These missing pages prove that the widowed queen stayed in touch with Pucelle, the artist who made her prayer book. How else could he know the information to put on the pages except from the queen herself? It is also rumored that he continued to work on the text until his death in 1355. This folio, which is in Pucelle's same style, might be part of that work and would prove that he was indeed the artist, especially if he signed one of the missing pages. My dear, why did our sweet Marjorie have this?"

"I don't know." I shot a look at Jack. He knew more than what he was saying, but I'd already tried and failed to get him to tell me. No sense in going over that rocky terrain again, so I turned back to Sumsion. "Can you read what the page says?"

He placed the folio down on his desk and grabbed his magnifying glass and a pencil and paper. "Latin is hard to translate because you need the entire context to understand what exactly is being said. Many get it wrong. A little word like *et* can mean *and* or *also* or *even*, and without the missing pages, it's hard to comprehend the full meaning. And I believe this is a mix between Medieval and Old Latin. But let me see what I can do." He picked up his magnifying glass again and turned all his attention on the project before him.

He scribbled some words on his yellow notepad, then continued studying the page. Again, more notations. He pulled out a cloth handkerchief, blew his nose, stuffed it back in his pocket, and went on with his work.

He huffed and leaned back in his chair. Again, the springs complained. Rubbing his chin, Sumsion said, "The ink has bled a little, and the scrolling makes it even harder to read. It would be impossible to translate this with one of those fancy apps the kids tout in class or even on a computer. Technology has its place, mind you, but some things need a human eye."

Jack stood behind Sumsion. He shrugged as if to say, "Yeah, we know that."

Sumsion studied what he'd written. "This seems to be directing us to Notre Dame."

That Sumsion considered himself part of our strange little team warmed my heart.

He picked up his legal pad, and translating the Latin into English, he said, "'Within the walls of the mother of Notre Dame lies a rose, a secret from the world. An angel holds an open book, the pages missing, a secret that one day may save our Scottish brothers and ourselves from the tyranny of King Edward.'" He glanced at me.

"Scottish brothers?" That didn't make sense. "I thought you said the *Book of Hours* was about Christ and Saint Louis. Why would Jeanne d'Évreux, a French woman, want to send a message to Scotland?"

"Maybe it wasn't Jeanne sending a message but that Pucelle guy, the artist who made the book." Jack said it like he was thinking out loud as he studied the page over Sumsion's shoulder.

"No, I think Skye is on to something." Sumsion placed his fingers over his lips, deep in thought, then said, "I don't think Jeanne had Pucelle make this text for Scotland but for her own countrymen she loved. Understand that France was in great turmoil because Charles didn't have a male heir. His closest male relative was Edward III, king of England. Edward's mother, Isabella, was Charles's sister. It was rumored that Isabella had had her father-in-law killed. A Machiavellian business, to be certain.

"Of course, French nobility could not abide being ruled by Isabella's son, so they gathered assemblies of French barons and prelates at the university and came up with a new rule that stated males who derived their right to inheritance through their mother should be excluded."

"Male chauvinism at its finest," I said.

"True. Sadly, history is full of it." Sumsion patted my arm. "The nearest heir through male ancestry was Charles IV's first cousin, Philip, the Count of Valois." Sumsion took a deep breath and let it out slowly. "Edward III reluctantly paid homage to his French fiefs, but he also reserved the right to reclaim territories the French confiscated. He could now concentrate on his war with Scotland. And so, my dear, Scotland was very much involved."

I looked at Jack. His homeland was Scotland. It couldn't be a coincidence that he was involved with this. He had already admitted that he knew more than what he was telling me. His eyes met mine and held my gaze as if to say, "I wish I could tell you, but I can't."

Oblivious to the tension between Jack and myself, Sumsion went on. "Actually, the friendship between France and Scotland went way back. They were allies and had signed a treaty during the reign of Philip the Fair, in 1295. Several years before he died, Charles IV formally renewed the treaty, promising Scotland that France would support them if England invaded their country. I guess Edward III hoped that with the death of Charles IV, the treaty would not be binding—a great miscalculation on his part, I must add."

"He miscalculated a great many things, like we all do." Jack had been looking at me, and I knew there was deeper meaning to his words. Did he think he'd miscalculated me or that I had him? It didn't matter.

What was most important was finding the other two pages so I could save Auntie. "Professor, as fascinating as history can be, we need to cut to the chase. Now, you said that you think the other page might be in Notre Dame?"

"It possibly could be there, though over the years, the cathedral has been rebuilt several times and added onto. But Notre Dame is a good place to start. Jack, can you get some help from CIA resources to confirm?"

I looked at Jack, waiting for him to answer. He stared back at me and clenched his jaw but then turned to Sumsion. "This mission is off the grid."

"He told me it was top secret," I added.

Sumsion gave Jack a curious look, then took a deep breath. "Okay, so we do this the old-fashioned way by going there. When do we leave?" He carefully placed the artifact between the cardboard and slid it into the envelope.

"Oh, no." Jack shook his head. "Professor, you can't come."

"Why not?" I needed him with me. I still didn't entirely trust Jack. I needed someone I knew who had Auntie's and my best interests at heart. Though staying home was probably in Sumsion's best interest, I didn't want Jack calling the shots. Sure, he was CIA and had been trained when it came to undercover, keep-yourself-alive work, and though he'd said his main mission was to keep me safe, something wasn't right with him.

Out of Sumsion's view, Jack glared at me. "Cos I'm going tae have a hard enough time keeping you safe, let alone the professor."

"Young man, I won't hold you up. Though I was but a clerk in the army, my study of history has taught me how to keep my head down and run like a Jacobite with his kilt on fire." He gave an abrupt nod to Jack, as if his last words were in honor of his heritage. "All kidding aside, my Marjorie needs my help. I have to go."

Suddenly, the enormity of the mission before us hit me. I wished I could talk with Auntie and know how she was.

I thought of the other thing the kidnapper had told me. *You're the one who hears the voice. Perhaps it will tell you.* When he'd said those words, my shock that he'd been with Auntie when I'd called had overwhelmed me. Now that I thought more about it, I wondered if there was something more about the voice. Something I didn't know but felt.

The voice had warned me about the death of my parents. And also about Auntie. Was there something more to it? Was it some type of telepathic communication with loved ones? Or with the dead? No! Not the dead. I'd spoken to Auntie after I had first heard the voice. And I'd seen her in that texted picture the kidnapper had sent me. I had to believe she was still alive.

"What's wrong?" Sumsion eyed me.

"Nothing. I'm just worried." I couldn't tell him. Better to keep my worries over the voice to myself. Besides, it was more like a premonition of something to come. A type of forewarning. Most everyone experienced it at one time or another. But was the voice I heard somehow different? I didn't know, but I prayed it would continue to help me.

CHAPTER EIGHT

Using my employee passes, we caught the red-eye to Paris. Fortunately, all three of us had our passports. Jack always carried his like I did, and Sumsion kept his in a safe in his office. Before reaching the airport, Jack wiped the gun he'd taken from the Frenchman and dropped it in a random mailbox.

As we boarded the plane, I realized I had only two first-class seats. The third seat was in economy. Jack graciously took it, but he didn't look too happy about being separated from us.

Before boarding, we'd purchased bare essentials for the trip at the gift shop. The selection wasn't great, but we didn't have time to be choosy. We each bought small carry-ons and items to put in them. I grabbed a kit for personal hygiene, a T-shirt with a picture of Utah's Arches on the front, and a fleece jacket.

Once we'd settled into our seats and the plane became airborne, I felt as though I'd come out of my skin, as worry for Auntie intensified. This flight would take at least nine hours. How long could Auntie go without receiving medical help? I nervously began to tap the armrest of my seat.

"You really should try to sleep, Skye." Sumsion leaned back. "Marjorie knows you're doing everything you can to save her. Your aunt is a tough woman."

"I know, but the—"

At that moment, Topher Simmons, a young male flight attendant I'd worked with several times before, stopped by. Odds were high that people I knew would be working this flight. Topher and I had gone out a few times, but we were just friends.

He smiled. "Skye, Elizabeth said you were taking time off. Are you and your grandfather going on vacation in Paris?"

Topher didn't know much about me. He didn't know that my parents were both dead and I'd never met my grandparents on either my father's or mother's side because they had passed on before I was even born. My only living relative was Auntie.

Desperation washed over me.

"Young man," Sumsion took Topher's attention. "I'm honored that you think I'm Skye's grandfather, but alas, I'm only her aunt's good friend." Sumsion held out his hand. "Name's Shepherd Sumsion. Do you work with Skye?"

"Yes, I do." Topher looked around us. "Where is your aunt? Isn't she traveling with you?"

What could I say? She's been kidnapped, and we're on a ridiculously impossible quest to find some ancient pages to free her. That sounded like a crazy person. Besides, he'd never believe me. "Ah . . ."

"Marjorie had to take an earlier flight. I couldn't leave with her, so Skye offered to accompany me." Sumsion rescued me once again.

I noticed a passenger's call light flick on a couple rows ahead of us. "I think you're needed." I pointed it out to Topher.

"Thanks. When things settle down, I'll come back, and we can talk." He scurried off before I could discourage him.

Sumsion leaned next to my ear. "He's a bit of a challenge, isn't he?"

"You don't know the half of it."

"Oh, I can tell he has a crush on you, if that's what you mean." Sumsion nodded like he might be old but he wasn't blind.

"It's that obvious?"

"As obvious as the crush Special Agent Duncan has on you." His gray, bushy brows raised.

"You're way off there. But funny you should bring him up." I had to set Sumsion straight on Jack and my relationship. "I don't know how to say this, but I don't trust him."

Sumsion folded his arms. "Tell me more."

"This entire day has been a nightmare." I spoke in hushed tones that only Sumsion could hear and told him how I'd heard the voice, how Jack had saved me from being run over, and how he had taken me home. "But when Auntie wasn't there, I knew something was wrong." I told him about searching for her, finding the safety-deposit key, and reading the creepy email.

"Do you suspect that Jack was behind the message?" Sumsion's hand went to his coat pocket where he'd stashed his pipe; then, as if realizing he couldn't smoke on the plane, he pulled at an eyebrow.

"I hope not, but I'm not sure." I told him everything that had happened to me today, and then asked, "Why do you suppose everyone is after the pages now? I mean, what's changed? Auntie had that page for years and years."

Sumsion shook his head. "That truly is a puzzle. Something must have happened though. Others want the pages as well, which doesn't surprise me. If that page in your possession is from the *Book of Hours*, it would be worth a fortune. And you well know now that there are many who would do anything, even kill you, to get their hands on it." He bit at his lip, deep in thought for a moment. "Keep it safe, my child. Its very existence has the power to stir up raw emotions long believed to be dead."

"What do you mean?" He was scaring me now, as if everything I'd been through hadn't already put the fear in me.

"Remember how I told you that France and Scotland were allies during the Hundred Years' War?"

I nodded.

"And for a while, it seemed there would be peace between France and England?"

"Yes."

"That didn't last long. Within a short time, King Edward assumed the title of King of France and England. Edward was fighting not only King Philip of France but also some of his own countrymen to hold on to power. After the Battle of Sluys, the English dominated the English Channel, which stopped the French from invading. But Edward ran out of money, and the war probably would have ended then and there if it hadn't been for the death of the Duke of Brittany. King Edward wanted John of Montfort to step into the position, while King Philip wanted Charles of Blois."

History had never been my subject. The names blurred together. "But, Professor, how does it all tie into this stupid little page that now has Auntie's life in danger? And how could it stir up emotions long believed to be dead? I don't understand." Frustration had built inside me until I thought I'd burst.

"It's only speculation on my part, but think about it. Jeanne d'Évreux had been watching all this going on since the death of her husband. Her daughter should have been queen, but because of some pompous, pious know-it-alls, they'd passed a ridiculous law that had stolen the throne from her. Jeanne's country was being pulled apart, the country her grandfather,

Saint Louis, had done so much for, let alone her husband. Perhaps in her own way, she wanted to make a difference. She wanted to strike back in the only way she could."

"By leaving these little pages behind that no one at that time even knew about? How does that make a difference? It doesn't make sense." A bone-tired weariness settled on me, and yet, I was wired. What Sumsion said wasn't helping. Kings, queens, and war. It all jumbled together. "What good comes from remembering the past anyway? We can't change what happened. Nor can we change the future."

"Don't rush to judgment. Do you know the history of the Israelites?" He tilted his head, waiting for my answer.

I really didn't want to go there, so to avoid another long story with names that meant nothing to me, I said, "Of course."

"Then you know that remembering their past brought them to the promised land. And maybe that's what Jeanne hoped for her people. Maybe she left the pages behind to guide them. The message they possibly contain could stir up a rebellion in France or Scotland or both. With contention in France over refugees from other countries and people upset in Scotland because of Brexit, a message from the past might remind them of simpler times and drive them to take action. There could be more riding on these pages than money. Powerful people may want them destroyed." After dropping that bomb, Sumsion yawned and patted my hand. "Let's not dwell on hypotheticals that are only conjecture on my part. Get some sleep. We're going to need all our energy once we touch down in Paris."

If Jeanne had hoped to leave a message for her countrymen, why bring up their Scottish brothers? Scotland had been an ally, but so what? My mind went around and around with the information Sumsion had told me. His daunting theory that powerful people could be after the pages as well was terrifying. I really couldn't handle it. Shoving the menacing thought aside, I decided to keep my focus on saving Auntie and not worry about other threats I could do nothing about. I pushed my seat back and closed my eyes as the words *promised land* echoed through my mind.

"Skye."

I blinked open my eyes. I must have slept for a while. Jack stood beside me in the aisle.

"What? Is something wrong?" I checked Sumsion next to me. He seemed to be dozing.

"I wanted tae let you know that I've made reservations for all of us at the Hotel Merci in Paris."

"Thanks. I hadn't even thought that far ahead." I motioned for Jack to bend over and lean closer so only he could hear. "I hope finding the page doesn't take too long. I'm worried about Auntie receiving medical help."

"Notre Dame is a big place. We're going tae have tae do some snooping, and sadly, that's going tae take some time."

"He's right." Sumsion had awakened and sat up. "We should have a control center. We may have our work cut out for us, and we'll need some place to recharge."

"Of course." My mind was still on Auntie. Was she recharging? Was she getting better or worse? Here I was stuck on this plane flying across countries and oceans while her well-being remained uncertain.

Jack leaned close, looking me in the eye. "Don't worry about your aunt. The kidnappers will keep her alive while they're waiting tae get their hands on the pages."

Sometimes Jack could be very perceptive.

"He's right," Sumsion added. "As long as you still have the page, they will keep my dear Marjorie alive. She's their leverage. They won't let anything happen to her until they have what they want." The older man's puffy eyes clouded over.

He'd been worried about Auntie, but I hadn't realized the extent of his feelings. By the sadness claiming his face, he not only loved her but was deeply devoted to her as well. Of course he was. He'd asked her to marry him at least once, that I knew of. But Auntie, for some reason known only to her, had said no. I hoped she hadn't set aside her own happiness, thinking she had to be there for me.

"We need to keep the aisles clear." Topher stood beside Jack, his arms folded.

I'd been so worried about Auntie and Sumsion that I hadn't noticed Topher walk up. How much had he heard? We'd been talking quietly, not wanting to draw attention to ourselves. And even though first class gave a little more privacy than economy, someone could have overheard. My heart sank.

"Sorry." Jack stood. "Just touching base with the rest of my party."

Topher looked between Jack and me as if surprised we knew each other and that I might be involved with this tall, dark stranger.

I didn't know what to say. And though Jack and I weren't involved, it might be best if Topher thought we were. At least then maybe he'd leave me alone for the rest of the flight.

Jack patted my shoulder. I put my hand over his before he returned to his seat. Topher stood there watching him go, then he seemed to gather his wits about him. "We have another hour before we reach Paris. Is there anything I can get you?" A coolness framed his words. His entire demeanor had changed. After all this was over, I'd tell him what was going on. Even though I had no desire to start something with him, I didn't like leaving things like this between us. For the time being, though, it seemed necessary.

"No, I'm fine. How about you, Professor?"

The older man shrugged. "Some Earl Grey tea would be nice."

"I'll get that for you." Topher left.

"My dear, I think you've crushed someone's heart." Sumsion watched Topher disappear into the galley.

"I know. Once this is over, I'll explain to him what's going on." The words *once this is over* echoed in my mind. At that moment, it seemed unending.

* * *

We arrived at Charles de Gaulle Airport in pouring rain and blowing wind. Standing at the curb, waiting for Jack to pull up in the rental car, I felt chilled to the bone. The jacket I'd picked up at the airport was doing nothing to stop the cutting chill. Sumsion wasn't faring much better. Both he and Jack had purchased thin, plastic rain jackets, which kept them dry, but that was all. Sumsion shivered, and I knew the frigid air must be cutting right through to him. Travel during March in Paris was always risky.

Jack pulled up, driving a small black Fiat. Sumsion insisted on getting in the back seat, so I climbed into the passenger seat.

"Who knew winter would sneeze all over us?" Jack said.

Sumsion chuckled and pulled the rain jacket hood off his head.

Jack entered the address of the hotel into the GPS and then merged into the stream of bumper-to-bumper traffic like it was no big deal, which surprised me. But it shouldn't have. He had probably traveled all over the world for his job and had learned to drive like the natives wherever he landed. I wondered how long it would take to check into the hotel and then go to Notre Dame.

I set my watch to Paris time. 12:30 p.m. How was Auntie? The image the kidnapper had texted haunted me. Had Auntie regained consciousness?

Did she know I was doing everything I could to help her? Were they feeding her, or was she even able to eat? How sick was she? Questions that had dogged my every wakeful moment now barraged me. "Jack, can I use your phone and check my email in case the kidnapper tried to get in touch while we were flying?"

"Sure." With one hand on the wheel, he dug his cell out of his pocket and handed it to me.

I tapped in my email information. No new message. Deciding to take matters into my own hands, I clicked Reply on the message the kidnapper first sent me and wrote, *How is my aunt?* and tapped Send.

"Well?" Jack asked.

The phone chimed. I glanced at the message. "A mailer daemon message saying my reply was unable to be delivered."

Jack didn't take his eyes off the road. "The kidnapper probably shut down his account. Don't worry. He will be in touch."

Disappointed, I returned his phone to him.

We reached the hotel. After finding a parking space, we sprinted for the building and were relieved to get out of the biting wind as we stepped past glass doors to the lobby. While Jack checked us in, I noticed that Sumsion looked a bit peaked.

"Are you all right?" I asked.

He straightened and seemed to stand taller than his five-foot seven-inch height. "Capital. I'm right as rain and ready to go."

He was lying, but I couldn't call him on it. We were going to need his help once we reached Notre Dame.

Jack joined us, handing us our room cards. "We're very lucky they let us check in so early, but we had tae take what rooms hadn't been stayed in last night. Professor, you're with me. Skye, I asked for an adjoining room tae ours, but they didn't have one. However, your room is next door. Or you could bunk with us?"

I shook my head. "I'll pound on the wall if I need help."

"Okay, then." Jack gave me a reassuring smile that said, if I pounded on the wall, he'd be right there. "Let's drop off what little stuff we have and get going."

We left the elevator on the ninth floor and proceeded to our rooms at the end of the long dimly lit hallway.

Once alone in my room, I refreshed myself, washed my face, and quickly redid my ponytail. I stuck my room card in my hip pocket and felt the manila envelope once again. There was a safe in the room next to the refrigerator. I wondered if I should put the page in there. As I searched for the instructions, I closed the door on the safe. Reading the code that would open it again, I punched the numbers in and tried to move the handle, but it wouldn't budge. *Oh, that's just great.* I was relieved I hadn't put the page inside before testing it out first.

The phone in my room rang.

Jack and Sumsion must be waiting for me.

I picked up the receiver. "Hello."

"I hope you had a good flight." There was no mistaking the tinny voice. The kidnapper knew we were in Paris.

CHAPTER NINE

"How did you know I was here?" My heart triple beat as my grip on the receiver tightened. I patted myself down, wondering if I had a bug planted on me but came up empty. Then I looked around the room for a camera or anything that seemed suspicious, but how in the world would he know I'd be in this room?

"What happened to the phone I gave you?"

My mind raced. I couldn't tell him Jack pitched it out the car window. Then he'd know I wasn't alone. "I dropped it, and it broke."

"You're lying. I told you I'm watching you." His voice of authority made my skin crawl. "You need to hurry. Your aunt . . ."

"What about Auntie?" I clutched the receiver with both hands, frantic to learn of her condition. "Have you hurt her? Let me speak with her."

"Not yet."

"When? I need to know she's still alive."

"After you find another page."

"Please, let me speak with her. She looked so bad in that text." I envisioned her tied up, beaten, and going without food.

"Your aunt will be fine as long as you do what you're supposed to."

I remembered who Jack suspected the kidnapper was and that if he got in touch with me again, I was to try to get as much information as I could. Hoping I was doing the right thing, I forged ahead. "Are you the Black Prince?"

A long pause followed.

Maybe I'd gone a step too far. What was wrong with me? I shouldn't be doing this. Auntie's life was in danger, and I was trying to . . . what? Be a spy? This was like playing chicken with a semi.

"The two men with you, who are they?" Anger crackled in his voice.

Panic coursed through my veins. I shouldn't have challenged him. But I couldn't take it back. However, I sensed I'd caught him off guard with my question, which meant I had the upper hand. I had to use this to my advantage, to Auntie's advantage. "I needed help to find the pages. If something happens to my aunt, I'll see that the world knows the Black Prince was responsible. Now, let me speak with her."

"No! You need to do more to hear her voice. And notoriety doesn't scare me. I crave it."

And that quickly, I lost the upper hand. The trembling that usually plagued me during stressful times started from within, making me shiver. What could I say? Something to assure him I was doing all I could, something to keep Auntie alive. "I should have the second page shortly."

"Don't test me, Ms. Armstrong. Remember, I'm watching you. The sooner you obtain the pages, the better. I'll be in touch." The phone went dead.

I sank down on the bed. I'd made him angry. No more was I doing what Jack told me to. A blaring beeping noise came from the phone, making me realize I still held it in my hand. I set it in the cradle.

Even though I'd played with fire, I'd learned that, indeed, the Black Prince, whoever he was, had Auntie. Also, reinforced in my mind was the heartlessness of the kidnapper. He enjoyed being cruel.

His voice had sounded a little clearer, not quite so garbled, and I'd detected an English accent. Why would a Brit want to kidnap Auntie? It didn't make sense, but I couldn't sit here and try and figure this out. I had to find the pages.

Plus, I had to tell Jack and Sumsion about the call. I rushed out the door and was about to pound on Jack's, when I saw him down the hall, intensely involved in a conversation with a tall, rather slender woman.

I stepped back into my room and peeked around the corner.

Whatever Jack had told her seemed to calm her. She rose on tiptoes and kissed his cheeks, first one and then the other. She paused a moment, staring into his eyes, then they both got in the elevator.

Who was she? And what had they been talking about?

The door to Sumsion and Jack's room clicked like someone was coming. It had to be the professor since Jack was in the elevator with the woman. I stepped out and greeted Sumsion but couldn't help glancing once again down the hallway.

No Jack.

No woman.

"Ready, my dear?" A caring gleam shone in Sumsion's gaze as he offered me his arm. I smelled the warm, sugar-berry scent of his pipe. He must have taken a few puffs to calm his nerves before heading out on our mission.

I took his arm. "I came out a second ago and saw Jack down the hall with a woman."

"Really? He told me he was going to pull the rental car around and wait for us."

I didn't want to bring up the kisses and sound like I was jealous, mainly because I didn't really know him and, most importantly, because I didn't trust him.

We'd reached the elevator. Sumsion pushed the down button. "Maybe she was a guest in the hotel who had become lost. It's easy to get turned around in these places."

"She kissed him on both cheeks." I couldn't believe I'd blurted what I'd just decided not to tell. And I was right. It did sound a bit jealous; however, it was valid information.

"That's a French thing, my dear. Maybe they are old friends."

"No. This was something more." Okay, that really did sound jealous.

Sumsion inhaled deeply. "There's the rub." A twinkle flickered in his gaze. "Jack is a man who probably has acquaintances all over the world."

The elevator doors opened, and there stood the woman I'd seen with Jack. She looked familiar—tall, slender, even athletic. And then I knew. She looked amazingly like the woman who had held me at gunpoint, except this woman had short blonde hair. My mind must be playing tricks on me.

"*Bonjour*," she said as she stepped from the elevator and we got on.

"*Bonjour*," Sumsion replied.

She looked at me for a minute, as though evaluating me. Maybe she was that same woman in a wig. If so, was she working with Jack? Or the Black Prince? And if that was the case, did Jack work for him as well? The kidnapper sounded English; Jack was Scottish, but that didn't mean anything, did it?

The elevator doors closed, separating us. I turned to Sumsion. "Did you see the way she assessed me?"

"I'm afraid I did." He seemed as taken back as I was. "I must say, she appeared a bit calculating."

"Professor, what if Jack is working for the kidnapper?"

The older man's brow wrinkled. "It does seem he isn't truly CIA."

"The kidnapper called my room."

Sumsion stepped back a little as if the information had pushed him. "Were you able to speak with Marjorie?"

"He refused to let me. Jack told me before that the kidnapper could be someone known as the Black Prince, so I asked him."

"Black Prince?" Sumsion stared off as if he were trying to remember something on the edge of his memory. "Did he say he was that person?"

"Not exactly, but he didn't say he wasn't."

"Oh, my dear." Sumsion rubbed his chest, making me worry that he might be having a heart attack.

What was I thinking, bringing him with us? "Are you okay?"

"A little angina. Nothing to worry about." He pulled a pill bottle from his jacket pocket and put a little white tablet in his mouth. "If the kidnapper goes by the name Black Prince, we may have more trouble than we expected."

"Why?" How could it possibly be worse?

"Because the title came from a very valiant fighter. If the kidnapper goes by that name, it doesn't bode well for our Marjorie." Sumsion chewed on his lip as though missing his pipe.

"What kind of valiant fighter was the Black Prince?" I really didn't want another history lesson, but right now, the information might be very helpful.

"Edward of Woodstock. He lived during the 1300s. He was the eldest son of King Edward III and was made Prince of Wales in 1343."

"Why did people call him the Black Prince?"

"After the Battle of Crécy, he was accoutered in black armor. But I believe it was more than that." Sumsion's face paled.

"Why?"

"Because he pillaged, sacked, and plundered the French countryside on his campaign to Aquitaine, taking no prisoners, killing men, women, and children. He ravaged the land. Some say such actions were all part of war and that the French performed atrocities as well. War brings out the worst in people. I will say this: the man never gave up." He paused a moment, looking to the floor, then gazed up at me. "And you believe our Jack could be working with this modern-day Black Prince?"

My heart sank. "I don't know. But Jack made the reservation. How would the Black Prince know where I was unless he told him?" I waited to see if Sumsion would come to the conclusion I had.

He took a deep breath. "In my day, I've traveled some and have made friends with all sorts of fascinating people. I have a friend in the CIA." The older man nodded as if to confirm that he really did. "Perhaps I should give her a call and see if she can enlighten us about our Jack." The elevator doors opened to the lobby, and there he stood.

"Come on. I left the car in the loading zone." Jack ushered us out of the hotel, through the pouring rain, and to the waiting vehicle. He opened the back door for Sumsion and me to crawl inside, then climbed in behind the wheel. And off we went.

I stared at the back of Jack's head. What was he up to? What was he not telling us about himself? I was grateful Sumsion had connections and could check into Jack, but I still wondered.

The bud of an idea blossomed in my mind. What if the kidnapper had sent him to keep an eye on me and to keep me safe until I had all three pages?

Now, that made sense. Jack could be the kidnapper's guarantee that he'd know where I went and what I did. That had to be it. Well, two could play at that game. Instead of becoming upset, I'd use Jack's knowledge and skills to my advantage and find the pages. My problem was, what would I do with him afterward?

And would he kill Sumsion and me once we finished?

CHAPTER TEN

JACK LET US OUT AT the curb in front of Notre Dame. Then he drove off to find a parking place. I gazed at the French Gothic cathedral that loomed ahead. Pouring rain mixed with a few snowflakes made the flying buttresses and spires of the building appear like a giant ship on a storm-tossed sea.

I pulled the collar of my fleece jacket up around my neck, trying to stay warm. Surprisingly, even in this frigid weather, a long line awaited admittance. Sumsion and I joined them as the deep gong of the cathedral bells rang out and vibrated in my chest. I checked my watch: 1:30 p.m.

Jack quickly found us and opened an umbrella he'd purchased somewhere along the way, giving us shelter. I gazed at his strong hand holding the umbrella handle. A manly hand. A hand that could become lethal. Did he actually know the Black Prince? I had so many questions I wanted to ask him but couldn't. I had to become as cunning and crafty as Jack and his boss. I stood closer to Sumsion.

Organ music eerily drifted from the large building.

"Are they having mass?" I knew Westminster Abbey in London didn't allow visitors during services, so would the French do the same?

Jack shrugged. "Sounds like it."

"And they're still letting tourists walk through?" I found that very hard to believe.

Jack leaned toward me. "The congregation is in the center chapel, facing the high altar. There's plenty of room for visitors tae walk around the periphery, light a prayer candle, or admire the other altars."

"Have you been here before?" I'd never pegged Jack as religious.

"Of course. Though I'm not Catholic, I do admire architecture. I'm sure the professor does as well. I'm surprised you've never been inside. I'm sure you've been tae Paris many times as a flight attendant."

"I've always had other things to do here." Yes, I'd been to Paris a lot. But when I had extra time for myself, I checked out the Louvre or the Eiffel Tower or even the Arc de Triomphe. I went to patisseries, fine restaurants, and pubs. But mostly, I crashed and got my rest for the next flight. "I've ridden by the cathedral but have never taken the time to go inside."

Here I stood outside one of the most famous cathedrals in the world, the cathedral that had stood through several wars, and I'd never toured it. Perhaps my not taking the time showed disrespect to all it represented. If only I'd known that within the walls a secret had been waiting to be discovered. I'd never dreamed this building would become so very important to me. Had it been protecting a page of the *Book of Hours* all this time, through air raids and angry mobs?

"This church has seen a great deal of history," Sumsion said, as if reading my mind.

Oh no. Sumsion was about to give another lesson. Yet, I needed to know all I could. Something had ignited this trouble, and maybe something in history would give me a clue as to why. A new, profound gratitude for Sumsion's wealth of knowledge flooded over me. I gave him my complete attention.

"If memory serves, the Cathedral wasn't completed until 1345." The professor's appraising eyes scanned the Gothic structure. "They'd worked on it since 1163, during the reign of Louis VII. Jeanne lived until 1371. She could have easily had one of her minions hide the page somewhere inside."

"Surely someone would have found it by now." I didn't want to play devil's advocate, especially when Auntie's very life depended on me finding the pages, but someone had to.

"Maybe, maybe not. They tended not to tear things down so much as to build upon them." Sumsion peered at the majestic façade. "Even the famous gargoyles were added later as a means to protect the building from water."

I peered up at one. Gargoyles had always frightened me. That was their intent—to scare. But mainly to scare evil away. More anxious than before, I changed the subject and asked, "How are we going to look for the page with mass going on?"

"I should have explained," Jack whispered, surveying the area around us as if worried someone might overhear. "This is a reconnaissance walk-through.

We'll look for likely places where the page could be and then come back later tonight when no one is here."

"Tonight? But we need to find it now. We can't wait. The Black Prince won't let me speak with Auntie until we have another page."

Jack's brooding stare focused on me. "You've spoken with the kidnapper again?"

"Yes."

"Why didn't you tell me?" His imploring eyes seemed so concerned.

A flash of guilt for thinking that he could be working with the kidnapper pressed down on me. I looked at Sumsion for help.

As if realizing my dilemma, he said, "Son, the truth is we were afraid you could be working with the Black Prince."

"Professor, I understand your questioning my motives, but"—he glared at me—"you? How many times must I prove myself tae you?"

Sumsion looked thoughtfully at Jack, as though he might have jumped the gun in his assessment of him. I was still waffling on my belief that Jack was a double agent, and I wasn't quite ready to abandon the notion. And now his acting had hoodwinked the professor.

I had to put a stop to that. I scowled. "Tell me, how did the kidnapper know to call me in my room? How did he even know I was in Paris? And who was the woman I saw kissing you?"

Jack reared back with my last question.

The line moved forward. People huddled closer.

"I haven't a clue how he knew, but like I've told you before, the Black Prince has vast resources. And there are others besides him who want those pages. As for that other woman, she's a friend. That's all. Please believe me, Skye. I'm on your side."

A couple cut in front of us, mumbling something that ended with *pouah, pouah.* They smiled like they were rubbing our noses in our mistake of not paying attention and leaving a gap in the line.

All the anger I'd kept bottled up for Jack now channeled toward that French couple who giggled to each other. "Did they just call us . . . poop?"

"Je vous demande pardon," Sumsion said to the couple. He seemed unruffled by their bad manners. *"Amoureux se querellent. S'il vous plaît a ouvert la voie."*

The couple giggled again and turned their backs to us. Jack smiled and pulled me close.

I wanted to shove him away, but we'd already drawn some unwanted attention. Instead, I forced myself to endure him. "What did the professor say?"

"He told them we were having a lovers' quarrel and tae please lead the way."

Sumsion shrugged and said, "It's a good cover story. Let's keep our quarrels private. Right now, Marjorie's well-being is top priority, and we must stay focused."

Crushed that Sumsion had chided me for not thinking of Auntie, I said nothing and withdrew from the conversation.

"I hate tae ask this, but I have tae know." Jack looked deeply into my eyes, and I supposed to other people, we appeared to be in a relationship. He went on. "When did the Black Prince contact you?"

"He called while I was in my room. Said he's watching me." I glared at Jack as if to say, "Like you didn't already know."

The line moved, but he kept his arm around my waist as we stepped forward, nearing the doors. I wanted to accuse him of being a double agent, wanted to call him out right there and then, but with so many people milling around, I couldn't. Not now. Especially since he seemed to have Sumsion on his side.

And the truth was, I needed Jack's help. Even if he was here because the kidnapper had sent him, I needed him to help find the page and to keep me safe from the other teams bent on killing me. When we actually had our hands on the prize, I'd make my stand. Until then, I needed to hold in any resentment.

I noticed Sumsion had been watching me and nodded as if he had read my mind and agreed with the conclusion. Which was good. Maybe later, Sumsion could call his CIA source to check on Jack.

We entered the amazing historic church. I scanned the interior, hoping to see something that might lead us to the page. Doubtful it would be above in the vaulted ceiling over the main chapel. Stained-glass windows rimmed the top, leaving no place to stash it. Two stories below them waited archways with Gothic pillars guarding each. The huge three-tiered candelabras that hung from every arch and appeared lit with real candles caught my eye, but mainly because they were so medieval looking.

A sea of parishioners sat in the entire middle section. The organ stopped for a moment as the father said a few words in French and Latin, and then the organ again played, and a choir of heavenly voices joined in.

Smoke came from the high altar and drifted over the crowd. The pageantry of the ceremony made emotion well up in me. I didn't know why. I wasn't Catholic. Maybe every Christian felt a kinship with the rituals and setting.

"Come on." Jack motioned for Sumsion and me to follow him.

We joined the steady stream of visitors flowing down the sides of the main chapel. We went from one altar to another, frantically reading descriptions of each. One was dedicated to Joan of Arc. Another Mary and the Christ child. Still another honored Saint Anne, the next Saint Denis, then Saint Mary Magdalene, and Chapelle Saint Louis.

Sumsion stopped here. "King Louis IX. This might be a likely place."

We trailed Jack into the small chapel. While Jack studied the statue, Sumsion and I tried to divert attention from passersby by pointing out other areas of the small alcove.

Jack rejoined us. "I don't think this is it. There's no place I can see where it could be hidden."

We left the chapel, joining the main throng of tourists slowly making their way around the center. We came to the Chapelle of Saint Charles and stopped again.

"Is this dedicated to Jeanne's husband, King Charles IV?" I said, hopeful this might be the place.

Sumsion pointed to the date. 1570. "The chapelle was built too late."

After that, we came to the exit. We had nothing to show for our effort except frustration. There had been the Chapelle of Saint Louis, but Jack had ruled that out when he'd searched it.

We stepped out into the rain mingled with snow, and I felt like a total and complete failure.

Jack stayed close, trying to shield all three of us from the elements with the umbrella, but he was more in the rain than Sumsion or me. Just when I had set my mind to put him in one category, he did something that made me rethink my judgement of him.

As the three of us walked down the wet, gray sidewalk, my spirits sank lower still. "Poor Auntie. There has to be something we can do."

"Don't be discouraged, my dear." Sumsion patted my arm. "Seeing the chapel of Mary and the Christ child in Notre Dame jogged my memory some. King Charles IV had a statue made for his wife, Jeanne, at pretty much the same time he commissioned the *Book of Hours*. I believe it's in the Louvre, which isn't far in that direction." He pointed with a knobby-knuckled index finger. "Though the page clearly said within the walls of Notre Dame, I wonder if something on that statue might give us further direction of where we could look in the cathedral. If you can stand the cold a little longer to walk over there, it might be well worth a visit."

"I parked the car in a plaza just over the river. It's on the way," Jack said.

At this point, even this little bit seemed encouraging. I gave in. "Yes, why not go?"

My hands felt frozen, despite my sticking them deep inside my jacket pockets. Even though my hair was pulled into a ponytail, my bangs and hair were wet and limp, and my teeth chattered. After crossing the bridge over the River Seine, we came to the car plaza. Jack paid the attendant, and we gratefully got inside the Fiat.

He drove past several busy streets until we arrived at the Louvre. "I noticed a parking spot not far." He braked and let us out.

As I closed the door behind Sumsion, Jack took off.

The Louvre never failed to impress, with the grandeur of its buildings and grounds. The line to go inside seemed to be one giant armada of umbrellas. As Sumsion and I walked toward them, Jack joined us.

"You got the prime parking spot?" I asked but knew the answer.

He nodded as if he'd won a trophy.

Sumsion motioned to us to follow him. "Stay close. I can get us in."

A guard stopped us, but Sumsion straightened him out in a flood of French that left my head spinning. However, when Sumsion finished, instead of making us go to the back of the line, the guard took us to the entrance and even handed each of us a map before leaving.

"What did you say to him?"

"I name-dropped several of the museum's most affluent donators, whom, I might add, I do know and have their permission to visit the site for free whenever I find myself in Paris." Sumsion cleared his throat. "However, I may have stretched the truth a mite by telling him that you are my granddaughter and Jack is your fiancé."

Jack smiled and looked at me.

He knew it irritated me to no end to be coupled with him.

"I'd endure anything if it means getting the pages so I can save Auntie, so don't get all cocky."

He shrugged, yet a playfulness remained in his eyes.

As we walked into the giant main lobby, three great portals were before us: *Richelieu*, *Sully*, and *Denon*. Hanging above a sweeping staircase to the *Richelieu* area was a huge poster of a golden sculpture.

"That's the sculpture Charles gave Jeanne." Sumsion pointed to the poster.

We hurried up the steps, stopping several times for Sumsion to catch his breath. His complexion grew paler. "I'm afraid the brisk walk to get in may have drained my energy somewhat."

"Let alone the tall tale you told the guard," I teased him.

He nodded and shrugged like he agreed but wasn't remorseful in the least.

"I'll go ahead and see if I can tell what direction we need tae take once we reach the top." Jack took off.

"You know, my dear. We may have misjudged the lad. He doesn't seem the type to willingly help us while deceiving us at the same time." The coloring in Sumsion's cheeks was returning. He started up the steps again. "I'll press him after we're finished here. Mark my word, I'll get to the bottom of who he truly is."

I squeezed his arm and then took his hand, giving him what support I could up the last few stairs.

Jack met us. "It's down this way." He guided Sumsion and me past several exhibits to a main walk-through, and a little farther down stood the golden sculpture within protective glass. The Virgin and the child.

"I've seen many shrines of the mother Mary holding her child, but this one is different." Sumsion spoke his thoughts aloud. "See how she smiles and seems affectionate, even playful with her son? The page spoke of a rose. The Christian symbolic meaning of *rose* is 'Mary,' after the Virgin."

I'd never heard that before. I stared at Mary's face, and he was right. She appeared happy, not solemn like she was usually portrayed.

Jack stood behind me, almost too close, but I didn't want to make a scene, so I devoted all my attention to the figurine before us.

"Look at the base." Sumsion pointed. "The separate buttresses are much like Notre Dame's. However, this has scenes of Christ: as a teacher and the Passion, with His crucifixion. *The Book of Hours* has similar scenes, but they aren't on the page we have."

The scenes were on a dark-blue background with figures in colors of emerald-green, yellow, and red on gilded-silver painted in a golden color. Four miniature lions bore the weight of the sculpture.

"Is she holding a fleur-de-lis?" Jack's voice startled me, even though I knew he stood behind me.

Several people walked past.

"Ah, yes. The fleur-de-lis is often used to represent French monarchy. It's also associated with the Holy Trinity or the Virgin Mary because it represents purity and chastity as well. That they are part of the statue means the figure is holy." Sumsion nodded as if this bit of history made total sense.

As I stared at the piece, my eyes were drawn to the child. His hand reached up and touched His mother's face in a loving, tender way. I couldn't help but think of my own mother. She had always been kind and caring. She had loved to cook, and on days when she'd made bread, she would cook frybread and smother it with some of her homemade currant jelly. I remembered watching her slender hands knead the dough.

"Look at how the gold folds with her clothes." Jack pointed to the veil around Mary's shoulders. "It seems tae drape her." He pointed to the bottom. "The base has words written in French, but I can't make them out. Professor, what does this say? Is it a clue tae where the other pages might be hidden?"

The older man leaned forward, studying what Jack had pointed out. "It merely states the obvious, that this is the mother and Christ child. There's something about Saint Denis. I believe the sculpture was first donated to the abbey of Saint Denis by Jeanne d'Évreux." Sumsion straightened. "Now that's a possibility. That's where most of France's nobility is buried, but the page we have plainly said Notre Dame." He looked up at me.

"Still, maybe there's something there that could give us a hint as to where the page could be hidden inside Notre Dame. It's worth a try. Before we break into the cathedral, we need to know exactly where to look. Where is Saint Denis Abbey?" I was ready to go there right now.

"The outskirts of Paris." Jack answered for Sumsion. He took several pictures of the sculpture with his phone.

"Let's go." I started to walk away but realized I was alone.

Jack had hung back. He nodded at Sumsion like I'd forgotten someone. "Chances are that it's closed by now."

Sumsion's face had turned pale again. It had been awhile since we'd eaten. Mix that with the long plane ride and both were taking a toll on the older man.

"How about we grab a bite to eat first?" I pulled out the map the guard had given us. "There's a bakery, a tea room, and even a restaurant with traditional French cuisine here at the Louvre."

"A capital idea, my dear," Sumsion said. "But I think this old man needs to rest a spell. Do you mind if we head back to the hotel?" Always the gentleman, even when he felt lousy, he held out his arm for me.

"Of course not." I took his arm.

Before making the turn to the staircase, I looked back at the statue. A knowing stirred inside me. We were on the right track. I wondered if Mother Mary and her child agreed.

The real question was, Would the kidnapper? Somehow, I had a feeling he'd been watching us all day. And as much as I wanted to think the best of Jack, something deep inside me told me he was the eyes.

CHAPTER ELEVEN

JACK LEFT AHEAD OF US to collect the Fiat and met Sumsion and me as we left the Louvre's grounds. Sumsion and I got in the back.

As Jack drove through the Paris streets, I gazed out the window through the rain sheeting the town. Every building looked the same. Well, not the cathedrals and churches, but the regular stores. They were all a buff, tannish color, and all had black roofs. I thought of my home. My home and Auntie's. The homeowners' association had definite guidelines of what residents could do to the outside of their homes. There must have been a pretty strict building code in Paris that went way back. I had a hard time placing where we were without being able to differentiate what each building was when I first looked at it.

Jack pulled up to our hotel, and I helped Sumsion out and offered him my arm. He chuckled and accepted, and we hurried inside out of the rain while Jack parked.

"I trust you had a good day, *oui?*" the concierge said. Did the man seem overly friendly, or was I just being sensitive?

"Capital, my good man." Sumsion gave him a nod.

As we reached the elevator, Jack caught up to us and got on. Though he'd closed the umbrella, raindrops leaked from it onto the floor. I tapped my room card on the elevator keypad, then pressed nine.

"Why don't you two go to dinner?" Sumsion looked at Jack and then me. "You could bring me back something to eat. I'm sure once I've had a nap, I'll be recharged and ready to go."

"We can wait for you." The kidnapper knew where we were. However, he wanted us to find the pages. And he knew Sumsion was helping me, so logically he wouldn't hurt him. The image of Auntie passed out came to mind. I really didn't know what the Black Prince was capable of doing. He might kill Sumsion just for kicks. Or kidnap him as well. And the other teams who had been chasing me wanted to kill me, so Professor Sumsion's life was also in danger. "I don't think it's wise to separate. The people who were trying to kill me back home could have followed us."

"Your concern over my well-being is very touching. But you, my dear, are the one they're after. Not this old man. I'll be fine. Please, go. Eat. And recharge your energy. When I awaken, we'll head to Saint Denis." The elevator doors opened. "I can see myself to the room, thank you." He stepped off and turned to me. "And I'll take care of that other matter we discussed earlier today."

Before I could reply, the elevator doors closed, leaving me alone with Jack. Sumsion must have meant he'd call his friend in the CIA. That was another reason for me to be alone with Jack, so Sumsion could set in motion the wheels to learn the truth.

"What was that all about?" Jack glared down at me.

"It's something he wanted to do for Auntie. No big deal. Where do you want to eat?" I hoped that would move him off the subject.

"I don't think we should go tae far from the hotel. I saw several open restaurants down the street. I'm sure we can find something." He guided me to the exit, and as we stepped out, he opened the umbrella, giving us both shelter as we made our way down the rain-slick sidewalk.

Pierre's Pizza Palace was the first one we came to. Jack looked at me. I shrugged.

"We're in Paris, yet pizza sounds good," he said.

"To me too."

We hurried inside. Jack released the tension of the umbrella and looked toward the rear of the building and the back door just as a waiter met us.

"Table for two?" The thick French accent belonged to a tall, slender young man, a white waiter's apron tied snugly around his thin middle. He looked all of eighteen.

Ah, someone who spoke English. Right away, I relaxed a little more as he guided us to a table for two not far from the door. A long bench seat went the length of the wall, with tables for two and four in front of it. Wire chairs rested opposite the tables and bench.

"Could we have this one, please?" Jack pointed to a table for four. The restaurant only had two other couples. The French normally didn't eat this early in the evening, so the main crowd hadn't arrived yet.

"Oui. May I start you with a fine bottle of wine?" the waiter asked as I sat on the bench seat facing the room and door.

Instead of sitting in the chair across, Jack came around and sat on the bench next to me. "Would you like some?" He acted as if sitting beside me was normal.

"No thanks."

Jack glanced at the waiter. "I think we'll pass."

The waiter handed us the menus and left.

Even though I was hungry, I didn't open it. "Why are you sitting right here?" It felt awkward to have him so close.

"We both need tae keep our backs tae the wall. You don't mind, do you?" He checked out the huge window looking out onto the street, then, satisfied, perused the menu without waiting for my reply.

Perhaps he thought the question rhetorical.

He pointed to a picture of noodles. "They also offer pasta dishes. Cheese ravioli with cream sauce looks good." Again, he checked out the window, ever on the alert.

"Do they issue you your CIA credentials when you're sworn in?"

He reached for the back pocket of his slacks and pulled out his billfold. "Let me see if there's a date on it. It bothers me that you don't trust what I tell you." His thumb rubbed the leather edge of his wallet.

"Why should I?"

He set the wallet on top of the menu on the table and folded his arms. His face bore a five o'clock shadow, making him appear a little scruffy. "Cos, while it is my job tae keep you safe, I want tae help bring you and your aunt safely home. And know this. I don't give up. Ever. Not until my mission is accomplished."

In the restaurant's dim lighting, accompanied by the flickering flame of the candle on our table, his blue eyes seemed darker. He seemed sincere and like he genuinely cared, so much so that I believed him and even wondered what it would be like to actually have a relationship with him. But I couldn't let my emotions rule my thoughts.

What was the matter with me? I couldn't afford to let down my guard. I had to snap out of it.

My gaze fell on his billfold. Trust but verify. I'd heard that somewhere, and it seemed to make a lot of sense right now. I could grab his billfold and study it for myself, but then I realized he was testing me. Why? I didn't know. Maybe in some strange way, he wanted to know if *he* could trust *me*.

Which was a crazy notion. Again, I wondered what I would do without Jack's help. I had Sumsion, but his stamina could only take him so far, and then he needed to rest. What Jack had just said about wanting to make sure Auntie and I returned safely home had touched my heart. If it was only my life and not Auntie's too, I could take the chance and trust his every word. But something stopped me.

I just wanted to feel better about him. I fisted my hand to stop from reaching for his wallet because at that moment, I wanted to grab the stupid thing and check for myself. Chiding myself for softening, I became irritated. How dare he test me? Who did he think he was, testing me, of all people?

"But you can understand my position, can't you?" I looked into his deep blue eyes, trying my best to be earnest. "I mean, with so many people wanting to get their hands on the page, combined with Auntie's kidnapping and my being shot at, you can surely see why I would want solid proof as to who you are. And you should know the date your badge was given to you."

He shrugged like maybe he understood a little, then said, "You still have the page, right?"

Having it on me for so long, I'd become used to it being there. "Of course. But there you go again."

"What do you mean?" He leaned against the wall. "I'm still here. I haven't left my seat."

"You're being difficult and trying to distract me. Open the stupid billfold and look at the date." I glared at him, willing him to give me this one request.

With a deep sigh, he picked it up. As he began to open it, the waiter returned, making him quickly fold it and stuff it back in his pocket.

"Have you decided?" The waiter looked to me and then Jack.

I hadn't opened the menu, and though I was hungry, my stomach felt raw and queasy.

"I'll have the ravioli. Does that come with a salad?" Jack pointed to the item on the menu.

"No, sir. But I can add it."

"Please do."

"Anything to drink?"

"You don't happen tae have sugar-free Irn-Bru, do you?"

A huge smile crossed the waiter's young face. "Oui. The manager has Scottish connections. But it is not sugar free."

"Okay. I'll have that."

"Very well, sir." The youthful waiter looked to me.

Not wanting to prolong his standing over us, I said, "I'll have what he's having."

"Very good, madam. I'll bring your drinks right away." The waiter retrieved our menus and left.

"Okay, hand it over." I held out my hand.

Jack tilted his head and gave me a lazy smile. "He's coming back. Wait until he delivers the soda, then I *promise* I'll show you."

I shrugged as if I didn't believe him, but whatever.

He gazed out the window again, checking the street.

The waiter returned with two orange cans and two glasses. He set them on our table. "Your dinner will be ready in a few minutes. Is there anything else I can get for you?"

"No, we're fine, thank you," Jack answered for both of us.

Alone again, he popped open my drink and poured it in my glass, his sad effort to soften me up.

Not to be outdone, I opened his can and poured his drink.

"Why, thank you." He picked up the glass to take a sip.

I did as well.

"Have you ever had Irn-Bru?" He looked at me, glass raised.

"No."

"You might want tae read the warning label." He took a long swallow.

I held the can close to the candle and scanned through the warning, stopping at: *may have an adverse effect on activity and attention in children.* I'd never seen such a warning. "What is in this?"

Jack set his glass down. "This drink makes kids hyperactive. Has lots and lots of sugar. But with everything we need tae do tonight, I thought it would be a good boost of energy."

I slowly took a sip. It tasted like very rich cream soda.

"Okay, now—"

Jack suddenly sat straight up. "That guy"—he pointed to a man in a hoodie and baggy jeans—"he's walked past four times. And each time, he's peered in at us. I don't like it."

I couldn't see the man's face. "What should we do?"

Jack stood and helped me to my feet. "Go out the back door. Walk slowly; we don't want him tae know that we're on tae him."

It was all I could do to not run, to act casual.

Jack hustled me forward. "He's coming in and has a gun. Run!"

Jack had ditched the gun he'd had in the States before we'd left. We were defenseless. I rushed forward and bumped into our startled waiter, making him drop a tray full of food. I wanted to stop and apologize, but instead, I lunged for the back door.

CHAPTER TWELVE

BURSTING THROUGH THE PIZZA PALACE'S back door into the rain-drenched alleyway that seemed to go on forever, I felt we would never make it to the main street and safety before the man caught us.

Jack's arm came around me, guiding me over the paver bricks, quickening my pace. Rain soaked our heads and ran down our faces. In our haste to leave, Jack had left the umbrella behind. I looked for a dumpster to hide behind, but there was none. What kind of alleyway was this? Not a single dumpster in sight.

Jack pulled me into a very small, darkened entryway on our right. We stood face-to-face, breathing heavily from running. His warm breath fanned my cheeks. I caught a whiff of Irn-Bru and wistfully thought of the relatively calm moment we had just shared in the restaurant.

A door slammed.

Angry male voices speaking French echoed up the alley. The man with the hoodie had an accomplice.

Jack moved closer, pinning me against the threshold as if to shield me should we be found. My heart raced, nearly exploding. A chill rippled up my spine, making me shiver.

Heavy footfalls slapped the pavers. They were coming.

I hoped Jack would know what to do if we were discovered, and then I prayed that the men would go by.

They passed us, running. By some miracle, they hadn't seen us.

I expected Jack to move away, but he didn't. He stayed where he was. Quietly, he said, "Let's wait a little longer until they're out of the alley."

His body heat warmed me, calming my nerves. I wanted to say something but didn't dare. I hadn't been this close to him since he'd saved me from being run over at the airport. And at the time, I hadn't known much about him. The fact was, I still didn't.

However, I did know I couldn't stay this close to him. I'd become keenly aware of his broad shoulders and muscular build. Keenly aware that his skin smelled like sandalwood, some kind of spicy berry, and . . . was that lavender? Whatever it was, the combination of the tantalizing scents made me want to draw him closer, to have him protect me for the rest of my life.

What?

"I think they're gone." He stepped away.

Disappointed, I snapped out of it when he motioned for me to follow him down the alley in the opposite direction the men had gone.

"We don't have a lot of time." Jack looked up and down the alley. "Chances are they'll come back when they realize they've lost our trail."

All notions of being attracted to him fled as we hurried down the wet alley. Coming out onto the busy street, we continued to make our way back to the hotel. We came to a grocery store, and Jack pulled me into it.

"We still need tae eat, and Professor Sumsion needs something as well."

"But what if the men who were after us have found him? The kidnapper knew where we were staying. I think we need to make sure he's all right first." A sharp something's-wrong feeling balled up in my gut. At least I hadn't heard the voice.

"It will only take a few minutes. If they have him, they'll be waiting for us anyway, and if not, we might as well eat something. Let's split up and meet at the check-out." He left me standing there before I could object.

Fine. I'll look for something to eat.

I grabbed a bag of croissants and a small jar of jam. The bread would help take the edge off our hunger, and sweet jam would be a nice complement. Next, I added several Snickers candy bars. A sad substitute for protein, but on the run, they would give us energy. I met Jack at the cashier. He had several large bottles of water and a bag that said Jack Link's Beef Jerky. Of course he'd go for the brand with his name on it.

We paid for our purchases and hustled out into the rain. It had let up a little and turned to a drizzle. Spying our hotel's sign a block ahead across the street, we cut over and quickly made our way in. Jack kept checking behind us. Again, I realized with sharp clarity that I really needed his help.

The elevator seemed to crawl to the ninth floor, but eventually we made it and flew down the hall to Jack and Sumsion's room. Jack pulled out his keycard and tapped it on the handle. The little green light flashed, and he opened the door.

The room was dark and had the warm, fruity scent of Sumsion's pipe tobacco.

If he was sleeping, of course the room would be dark, but if someone were holding a gun to him, it could be dark as well, especially if they were waiting to ambush us.

Jack looked at me. "I'd say ladies first, but I think in this case, I'll go in ahead of you."

"Be my guest. It's your room." I gladly let him pass.

"Is that the troops come to retrieve this old man?" A light clicked on near the twin bed as Sumsion sat up. His cheeks had more color, and his eyes weren't quite so puffy from lack of sleep.

Once we set the groceries on the desk, Jack disappeared into the bathroom. This was my chance to talk with Sumsion alone. "Did you call your source in the CIA?" I whispered.

A grim expression wrinkled his brow. "Indeed, I did, my dear. She could not substantiate that he worked for the agency. But she reminded me that some agents are on secret teams, kind of like black ops. Maybe that's what Jack is."

I sank down on the bed beside Sumsion. "I think he genuinely wants to help me and Auntie. What are we going to do?"

He slipped his stocking feet into his brown Florsheim shoes and tied them. "I suggest we play along. If he has another motivation, we'll find out soon enough. In the meantime, we need to do all we can to save our sweet Marjorie."

I knew he was right because I'd pretty much arrived at the same conclusion. I noticed that the pill bottle with his little white tablets rested on the night stand between the twin beds. It read nitroglycerin.

Sumsion checked the grocery bags and pulled out the croissants and jam. "Dinner, I suppose?"

Trying to act like I hadn't noticed his medication, I said, "We ran into a bit of trouble at the restaurant." As he opened the bag and jar, I told him about the men who had chased us.

"You two were blessed to get away." He set the food on the desk and rubbed his chin. "Could I take another look at the page? I thought of something just before I took my nap, and I want to check it out."

I pulled the manila envelope from beneath my shirt. The drops of blood from the man who'd ordered me killed had now stained it with brownish-red streaks.

Jack came back. His eyes went to the page. "What's going on?" he asked as he stepped to the sink in the wash room to clean his hands.

"I wanted to check something." Sumsion slipped on his bifocals, turned on the desk light, and studied the small page beneath the plastic page protector.

I was still amazed by the artifact's beauty and the intricate details on such a small piece of vellum.

"I thought this said within the walls of the *mother* of Notre Dame. But it doesn't. I thought that right there"—he pointed to what looked like an *m* with all the scrolling—"I think that's a *p*, so instead of it saying within the wall of the *mater* of Notre Dame, it says the *pater*, which in Latin means 'father.' And that's an entirely different direction." He nodded, and the tiny flyaway hairs on top of his silvery head moved back and forth.

"What difference does that make?" Jack peered over Sumsion's shoulder at the page.

"It means, my dear boy, that we went to the wrong church. We should have gone to Sainte-Chapelle." Sumsion carefully placed the page back between the cardboard and slid them into the envelope, handing it to me. I returned it to its hiding spot.

Sumsion picked up his croissant that he'd abandoned and gave a wistful look at the jam.

Jack pulled a handy gadget from his pocket that had several blades and drew the longest one out, giving it to Professor Sumsion.

"Where did you get that? You didn't have it when we got on the plane." I knew he'd never be allowed on board with something regarded as a weapon.

"I have my ways." Jack opened the jam and set it down so Sumsion could garnish his bread.

Jack Duncan had *many* ways about him I didn't understand; it was driving me crazy.

He sat on the other twin bed. "Where is this Sainte-Chapelle?"

"That's the thing." Sumsion dramatically rolled his eyes. "We passed it as we made our way from Notre Dame to the Louvre. It's on Boulevard du Palais." Sumsion licked jam off his fingers.

I picked a croissant for myself. "It's probably not open now. It's 9:00 p.m."

"Doesn't matter. I can get us in." Jack chose a croissant for himself.

"You mean break in?" I looked at Jack.

He shrugged his shoulders.

Then I looked at Professor Sumsion.

The older man nodded. "Sorry, my dear, but he's right. It's probably best that no one else be there." Sumsion got another croissant.

"But there have to be guards." I wasn't trying to throw up roadblocks. I wanted to find the other page more than anyone here, but we also couldn't find it if we were thrown in jail.

"Leave the guards tae me." Jack consumed his croissant in four bites. After he swallowed, he said, "But we better get a move on. Those two goons who tried tae catch Skye and me at the restaurant will probably be banging on our door any minute now. It would be best if we were gone before they arrived."

No wonder he'd snarfed down his food.

Again, the knot in my stomach twisted. This nightmare was far from over, but we were getting closer. At least, it felt like we were. Jack stored the jerky in his jacket pocket. I slipped into flight-attendant mode and hurriedly brushed crumbs off the desk and stuck the empty bag in the garbage.

I handed Sumsion and Jack a candy bar. "Just in case we need to eat something. Who knows what's going to happen to us next?"

Sumsion's eyes grew big at the sight of the candy. He stored it in his jacket pocket. Snickers must be his favorite.

"Maybe I should check my room, make sure I haven't left anything," I said as we exited.

At that moment, the elevator doors opened. Two men got out and headed our way.

"No time." Jack shoved me toward the emergency-exit staircase.

CHAPTER THIRTEEN

WE SPRINTED DOWN THE RUSTY metal stairs a couple of floors, then Jack had us dodge back into the hotel and hurry to the elevators. It seemed to take forever as we waited for one to arrive. Worry nagged me. What if the guys chasing us were in the elevator?

It dinged. The doors slid open, and the compartment appeared empty.

We got in, and as I pushed the ground-floor button, Jack said, "I'll get the car. You two don't wait; start walking down the street. I'll find you."

The doors slid open on the ground floor. Jack bolted through the lobby and out the front door while Sumsion and I hastily followed. The tall, meticulously dressed concierge looked at us with concern. "Is everything all right?"

"Oui. We're out to see the city," Sumsion said as we passed without stopping to chat.

"Have a good time." The concierge smiled. "The rain has stopped. Paris is beautiful at night."

We pushed out the doors. No sign of Jack.

"Let's do as Jack said." I guided Sumsion down the street, the heavy scent of rain all around.

I checked behind us, looking for the black Fiat and also knowing that at any second the two men after us could appear.

Headlights reflected off the puddled road, heading our way. Jack pulled to a stop, and we climbed in, but this time, Sumsion sat in the front with Jack. We sped off just as a couple of men dashed out of the hotel.

Jack peered into the rearview mirror, then leaned back in his seat. Since he relaxed a little, he must be confident no one was following us.

"I imagine you plugged our destination into the GPS?" I had to double-check.

"Of course." Jack fell quiet.

None of us spoke as he skillfully drove through the ever-confusing streets. The night concierge had been right. Paris lights reflecting off the wet road seemed dazzling.

"The city really is quite beautiful, isn't it?" I said.

"There's a reason they call it the City of Lights." Jack peered out the window and once again checked the rearview mirror.

Sumsion turned in his seat, trying to look at us both as he spoke. "It might interest you to know that the city actually earned that reputation because Paris was the birthplace of the Age of Enlightenment. However, I must admit, in modern times, the title comes more from the wattage perspective."

Leave it to Sumsion to even know about Paris history. The man was a wealth of knowledge. My thoughts went to Auntie. Again, worry grew. This entire quest to find the pages was taking longer than I would have liked it to. I needed to get to Auntie. Was the kidnapper a doctor? Why would a doctor be involved in this? For that matter, why were Auntie and I involved?

Auntie had the page, so I had one answer, but it only multiplied my questions. Why? Why did she have the page? Why had she kept it a secret? Why? Why? Why?

Jack pulled over and parked. We'd arrived at Palais de la Cité. As I got out, I studied our surroundings. A huge Gothic building with fencing loomed to the right. But nothing looked like a cathedral. Maybe I was searching for something as foreboding as Notre Dame, which automatically drew the eye. Just as I thought this, midway in the complex, I saw a dark, towering steeple above a cathedral basking in light. That had to be it.

Sumsion noticed me staring. "Not exactly as awe-inspiring as Notre Dame, but wait until we get inside."

"How are we going to do that?" Movement across the street drew my attention. A man in a hoodie stood in the shadows. He wasn't as tall as the other men who had chased us. And he was merely standing there, watching. I nudged Jack's arm and tilted my head in the man's direction.

Jack understood and looked, then leaned over, speaking with both Sumsion and me. "We're being watched. You and the professor act natural and start walking down tae the church. I'll discreetly hang back and take care of him."

What did he mean by "take care of him"? Kill him, like he had the Frenchman in Elizabeth's house? I hoped not.

Sumsion took my arm and looped it with his, and we all three began to walk down the sidewalk. "Did you know that Palais de la Cité was the residence and seat of royal power at one time?" Sumsion was trying to take my mind off the ugly business Jack had to do.

In fact, Jack had slipped away already, leaving Sumsion and me vulnerable.

Stop.

I couldn't think like that, so I played along with Professor Sumsion. "I had no idea." I wanted to look behind us to see what Jack was doing but didn't dare.

"Yes." Sumsion cleared his throat. "I believe it was King Louis IX, who, by the way, became Saint Louis, and his likeness is said to be in Jeanne's *Book of Hours*, but I digress. Anyway, he had Sainte-Chapelle built to house his relics of the Passion of Christ, the most famous of which was the Crown of Thorns. That one artifact cost the king more than building the entire chapel."

I would have been more fascinated with the story if I hadn't been so concerned with what Jack was doing. What if the hoodie guy had overpowered him? Then Sumsion and I would be on our own.

"Louis IX added prestige to France, and Paris was viewed as the New Jerusalem and became the second capital of Christianity."

"You don't say." Where was Jack?

"During the French Revolution, though, a great deal of damage was done to Sainte-Chapelle because it became a symbol of divine-right royalty. However, the stained-glass windows remained intact. Even during the bombing of World War II, they were spared."

I heard a scuffle behind us and whipped around. Jack and the man trailing us were going at each other. But it looked like the man was merely defending himself and yelling, "*Arrêtez! Arrêtez!*"

Jack stopped his arm midswing. "Raphael? Is that you?"

"Oui!"

"What the . . . ?" Jack threw his arms around the man, who stood a half foot shorter than he. He motioned for us to join them.

Not knowing what the deal was, we retraced our steps.

"This is my friend Raphael Dubois."

I nodded hello while Sumsion shook the man's hand.

"But that wasn't you chasing us at the restaurant or in the hotel?"

"Ez possible. Could be my men." He spoke with a bit of a French accent.

"But why?" Jack did not sound as baffled as I felt.

"One of them see you in zee airport. Never good for business when agent from foreign authorities visits Paris. We watch you, but so do many others. Zee concierge at Hotel Merci has men who also watch you."

I thought of the tall meticulously dressed man who had wished us well tonight. Bad guys were everywhere. But what did this guy mean by foreign authorities in reference to Jack? Unable to contain myself, I asked, "What's he talking about?"

"I'll explain later." Jack turned back to his friend. "I actually could use your help. We need tae get into Sainte-Chapelle."

"This night?" Raphael looked at all three of us like we were crazy.

"Has tae be tonight. Someone's life depends on it. And once we find what we're after, we'll leave town."

The man pulled at his bottom lip, shifting from one foot to the other as he thought. He stopped. "Others chase you, no?"

Jack tilted his head. "Quite a few people, actually."

"You seek treasure?"

"Come on, Raphael. You owe me. I saved your bacon in Monte Carlo. That casino owner would have fed you tae his dogs." Jack folded his arms.

The man shrugged as though Jack had made his point. "Un moment." He hurried down the street, leaped up on the fencing, and catapulted over the top, then disappeared into the shadows.

"Just who is this guy?" I asked Jack.

"He's helped me before." Jack peered through the darkness as if trying to see him.

I tried to see him as well but could only make out inky darkness.

"Can he be trusted?" Sumsion asked.

"He knows if he crosses me, it would be bad for his business." Jack still stared off into the darkness around the cathedral.

"What kind of business?" I asked.

Jack turned to me. "He and his men operate on the shady side of the law."

"You've got to do better than that. My aunt's life is at stake here."

"He's a con man and is also into petty theft. Nothing big—more annoying, if anything. And since his business has never been a threat tae national security, I've used him a couple times tae help me. And in exchange, I sometimes turn a blind eye tae what he's doing."

"Nothing like being vague."

"That's part of my job, being vague. It's usually for your own good."

We heard footfalls, and then Raphael was unlocking the gate and letting us inside. He quickly closed it again and led the way to the chapel's ground-floor entrance.

He opened the heavy door with keys he'd gotten from somewhere or somebody. I didn't ask.

Jack handed Sumsion his cell phone with the flashlight turned on. I followed Sumsion in. But Jack remained behind.

"Thanks. I owe you," he said to his friend.

"Oui, you owe me, so I come with you." Raphael closed the door behind us.

"Okay," Jack begrudgingly agreed. "But you cannot tell anyone what you see us doing."

Raphael shrugged.

"No, my friend. You must promise," Jack pressed.

"Promise." He held up his hands, palms facing Jack.

At the end of the room, a light shone on a statue that stood about as tall as Jack. I felt drawn to the figure, mesmerized. "Who is this?" I asked Sumsion.

"Could be King Louis since he is the one who had the building constructed. A pity that over the years, his hands have been broken off. This is the lower chapel where the king would have his servants worship." Sumsion shined the flashlight around the room.

Along both walls, the pillars had blue background with gold fleur-de-lis symbols all over them. They supported small archways. Behind the archways stood a wall—the top half of which had been painted with what looked like dark-tan and white flowers with blue centers; the bottom half had red and green circles with Gothic-looking lions and eagles on them. As I moved deeper into the room and closer to the illuminated statue, other pillars appeared to be painted red with what looked like tiny golden crowns.

"I don't see a place where the pages could be hiding down here. Why don't we try upstairs?" Jack had stayed behind and had somehow found an entrance to a very small circular stairway.

Sumsion and I hurried over. I had Sumsion go first, wanting to make sure he was okay and not left behind. Besides, only he would know if we were on the right trail or not. He paused several times, catching his breath, but we made it to the second floor and stood in a vast cathedral chapel. The building's night lights hitting the cathedral from outside illuminated the stained-glass windows that lined the room nearly to the top of the arched wooden ceiling. Sumsion directed the light over them, intensifying their rich colors. Awestruck, I gazed up at the spectacle.

At the end of the cathedral stood a platform with beautifully carved archways around it. In the center rested a grand piano with a blue covering draping it. Sumsion moved the light to the floor. Intricate tiles with pictures of scrolled flowers were on backgrounds of reddish-pink colors, while others had backgrounds of green with scrolling around a dog. These made a type of frame around the white-tiled floor, with green squares in each corner. Another area of the floor had bigger tiles with castles and fleur-de-lis designs.

"Where could the pages be?" Jack asked as he studied the room.

"Pardon?" Raphael asked.

As if irritated that his newfound friend questioned him, Jack pointed to the stairs we'd just come up. "Why don't you keep watch?"

Raphael grumbled to himself as he retreated down the steps.

"*Look up,*" a voice close to me said. I recognized it right off but had to be certain. I turned. Sumsion's attention was elsewhere. So was Jack's.

I looked above the other end of the cathedral where a rose stained-glass window was set high in the wall. Lights from the outside reflected through. The words on the page pressed against my back said something about a rose and a secret from the world.

Biblical scenes were portrayed in each petal shape. Mesmerized, I walked toward it.

"What is it?" Sumsion shined the light up.

"Do you suppose that is the rose from the page?" I stared at him.

He stared at me and then the window again. "Yes. It also mentions an angel holding an open book, and look." He pointed to a petal above us with an angel and a book. "'What angel wakes me from my flowery bed.'"

"What are you going on about?" Jack joined us.

"A phrase from Shakespeare seemed appropriate." Sumsion gazed at me. "Maybe not." He turned his attention back to the quest.

Jack stared at the window as well. "But what does that mean?"

"It means, my dear boy, we are in the right place. Now the challenge is, where would the queen have hidden the page?" Sumsion moved the light down the walls.

I still remained focused on the angel holding the book. "Is she pointing to something?" Jack had Sumsion shine the light where he thought the angel was looking. But her gaze seemed directed at another stained-glass window with a king.

"That's King Louis." Sumsion rubbed his chin with his free hand.

"Didn't you tell me that King Louis had this cathedral built?" I didn't know where I was going with this train of thought, but I felt like I was on to something.

Sumsion nodded.

I thought of when we'd first entered the building. "And wasn't there a statue of him on the ground floor when we came in the lower chapel?"

Jack started for the circular stairs, with Sumsion and me hot on his heels. We thumped down the steps to the chapel. When we came near, we slowed, almost in reverence and awe, as we made our way to the illuminated statue.

"What do you think the base he stands on is made of?" Jack reached to touch it, but Sumsion stopped him.

"Wait, my son. There might be alarms attached."

"*Non.*" The voice came from behind. Raphael had joined us. "No alarm. I checked."

I didn't like that Raphael was with us but could do nothing about it, and we were so close to discovering another page, I didn't want to stop and worry about him. Jack didn't seem concerned with his friend being here.

Jack tapped on the base of the statue. It sounded hollow. "Raphael, come help me."

"What are you going to do?" I watched as Jack got on one side of the statue and Raphael on the other.

"We're going tae lift the king off the base and see what's inside, if anything." He gazed at the statue as though looking for a good place to hold. He grabbed an arm and leg. "Seems like in seven hundred years the statue would have been moved before. If something had been inside the base, it would have been discovered, but we need to know for sure."

Jack and Raphael tried to lift just the statue, but the base was attached. Actually, it looked like part of the statue itself, so why did it sound hollow?

They carefully set it back in position.

"You're right, my boy." Sumsion stared at the base. "It would have been moved for renovation or even to clean. But I wonder . . ." He knocked near the bottom, like Jack had before. It definitely sounded hollow. "Would you good fellows lay the statue down on the floor?"

Jack and Raphael did as asked, very carefully tilting the statue over until it rested on the tiles.

Sumsion shone the light on the bottom of the base. It appeared solid, no lines. "Anyone have a hammer?"

"Professor, you can't be thinking of smashing the bottom open." If this statue was made when the chapel was built, it too was priceless.

"You'd better believe I am. I'd break the statue in half if I thought it would help save Marjorie."

He was right. What was I thinking? My poor Auntie could already be dead, but if she wasn't, she was certainly near death's doors, and if the other page was inside this statue, then yes, the bottom needed to be opened. "But what if we're wrong?"

Jack and Raphael searched around the chapel. By the small merchandise stand where tourists could purchase little tokens to remember their visit, Jack found a screwdriver. "This might help."

He brought it over, handing it to Sumsion.

"Here, my dear, hold the light." He handed me the cell phone to shine the light while he worked.

Jack and Raphael squatted beside Sumsion as he knelt and started chipping a small hole in the bottom.

I heard a noise outside the building. "Someone's coming."

Raphael leaped up and scurried out the door.

"Don't worry. He'll take care of it." Jack grabbed my hand, redirecting the light where Sumsion worked.

He finally broke through. The hole was big enough for him to stick a few fingers inside. "I feel something . . . like a clay jar." Sumsion's hand started shaking. Either he was having regrets about defacing an antiquity, or he was excited.

Jack took the screwdriver from him. "Let me have a go at it."

"Be careful. I don't want to cause any unnecessary damage." Sumsion sat back and let Jack continue his work.

He was just as careful as Sumsion, which surprised me.

I hadn't heard anything since Raphael had disappeared. What was going on out there?

Jack worked and worked until he was able to put his hand inside the base. "You're right, Professor. There is a clay jar." He pulled out the ancient-looking vessel, and small bits of grit and grime fell to the floor.

He handed it to Sumsion. He took the lid off the wide-mouthed terracotta jar, then looked up at me. "My dear, could I see the light?"

I handed it to him. He shined it inside the small container. "Success! It appears another page is within. And in very good condition."

"I don't like that Raphael has been gone so long. Let's clean this up and get out of here." Jack stared at the door as if he thought at any moment we'd be found.

I took the jar. I couldn't very well put it in the same place I had the envelope, but I could shield it a little by hiding it beneath my fleece jacket.

Jack and Sumsion struggled to right the statue and smooth away evidence of our work and barely managed just before Raphael rushed in.

"*Flics!*" he said.

"What are *flics?*" I asked with the underlying suspicion that this was going to be very bad for us.

"The police." Jack stared at the door.

CHAPTER FOURTEEN

"WHAT ARE WE GOING TO do?" I scanned the small chapel, seeing no way out.

If they found we were stealing a priceless antiquity from the chapel, we'd go to jail, plain and simple. We were going to be arrested.

"My dear, don't panic." Sumsion put his arm around me. But I could see fear in his eyes as well. If we were caught, his reputation would be in tatters. His life's work ruined.

Jack turned to Raphael. "You know your way under, over, and around this city. How do we get out of here?"

The slender Frenchman thought for a moment. "I not certain. But this cost you."

"That's a given." Jack glared at him.

Raphael went to the circular stairs leading to the upper chapel. "Follow *moi*. A secret passage zee king used may be hidden in upper chapel."

"Of course." Sumsion followed, with Jack and me close behind.

We trailed Raphael to the far end, up on the platform where the grand piano stood. Starting on the east side, he pressed his ear to the wall and knocked, then moved and knocked again, then did it over and over until he stopped directly in back of the piano. "Ez here." He started moving the grand piano, and Jack readily assisted him, pushing it only a foot or two so he could open the hidden door.

The foul smell of dust and something rotten billowed from within. Jack shined his cell light in the entrance, illuminating a stone passage covered in cobwebs and soot.

"Where does this lead?" I hoped it didn't take us to the royal palace or something like that. But if the king used it to get to the chapel, it made sense that it would.

"Doesn't matter. We have no choice but tae find out." Jack stepped over the threshold.

A ruckus came from the lower chapel. Raphael motioned for us to hurry. Jack led the way with the light. Footsteps rushed up the circular stairs. Being the last one, Raphael eased the door panel back in place. "Pray they no see zee piano ez moved." He motioned us forward.

We shadowed Jack through the musty tunnel. It turned and seemed to head downward. The squeaks of rats and dripping water had me keeping my gaze forward. At any second, I fully expected to feel a cold draft and hear eerie sounds. But my fear of being caught by the police and sent to prison outweighed my worry over stumbling into the world of the supernatural.

The tunnel came to an abrupt end. The passage had been walled up with thick slabs of rough wood. Cobwebs hung from the rafters.

A deep rumbling made the ground shake. Jack shined the light on Raphael. "How far do you think we are from the Metro?"

He thought for a moment and put up his hands. "May be on other side."

Jack drew a deep breath, then kicked at the wood.

"What are you doing?" It looked like a futile effort.

"We can't very well return the way we came. If we can break one of these planks loose, I think we can scramble through. When they built the Metro, they probably partitioned this off, never thinking anyone would come down here. If a bit of luck is with us, we'll find ourselves near a platform, where we can take the train."

After all we'd been through, could it be that simple? I hoped so.

Raphael and Sumsion started kicking the wood as well. There wasn't room for me to join in. Plus, I held the jar beneath my fleece jacket and was afraid I might drop it.

The wood creaked, the grain showing fractures with slivers of wood popping up. They kicked again and again until they broke through.

Jack jerked the wood, pulling it out of the way. He flashed the light into the dark unknown, then handed Raphael the cell light and belly-crawled through. "Skye, you come next."

I handed Sumsion the jar, knowing he'd keep it safe. Raphael stared at it. I shouldn't have done that, but I couldn't very well carry the jar. I got on my hands and knees, then eased down farther still and belly-crawled.

A hand took hold of my arm, pulling me to my feet. "I've got you." Jack stood next to me, and for a second, I wanted to grab hold of him and hang on. I'd never seen such darkness in my life, like I could reach out and touch it.

The scurrying of rodents came from the darkest reaches of the tunnel.

Trying to ignore the sound, I got down on my knees. "Professor, hand me the jar and then crawl through."

My eyes were drawn to the cell light. Shadows showed Sumsion kneeling and leaning forward with the jar. I took the vessel and immediately covered it with the front of my jacket, then stood up while Sumsion made his way through.

"Thank you, my good man," Sumsion said as Jack helped him to his feet. Seeing me, Sumsion said, "How are you, my dear?"

"Good. And you?"

"Good." His voice sounded a bit gravelly, like he'd grown extremely tired. But he'd soldier on because of his love for my aunt.

Raphael quickly shimmied through, handing the light back to Jack.

Jack immediately took the lead. "Now, let's see where this takes us. Keep your fingers crossed that I'm right."

Again, a tremendous rumbling shook the ground. Sumsion took hold of my arm. He had to be worried about me and probably the jar too.

The tunnel went farther down, and then, in the distance, flashing lights lit the darkness, as if a train were rushing by. The tunnel came out not at a platform but to the tracks. The platform stood about thirty feet away. A very small lip-of-a-walkway against the subway wall gave rail workers who maintained the Metro a path.

Jack again took the lead as we navigated the walkway. "Don't look down. Keep focused on me and take baby steps."

Sumsion gave me a nod that he'd be right behind me. I stepped out onto the lip.

A rush of wind from the tunnel made hair that had escaped my ponytail whip my face. I ignored it and did as Jack said, looking at him and taking small steps. I clutched the jar against my stomach and felt the envelope against my back. The enormity of my mission weighed heavily on me. I prayed with each step that my foot wouldn't slip.

The constant fear of a train finding us pushed me on. I checked to see how Sumsion fared. He lagged behind, but Raphael stayed with him, encouraging him.

A hand pressed against my back, drawing my attention. Jack gave me an I'm-here-for-you look. "The platform is only a few more yards."

Our strange little troop inched our way until at last we ambled onto the platform, exhausted and grateful. Only a few people waited for the next train. They paid us no mind. Sumsion found a seat on a metal bench, holding his chest with one hand while his other hand searched his jacket pockets.

"What is it?" I asked.

His face had paled yet again. "I left my heart medication in the hotel room." He cast a futile look at Jack, as if ashamed.

Jack paced. "We shouldn't go back there. They'll be waiting for us."

"But Professor Sumsion needs his medicine." I knew Jack was right, and as much as I didn't want to have another run-in with the guys who had chased us from the hotel, I also didn't want to face my aunt and tell her her boyfriend had died because we left his medication behind. "He might have a heart attack without it."

"I'll be fine." Sumsion tried to make light of the situation.

"No, you won't. You depend on those pills. I saw you take one before we went to Notre Dame."

He scoffed. "That was only a precaution."

"I don't think nitroglycerin is a precautionary tablet." I wasn't going to let him put down the importance of medication he needed to stay alive.

"Nitroglycerin?" Jack's attitude abruptly changed. "My mother had tae take that when her heart gave her trouble." He zeroed in on Sumsion. "I'll figure out something, but we can't go back."

"Zee answer ez obvious. Send moi." Raphael stepped forward. "I text my men. They not at your hotel. If your chasers were my competitors, I may still be able to fetch zee medicine with persuasion."

Jack thought for a moment but seemed to realize this was the only thing we could do. "Okay. We'll get a room down the street at the dive next tae Moulin Rouge."

Raphael nodded like he knew the place.

Though Sumsion had tried to convince us that he'd be all right without his meds, the worry lines on his face receded now that he knew Raphael would retrieve them.

"Besides—" Jack paused a moment in front of Sumsion. "We're going tae need you tae interpret the page we just found; plus, we still have one more page tae find. We can't do either without you." A playful glint showed in his gaze.

"Perish the thought." Sumsion put his hand over his heart, playing along. I could tell he enjoyed the banter and seemed relieved.

"Excuse me a minute while I check which train we need tae take." Jack headed over to the huge Metro map filled with colorful lines and squiggles detailing the different trains and routes.

I went with him. "What about your rental car?" I'd much rather have Jack drive us.

"Cops will be all over it."

Fear welled up inside me. "But won't that lead them to us? You rented the car."

"You don't think I used my real name, do you?" He scoffed and pointed. "We need tae catch the train on the other side tae return tae the hotel."

Obviously, he'd covered all the bases, so I dropped the rental car. We went back to Sumsion. Jack lent him an arm, and it touched me that now he knew of Sumsion's precarious health, he doted on the older man. It made me wonder what had happened to Jack's mother, but I didn't ask. I'd wait until later.

Without a word of complaint, we trailed Jack through hallways, up and down stairs, and on an escalator until we arrived on the right platform.

The other worry shadowing us was Raphael. Could he be trusted to get the medicine and return to us? And after . . . What then? I hoped Jack had a plan for dealing with his friend when he made his move, whenever and whatever it was going to be. The clock on the wall above posters of bold-colored advertisements read 11:30 p.m.

My arms and legs became heavy. The small nap I'd had on the flight over had worn off long ago. I hadn't felt tired as we were being chased, but stopping and waiting had allowed my fatigue to catch up with me. Jack had Sumsion sit on a bench to wait. Though the older man's eyes were closed, I could tell he was fighting off pain. He needed his pills.

With a loud swoosh and hiss, the train pulled to a stop at the platform. The train was packed despite its being the middle of the night, so we waited while passengers got off. Did this city never sleep?

Raphael woke Sumsion and helped him to the train. Jack stuck close to me. As I stepped into the car, he directed me to a seat, which would be an easier ride than hanging on to a handrail while holding the jar as well. Fortunately, there was a seat next to mine for Sumsion. Raphael guided him to it, then Jack and Raphael remained standing.

The doors folded closed, and the train was off.

Jack leaned over. "We have four stops before we reach our destination, so relax while you can." He surveyed the people in our car, always on the lookout for the unexpected.

Sumsion patted my leg. "Are you all right, my dear?"

"Yes, and you?"

"These old bones still might have some moves left in them." His shoulder nudged mine.

A wellspring of gratitude for his companionship during this ordeal gave me great comfort. Of the three men with me, Sumsion had become my rock.

I looked up at Jack. His gaze met mine and made me feel safe. It would be easy to fall for him. Not only was he handsome, but he seemed to truly care too. I wanted to trust him so badly. I truly felt he was a good person, but a nagging doubt stopped me from having complete faith in him. I smiled, and suddenly, a yawn found me.

He smiled back, and the dark-blue in his eyes held . . . affection.

Really? I must have misread it. Unnerved by the thought, I turned away and looked at the stops outlined over the door of the car. A light blinked, telling passengers of the next stop. The train slowed and halted. Passengers got on and off, and then we were moving again.

The rocking of the train lulled me to sleep, and before I knew it, Jack tapped my shoulder. "The next one is ours."

I swiped my palm over my face and blinked a couple times. Sumsion slowly rose. Making sure I had a firm hold on the jar, I did as well.

The train came to a stop. Jack guided Sumsion and me off, with Raphael next to him. We walked down the passageway to the stairs that would take us to the street.

Jack hung back, spoke to Raphael, and handed him something, probably his key card and money. And then the Frenchman took off.

"We can trust him," Jack said.

I hoped he was right. Guilt for wanting the Frenchman to leave us alone blossomed, but I tried to ignore it the best I could.

The windmill of Moulin Rouge reflected on the wet street and amplified lights of red. The chillingly cold wind made us walk faster. Even Sumsion.

Jack led us through the sliding glass doors of a seedy hotel. The smell of liquor and smoke nearly dripped from the walls. A couple of well-worn chairs rested against one. I guided Sumsion to them, and Jack dealt with securing us a room.

He quickly returned. "Unfortunately, the elevator is out, and we're on the third floor."

We tracked him to the frayed, carpeted stairs.

"This looks like a place that rents rooms by the hour," I said to his back.

"Beggars can't be choosers." Jack got on the other side of Sumsion as we started to climb.

None of us spoke as we made our way up, stopping every once in a while so Sumsion could catch his breath, then continued. Once we reached the third floor, Jack checked before allowing us to move down the hallway to our room.

He swiped the key card and opened the door. He motioned for us to wait a moment while he checked inside. Then he called out, "It's clear."

I entered the room and went to the desk, setting down the terracotta jar, glad to have that burden off of me for the time being.

Sumsion eased into a chair. He put on a brave face of fending off pain. "I need a small mirror that I can put inside the jar and a flashlight." He pulled his magnifying glass out of his coat pocket.

"I have one, but it's in my room at the other hotel." Along with other small toiletries I'd grabbed at the airport.

"I'll message Raphael and see if he can get it while he's there."

"But I didn't give him my room card."

Jack looked at me as if to say, "Amateur." "He won't need it. If you haven't noticed yet, Raphael is very resourceful."

"Oh, I've noticed. Again, I have to ask, are you sure we can trust him?" A nervous flutter churned in my gut.

"You don't understand the world I live in." Jack leaned close to me. "There may be no honor among thieves, but between a spy and his partners, there's a true understanding that we're in this together."

I hoped he was right.

CHAPTER FIFTEEN

A HALF HOUR SLOWLY TICKED by, with me doting on Sumsion, getting him water to drink and trying to take his mind off his pain by turning on the TV. Most every station was in French, except a couple: a weather station and reruns of old TV series. Jack kept surveillance, staring out the window.

A knock on the door made me jump. I didn't know whether to answer it or not. Jack beat me to it.

In rushed Raphael. Not only did he have Professor Sumsion's medicine but my bag and a bucket of Kentucky Fried Chicken as well. Who would have thought KFC was in Paris or that a Parisian would choose that place to eat? The aroma made my stomach growl.

Sumsion quickly took a pill from the bottle and placed it in his mouth.

"Did you see anyone?" Jack asked as Raphael set the food on the desk and handed me my bag.

"Non. But someone had visited Skye's room."

I couldn't believe it.

"Oui." Raphael nodded as if to emphasize what he'd said. "Tore apart zee room and stole zee safe."

I didn't know if Raphael was lying or not. If the other group of Frenchmen led by the hotel's concierge was after the page, he'd have a master key to the safe. Why steal it? Unless he was afraid management would find out.

Jack shot me a worried look.

"I still have the page. I tested the lock on the safe, but when I couldn't get the thing to open again, I gave up." I was grateful I'd thought better of using it and had kept the page on me.

"Good." Jack turned his attention to Sumsion. "You okay, Professor?"

He nodded. His complexion looked better, and the pain lines that had creased his face were already disappearing.

Jack patted his back. "Whoever took the safe has bought us a little time. Hopefully, it will be enough for you tae translate what is on the page in the jar before we have tae leave."

I rummaged through what little makeup was in my bag.

"I get your things off zee washroom floor. They broken, no?" Raphael seemed worried that I'd blame him.

The compact had been crushed, and the mirror had sustained a crack down the middle. I held it up. "It's okay. I think it's still usable."

"Well, it's all we've got." Jack went back to the window. "And we're running out of time."

"Best I hurry, then." Sumsion had the hotel's complimentary notepad and pen ready to take notes. He eased the mirror inside the jar. "Skye, my dear, could you shine the light inside?"

I picked up Jack's cell phone, tapped on the flashlight, and tried to direct the beam where Sumsion wanted without blocking his view.

With his other free hand, he held the magnifying glass just so. "I think this might be easier than I thought." He scribbled some notes, then tried again.

Raphael opened the bags of food and looked up at me as if for permission.

Sumsion persisted with his work, making notes and then peering inside the jar.

I stayed with him, dutifully holding the light. "You guys go ahead and eat. Once the professor is done, we'll get some food." I smiled at Raphael. I still didn't know if I trusted him or not, but he'd done a good thing in collecting our belongings from the hotel and even buying food.

He and Jack quickly did as I'd asked and got something to eat.

After what seemed forever, Sumsion leaned back in his chair and set down the magnifying glass and the mirror. He rubbed his index finger and thumb over his eyes and yawned.

I flipped off the cell light. "What does it say?"

Sumsion peered at Jack and then Raphael. By the concerned expression on his face, he didn't know whether to trust the Frenchman or not. I wasn't alone in my misgivings over our situation.

Jack seemed to understand. Wiping his hands off with a napkin, he said, "I think Raphael has proved his trustworthiness. Besides, he knows if he double-crosses us, I'll track him down."

Raphael nodded like he totally understood and agreed to the terms of his staying.

As if against his better judgment, Sumsion hesitated only a moment. "I'll forego the Latin and just give the English translation." He read, "'An angel holds the promise not in New Jerusalem. But hidden away with the heart of an allied land. A new hope lies buried, waiting to be free. Soon justice will prevail, the rightful heir will take the throne.'" Sumsion gave a deep sigh.

"Is that it?" Jack peered over Sumsion's shoulder, a look of disappointment lining his face.

"That's quite a lot. And I'm not sure I got it all, but I deciphered what I could." Sumsion stretched and left his chair, going over to the chicken, which was a good sign that he felt better.

"What do you think it means?" My stomach now demanded to be fed too.

"Let me ponder on it for a while." Sumsion pulled out a chicken thigh and grabbed a napkin.

Jack took the chair Sumsion had vacated at the desk, poring over the notes. "Think this angel is the same one mentioned on Skye's page?"

Sumsion shot him a menacing look. "Son, please wash the grease from the chicken off your hands before touching anything over there."

Jack immediately went to the wash room and did as he'd been told.

Sitting beside Sumsion on the twin bed, eating, I said, "We already know New Jerusalem is Paris." I finished off my piece of chicken and went back to the bag for a biscuit. Professor Sumsion's eyes lit up, so I grabbed him one as well and brought it over.

Jack returned and sat once again in the seat at the desk, looking over the notes. "We don't know who this angel is who holds the promise."

Sumsion finished his biscuit and went to the bathroom to clean up.

"Does it speak of France's throne?" Raphael returned to the chicken and pulled out a wing.

Sumsion came back, wiping his hands with a paper towel. "I believe so."

"But we are like America," Raphael said. "We have no throne." He took a bite of his food.

"At the time this was written, France did." Sumsion studied Raphael as if measuring the man's knowledge merely by appearance. "If Jeanne d'Évreux was the one who commissioned these pages to be written, that was nearly four hundred years before Napoleon came crashing on the scene, thus, before the French Revolution."

Raphael nodded, but a question still remained. "Who drew zee pages?"

"Looks to me like the same Jean Pucelle who made the *Book of Hours*." Sumsion appeared quite confident.

Raphael's eyes lit up. "Oui. Pucelle. He ez *magnifique*." He brought his fingers to his lips and kissed them.

Sumsion and Jack turned their attention to the notes. I looked at Raphael. He didn't know I was watching him, and for a second, a hardness settled on his easy-going Frenchman's face. I wondered if the man could be as calculating as we had first thought.

"Who do you suppose the angel could be?" Jack turned to Sumsion.

"Important question, indeed." Sumsion pointed to something on the page. "And even more importantly, who did Jeanne think could be the rightful heir?" He started to pace, and the flyaway silver hairs on top of his head tousled about. "Jeanne and King Charles had three daughters. The first two died young, and the third, Blanche, never had children. So the king and queen had no heirs."

"We don't have the luxury of sitting here tae try tae figure this out," Jack said. "Whoever ransacked Skye's room will be looking for us once they get into the safe and realize her page isn't in there." He took a deep breath. "With Scotland being an ally to France, it looks like our next stop is there, but where exactly?"

I stuffed the discarded sacks and used napkins into the trash. Jack was from Scotland, so of course he probably studied how France was his country's ally in school. But he knew more than he was telling us. We'd been running for our lives all over Paris, following him from one hot place to another. And even though he'd shown me his credentials, I still worried that he wasn't who he said he was. Sumsion's friend in the CIA didn't know him either. And now his friend Raphael was working with us like we were one big, happy team. Could my emotions and desire to trust Jack be wrong and my skeptical mind right? I focused on Jack and a sudden flush of betrayal and fear overcame me. All at once, I said, "I just bet you don't know."

As though completely caught off guard, Jack raised his dark brows. "What are you accusing me of now?"

"I find it too coincidental that your homeland is Scotland and that's where we're heading. Professor Sumsion called a friend in the CIA, and they don't have a record of you."

"Of course they don't." Jack's no-duh expression stopped my self-righteous vent. "Only those in the top tier know."

"Convenient." I didn't know why I'd decided to make this stand here and now when I should have held off until we'd found all three pages. No, I knew. I needed to protect myself from the growing attraction I felt for Jack. I had to harden those feelings. This was bigger than my heart being broken. This was about Auntie and her very life. I had to be ruthless. Anger pulsed through my veins, giving my mouth a mind of its own.

Raphael chuckled into his hand.

Jack glared at him like he wanted to shoot him on the spot.

"I don't know what you're laughing at." I folded my arms. "But I don't find this funny at all." I wanted to punch them both. First Jack, then Raphael, and then Jack again.

Jack stood, his dark-blue eyes glaring at me like lasers. "This conversation can wait until another time. We need tae get going."

"No! It can't." For better or worse, I was making this stand.

This made Raphael laugh out loud, which annoyed me even more.

"And you've compromised my aunt's safety by bringing him"—I pointed at the Frenchman—"in on this. Auntie's life is in danger. I don't have time for your lies anymore, Jack. Are you working for the Black Prince?"

The last two words wiped the grin off Raphael's face. "Zee Black Prince ez involved?"

"Didn't really know what you were getting into, did you?" I said. The surprise on the Frenchman's face fueled my fire. "Your friend Jack has been keeping many secrets to himself. And I, for one, am tired of it."

"My dear, this might not be the right time." Sumsion shook his head, trying to calm me down.

"Right time or not, I'm not going to Scotland or anywhere else until he tells us the truth." I returned my focus to Jack.

His shoulders slumped as he rubbed his brow. He bit his lips together as if trying to find the right words; either that, or he was formulating a new lie, which I wouldn't put past him.

"Tell her," Raphael encouraged him.

They were cohorts? Had Raphael's finding us at Sainte-Chapelle been staged? Now, I really was confused.

Jack glared at his friend like he regretted having him here, then turned to me. "You're right." He swallowed as if this was the hardest thing he'd ever had to admit. "I haven't told you the truth. I don't work for the CIA."

Glad to have him come clean, I pressed him. "Who *do* you work for?"

"Scotland Yard."

I wanted to believe him, but deep in my heart, I knew he was lying again.

CHAPTER SIXTEEN

J ACK CHECKED OUT THE WINDOW like he didn't want to discuss the topic anymore. "I think whoever took the safe is on tae us. A couple of shady-looking guys are coming in the back way."

We had to get out of the hotel fast. I reached for the jar with the page in it at the same time Jack did. The collision of our hands bumped the jar, and it fell to the floor in slow-motion.

Unable to move fast enough to catch it, I helplessly watched as it crashed against the leg of the desk and broke into a million tiny pieces.

I couldn't breathe. What had I done?

"I'm sorry." Jack's face paled.

Sumsion gasped and hurried over to see the damage. He pulled the small vellum page out of the rubble as delicately as he could. Parts had torn away on the edges, but the bulk of it remained. "Skye, quick, the envelope."

I tugged it from my waistband.

"Open it." He stood there holding the page.

Meanwhile, Jack went to the door and pressed his ear against it. Raphael wrung his hands as he watched Sumsion and me like he couldn't wait to see the page I'd kept safe.

Mistrust reared its ugly head, but I didn't have time to question, didn't have time to do anything, really, except what Sumsion told me to do.

I pulled out the cardboard, drew the pieces apart, and laid them on the bed, exposing the vellum beneath the page protector.

"Open it, and I'll slip this in with the other one." Sumsion waited while I did his bidding.

I carefully opened the transparent sheeting wide enough for him to slide the curled folio within. As the protective covering closed, it flattened the second page, and it rested next to the first one.

I placed the cardboard back together, put it inside the envelope, and returned it to my waistband. Once done, I realized while I'd been busy, Raphael had replaced Jack at the door. Jack stared at his phone.

Sumsion retrieved his pill bottle from the desk and patted the pockets of his black leather jacket as if to make sure he had everything he might need. Spying the notepad on the desk, he added it to his pocket.

"We need tae take the train tae the airport. I don't dare call an Uber driver. With our luck, whoever showed up would be part of the other French group after the page," Jack whispered. "The Metro is close. There are so many people coming and going at Moulin Rouge that we might go undetected." He joined Raphael, making him step aside. Jack cracked open the door and looked out. Relief washed his face, and he motioned for us to leave.

We hurried down the stairs, then Jack herded us out the door and down the busy street. Music from Moulin Rouge thrummed the air. We joined the flow of people, and Jack guided us to the Metro entrance. I looped my arm through Sumsion's, grateful he was with us. Despite his ailing health, he seemed to know what to do when things went wrong and tried to bring order when anger flared. I needed to listen to him more and quit letting my emotions rule.

The four of us hurried down the tunnel steps. People milled about. The rumble of trains echoed through the white-tiled halls. Luck finally found us, and we arrived at the airport train's platform just in time. We picked a car that wasn't crowded, and all four of us were able to find seats together. We were off with no sign of the bad guys.

I took a deep, cleansing breath.

Jack leaned over and looked past me to Sumsion. "What's our destination in Scotland?"

"I've been thinking about that. Before King Charles IV died, he firmed up France's alliance with Scotland, promising to fight the British should they attack them. The leader of Scotland at the time was Robert the Bruce."

"That means Edinburgh is our destination." Jack sat back.

I glared at him, fragments of our previous argument catching up with me. "You've known all along that's where we'd end up."

He shrugged. "Let's say I had a good idea but wasn't certain."

"What else have you had a good idea about?" I felt Sumsion pat my arm, his attempt to calm me down.

Jack turned in his seat and peered directly at me. "You."

Speechless, I didn't have a ready comeback. I squirmed in my seat. He had said he'd been sent to protect me. When he'd said it, I'd thought he worked for the CIA, and it had made a little sense because I was an American. But now, what did keeping me safe mean? I had so many questions I wanted to ask, needed to ask, and had to have the answers to for my own peace of mind. However, it might be best to let him do the talking. "Explain that to me."

He leaned close so only I could hear. "I want tae keep you safe."

"You're a broken record; do you know that? I'd ask to see your Scotland Yard credentials, but what's the point. They could be phony just like your CIA ones. There's something going on here that you're not telling me." I itched to ask him more, like why would Scotland Yard want to keep me, an American, safe? It had to have something to do with the pages. Of course they wanted the pages just as badly as the Black Prince. But why? Though I wanted to ask him, I didn't. I wanted to interrogate him when we were alone, with no holds barring us and away from Sumsion and Raphael. Without the other two, there would be no interruptions, and I could keep at him until I was satisfied that he had told me the truth.

However, I'd need some type of leverage to get him to talk. Whatever agency he worked for had trained him not to give away secrets, so I'd have to come up with some way to get him to spill the truth.

"I've told you all that I can. But know that keeping you safe is my main goal." He paused, waiting for me to reply. When I didn't, he added, "You have nothing tae say tae that?" His eyes searched mine.

"I have a lot to say, but not now. Later." It killed me not to tear into him with my barrage of questions, but I also felt more in control holding back. It felt good.

* * *

At the airport, I booked all four of us on a flight to Edinburgh. For some reason, Raphael insisted on coming with us. Too tired to argue, I didn't question him. Even though I had grave concerns about who he really was, I had to admit that his stealth and knowledge had come in pretty handy at Sainte-Chapelle. Before this quest was over, we might need him again.

Surprisingly, he had his passport on him. I always carried mine out of habit and because of my job, but it amazed me that he did. He and Jack sat together on the plane a couple of rows behind Sumsion and me, which was a relief because I knew if I sat next to Jack, we would end up arguing. I didn't want to do that. Not yet.

"My dear, Jack has many flaws, but I believe his heart is in the right place." Sumsion's bloodshot eyes searched mine.

"I hope so." Wanting to change the subject, I asked, "Tell me about this Robert the Bruce." Talking about history would take Sumsion's mind off Jack and me.

"Oh, yes. The king who played with spiders." He smiled.

"What?"

"'Tis so." A twinkle came to his eyes. "But his story starts before he became fascinated with arthropods. To give a detailed account, I'm afraid would bore you, so I'll gloss over it and give you only the essentials. In 1298, his father resigned the throne because of quarrels with John Comyn, Lord of Badenoch, and William Lamberton, the bishop of St. Andrews, which then made John Balliol, Lord of Galloway, king."

"Okay, you're confusing me." How were they all connected?

"It's a long story. Just believe me that that is what happened. However, King John's nobles tried to negotiate a treaty with France against England, and when King Edward Longshanks heard about it, he became furious, and decades of intermittent warfare began. It was known as the Wars of Independence. Edward stripped John Balliol of his crown. As you can imagine, this infuriated Robert the Bruce."

"I think I remember a movie about this. *Braveheart*, was it?" It had been awhile since I'd seen it, so I wasn't sure.

Sumsion sighed. "That portrayal was full of inaccuracies and was based on a poem instead of the hard facts of history." He cleared his throat and sat up a little straighter. "For one thing, the actor who played William Wallace—"

"Mel Gibson," I quickly added, happy I'd remembered something more.

"Fine actor, don't get me wrong, but William Wallace was a huge, strapping man believed to be the height of six feet five inches, at least. His two-handed sword stood taller than Gibson. And the way they portrayed Robert the Bruce? Intolerable if you're a Scotsman." Sumsion shuddered.

I wondered what the professor's roots were. "Were some of your ancestors from Scotland?"

"Sadly, no. My family were Brits. Some believed they were from Wiltshire; however, it's hard to prove since at that time, there was enforced clearing and dispersal of inhabitants to make way for sheep pastures; plus, there were natural causes, such as the Black Death. However, I must admit, I favor the Scots." He winked. "How about you? Where did your ancestors hail from?"

"I have no idea. That's why about a month and a half ago I sent my DNA in to that company that traces your roots. I saw an envelope from them on the kitchen desk. My mind was on Auntie and finding her when I was home, so I didn't open it." A chill rushed down my spine. My aunt's kind, wise face came to me. I bit my bottom lip, trying to suppress tears. Sumsion had grown quiet. Compassion reflected in his gaze.

I sighed, remembering how I'd gone against my aunt's wishes. "The funny thing was, Auntie never wanted me to do it. She got all upset when I brought it up. First, she'd argue that the government could use the findings against people who sent in their samples. And when I'd tell her how ridiculous that was, she'd say how ridiculous it was to learn of people in the past. They are dead and gone."

"If she didn't want you to send in your DNA, why did you do it anyway?"

"I guess I did it for her. I wanted her to see how silly she was being."

"Maybe you can show her once we have her safely with us again." Sumsion tilted his head, a sympathetic expression on his face.

"I hope so." Sadness settled on me. What if we failed? What if Auntie never made it home?

Sumsion's face seemed frozen, making me think he'd had the same thought I had. Then he scrubbed his palm over his face. "Let's think of something else, shall we? Let's revisit the subject of that *Braveheart* movie. I want to give you a word of warning: never take a film such as that at face value. It's always best to do your own homework and seek many sources to back up historical claims." He rubbed his chin, his other hand hovering over the pocket that held his pipe. "I could name film after film where some 'historians' have whitewashed history in their movies. Right criminal, it is."

The flight from Paris to Edinburgh took only an hour and a half, and who knew what would happen to us once we touched down. I decided to go back to the history at hand. "So, how did Robert the Bruce retake the crown?"

Sumsion nodded like he believed his point over the movies had been made and it was time to return to the most pressing matter, imparting his historical knowledge to help save Auntie. "An awful business, it was. In 1306, he killed John Comyn in the heat of an argument and moved quickly to seize the throne."

"How horrible."

"Don't judge too quickly. Comyn betrayed an agreement with Bruce to King Edward. So when Bruce and Comyn met at the Monastery in Dumfries, Bruce accused him of treachery. They came to blows, and Bruce stabbed Comyn before the high altar. Also, keep in mind that leading up to that time, Robert the Bruce didn't know who to trust. He'd had to flee for his life in the dead of night quite often. And by that time, his friend William Wallace had been captured, hanged, and drawn and quartered. Plus, Bruce had been forced to watch as many clansmen lost their homes and their lives due to King Edward's rule over them.

"When Longshanks learned that Robert the Bruce had killed Comyn, he came after him. And again, Bruce had to flee for his life." He shook his head as if in sympathy.

"Where did he go?"

"Some say Ireland, others the Hebrides. And this, my dear, is when the legend was born about him and the spider." Sumsion rubbed his hands together as though excited to tell me this tidbit. "He hid in a cave during the winter months and observed a spider spinning a web. The arthropod worked to connect one area of the web to the cave's roof. He watched the spider fall many times. But the creature was persistent and would merely climb back up to the web and try again.

"This, they say, inspired Bruce. When he returned to the mainland and fighting commenced in earnest, he would think of that spider and how eventually it succeeded in its task. Bruce believed he would as well. Thus, the saying, 'If at first you don't succeed, try, try, again.' And it worked for Robert the Bruce as he led the Scots to victory."

The flight attendant stopped beside Sumsion. "Would you care for a drink, some coffee or juice?"

"I'd appreciate a good cup of Earl Grey, if it's not too much bother." Sumsion gave her his famous smile.

"Not at all. And for you, ma'am?" The flight attendant, with hair coiffed in a twist, looked at me.

"I'm fine, thank you." I'd purchased a bottle of water before boarding, so I was good.

She left.

There was still so much I needed to learn from Sumsion. "How did Scotland become an ally to France?"

"I told you about King John Balliol?"

I nodded.

"He signed an alliance with Philip IV of France in 1295. The terms were if either nation was attacked by England, the other country would invade English territory. It's one of the oldest alliances in history."

"Is that why Jeanne d'Évreux looked at Scotland as a brother of France?"

"Probably. You might be surprised to learn that the alliance has never been revoked."

"Never? After all this time?"

"No. Remember only a few years ago when there was contention in Scotland and some wanted to break away from Great Britain? Protesters in France were very supportive and assembled in support of their ally."

"I had no idea." But then I thought about it. "Well, actually I'd heard a little on the news when England voted to leave the EU. Once that was settled, it kind of quieted down; at least, I assumed it did."

"Which is exactly what Britain wanted everyone to think. But a storm is brewing; mark my words. All Scotland needs is another William Wallace or Robert the Bruce to ignite a fire in their hearts for freedom and the UK will have a major problem." He nodded his head as if agreeing with himself.

It made me smile.

"Here's your tea, sir." The flight attendant had returned with a steaming cup.

Sumsion let the small table down from the seat back in front of him. She set the tea upon it.

"Can I get you anything else?"

"Not that I can think of right now." He smiled up at her.

She hurried off.

"Once we reach Edinburgh, where do you think we should go?" My legs felt jittery and my stomach queasy. The thought of the monumental task awaiting us seemed overwhelming. Yet, we already had two of the three pages, so we'd made progress. But it was taking so much time.

"I think Stirling Castle should be our next destination. William Wallace won a major victory at the Battle of Stirling Bridge, fighting off English forces over the River Forth. We might find a clue there as to where the page could be." He blew on his tea and took a sip.

The aroma of Earl Grey wafted to me.

"All right. I just hope Jack goes along with it." I craned my neck to take a look at Jack and Raphael.

Raphael sat in the window seat and seemed occupied with looking out at the clouds. Jack, however, stared right at me and held my gaze.

I had a feeling he wanted to talk to me alone just as much as I wanted to talk to him. But with Sumsion and Raphael here, I wondered if we would ever find the time.

And more importantly, could we ever clear up the contention between us?

CHAPTER SEVENTEEN

AFTER TOUCHING DOWN AT EDINBURGH airport, Jack rented a BMW. We piled in, Jack and Raphael in the front, Sumsion and I in the back. We took a collective deep breath, as if relieved we'd made it this far.

Jack's cell phone rang. He pulled it out of his pocket. "Says no caller ID."

I sat directly behind him but could see his expression in the rearview mirror. By his puckered brow, this was a surprise. But surprise or not, he swiped the phone, taking the call.

"Yes?"

Anxious to know who it was, I pulled myself closer to the front seat. Sumsion sat on the edge of his seat as well.

"Just a minute." Jack handed his cell phone to me.

I glared at him as if to say, "Who is it?"

"The kidnapper," he mouthed.

A coldness swept my skin. How? What? My mind had to stop stuttering. I had to talk with him. Sucking in a deep breath, I took the cell and said, "Hello."

"Your aunt wants to speak with you." The kidnapper sounded more English than before. I heard movement in the background, shuffling, and a moan.

"Skye?" Auntie's voice sounded raspy, barely audible.

"Auntie! Are you all right?" I pictured her strapped to a bed, unable to move or do anything.

Sumsion stared intently at me, deep lines creasing his face. Tears puddled in his eyes.

"Skye." This time her voice sounded relieved.

"I'm coming, Auntie. Hang on." If only I could reach into the phone and touch her cheek. I could almost smell her perfume of choice—a whiff of violet, rose, apricot, and lily of the valley—Charlie Red.

Noises of the phone being moved signaled my time of speaking with her had come to an abrupt end.

The kidnapper came back. "As you can tell, your aunt is in a bad way. You need to hurry."

I desperately wondered how I could keep him on the phone long enough to find out more about her condition. Jack stared at me in the mirror. I put two and two together. "You already know I'm doing the best I can, Black Prince. Your spy has kept you well informed."

Jack rolled his eyes and shook his head.

"Spy?" The kidnapper's playacting wasn't fooling me.

"How else did you know to call Jack's cell?" There, the truth was in the open, where it belonged, where everyone could look at it and digest it.

"You're correct. My spies are very close to you. But instead of wasting time chatting with me, you might want to get a move on. Your aunt's health is failing fast, and if you want to see her alive again, you need to find the last page." And then silence filled my ear.

I stared at the phone, then looked at the mirror and Jack. "So you ditched the phone the kidnapper gave me, but you kept yours. How convenient. Have you been texting him, keeping him up-to-date?"

Jack gave a deep, self-deprecating sigh. He held out his hand as if wanting his cell phone back.

I placed it on his palm.

"Like I told you, I work for Scotland Yard. They told me my mobile was untraceable." He opened the door, smashed the cell against the concrete, and chucked it into a nearby garbage can. He got back in and started the engine. "I probably should have kept it, but in case the kidnapper wants tae call again, it's best not tae. If he found a way tae get my number, he'd probably use the phone's GPS tae track us." Then, as though the argument was over, he asked, "Where tae, Professor?"

The nerve. He had more explaining to do. I was about to verbally pounce on him when Sumsion reached up and patted Jack's shoulder like he agreed that we needed to carry on. "Stirling Castle, my good man."

I felt someone's eyes on me. I looked up, expecting to meet Jack's gaze in the rearview mirror, but he seemed intent on driving.

My eyes went to Raphael. He had been quietly watching and listening to everything. Though the kidnapper had denied that he had a spy with us, he did say his spies were near. I now wondered about Raphael again.

I barely knew the man. And even though he'd come to our rescue in Paris, there had to be another reason why he wanted to come with us, other than being a good friend of Jack's.

I looked away from him and out the window. Auntie's haunting voice came back to me. Her breathy tones concerned me greatly. If only I could have seen her. All this travel and searching for the pages seemed to take too long. Yet, we'd made good time, considering the long flights and other obstacles. And there was nothing I could do about that. She had to know I was doing the best I could. She had to know I'd move heaven and earth if I thought it would save her life and bring her back to me. I bit at my bottom lip and once again stared out the window, trying to take my mind off things I couldn't change.

We passed two huge metal sculptures of horses' heads.

"Those are kelpies," Jack said as he drove. He must have noticed that they had caught my attention.

"They look like horses to me," I said in a deadpan voice.

"A kelpie is a demon in the shape of a horse," he replied.

"Really? I guess it takes one to know one." As the words left my mouth, I realized how childish they sounded and immediately wished I could take them back. What was wrong with me? I should let up on Jack. Sumsion seemed to believe him. Why couldn't I? Deep down, I knew. If I believed him wholeheartedly, I might get my heart broken when this was all over.

Sumsion moved in his seat. "Actually, if I'm not mistaken, a kelpie can take human form but retains his hooves." He wiggled his graying eyebrows, making the point and attempting to add some levity to the tension.

"You're right, Professor." Jack stomped the floor like a horse.

Raphael chuckled out loud.

"Ha, ha. Very funny." I was in no mood to joke around. "Auntie's voice sounded weak. She could hardly say my name. She might not have much time, yet we're discussing kelpies." Frustrated, I wanted to kick the seat in front of me or scream at the top of my lungs. But I couldn't. Despite my pent-up emotions, I held it together.

"Sorry, Skye." Jack's voice sounded repentant. "I wasn't thinking, just trying tae lighten the mood."

Jack's expression sobered in the rearview mirror. His concerned deep-blue eyes stared back at me.

And though I still clung to the grudge I carried against him for lying, I caved. "It's okay. I'm just worried."

The car fell quiet for a while.

Jack turned off the freeway and drove through meandering streets that started to climb.

"There it is." He pointed out the window. A mighty fortress, Stirling Castle, crowned the hilltop.

"It's big," I said, unable to think of anything else to say.

"Aye, it is. You didn't have the chance tae see the castle in Edinburgh before we left. It makes quite an impression as well." There was pride in Jack's tone.

The road switched back and forth and then opened to a huge parking plaza. Jack paid the attendant, and we parked the BMW.

I zipped my fleece jacket, double-checking that the envelope was safely stored in my waistband. I felt like Frodo, the keeper of the ring, except I was the keeper of the pages. I was grateful they weren't making me ill like the ring did him. No, instead, their very existence made me paranoid and seemed to have left Auntie in very grave health.

We walked up a cobblestone path through a gateway. "Is this the main entrance to the castle?"

Sumsion looked around. "More likely the main entrance for tourists. The castle's would be more distinct."

Once through, Jack noticed a ticket office to the left. He and Raphael went to it and spoke with a lady. Jack gave her some money, and she gave him a couple of booklets.

The two men joined us once again.

Jack handed one of the booklets to Sumsion and said, "This should give us the lay of the land."

Sumsion thumbed through it, stopping at a map. "Ah, where we are right now is called the Esplanade, built so the military could parade the grounds. But that was much later than Jeanne d'Évreux's time. It appears that we need to follow the cobblestone walkway in this direction." He pointed in the only way we could go unless we went back to the car.

Well-manicured gardens lay to our left. Sumsion said something about it being Queen Anne's garden. Ahead stood two towers beside a gate—the castle's entrance.

We trudged up the hill, walking through it to the principal courtyard, where Sumsion stopped. "I doubt we'll find anything of value here." He studied the map and then looked to the buildings. "What we need to check out is the palace, the great hall, and the north gate. I feel like something in those areas might point us in the right direction to find the last page."

"This is going to take forever," I mumbled, feeling overwhelmed with the task and worry for Auntie.

"Why don't we split up?" Jack didn't wait for an agreement. "Raphael, go with Professor Sumsion and cover the palace. Skye and I will check the great hall. We'll meet by the tunnel that takes us tae the north gate in, say"—he checked his watch—"a half hour?"

"Is fine with moi." Raphael motioned for Sumsion to lead the way. But the professor didn't move, as if reluctant to do what was suggested.

I felt reluctant to separate as well, but Jack was right. We wasted time by staying in a group.

"Watch for an angel or heart, the words *promise*, *New Jerusalem*, or anything about Robert the Bruce." Sumsion's gaze held mine. "And be careful."

"We will." I smiled at him, wanting to reassure the older man that I'd be all right. And I would be. Actually, this would give me time alone with Jack. I had a few things I wanted to get off my chest.

Jack led the way to the great hall. Our footsteps echoed off the wooden flooring and bounced off the great cathedral-like ceiling made of wood. A balcony of sorts stood at one end of the hall, and several displays explained how the people worshiped at Stirling Castle, how Mary Queen of Scots had James VI baptized here, and what the altar cloths were. Nowhere in the hall did I see anything resembling a heart, an angel, or anything about Robert the Bruce.

"This is disappointing." Jack turned around, gazing at the long space. "I think the palace will take the professor and Raphael a little longer. Why don't we head down tae the kitchens? They are near the north gate, where we're supposed tae meet them." Jack stepped to the side as if waiting for me to walk by.

We were alone. Now was a good time to bring up the questions that haunted me. I tried to think what the best approach would be. I really didn't want to get into another argument. I just wanted the truth from the man, if that was possible. And the best way to get a guy to fess up was not to accuse but to listen. A calm question might make him open up. Yes, a question could do the trick.

The cobblestones gradually sloped down toward a tunnel. Watching where I was going and hoping not to slip, I asked, "What part of Scotland do you call home?"

He reared back. I'd truly taken him by surprise. He chuckled. His penetrating eyes that I imagined would make any other woman's heart skip a beat stared at me. "I see what you're doing."

"What?" I tried hard to appear genuine and innocent of any manipulation whatsoever.

He shrugged as if deciding to play along. "Near Aberdeen, which is northeast from here."

Good. I was making progress. "Does your family still live there?"

"Aye." And he seemed happy to leave it at that.

"Your parents, siblings, or . . . fill in the blank?" I tried to sound earnest and not calculating.

We walked through the tunnel, coming out near an older structure. We both stopped. Jack thumbed through his pamphlet. "Says that this gate was built during the 1300s." The last words made us both do a double take.

We stepped closer to the old structure, desperately looking for something that might give us a clue. After several minutes of searching the wall and even the ground, we both came up with nothing.

Discouraged, I quit searching. Jack came to join me, reading again in the pamphlet. "We might as well check out the kitchens, like we were going to. Says here that when they were renovating this section of the castle, they came upon the kitchens. They believe they were used for the kings hundreds of years ago."

A new spark of hope ignited.

"Looks like it's down those stairs we passed just before the gate." He walked toward them.

We took the stairs to a large cave-like room. I stopped, reluctant to keep going.

"What's wrong?" Jack asked, as if eager to move.

"I hate caves."

"This isn't a cave. It's a kitchen." He coaxed me on.

I focused on the lights illuminating different areas where mannequins dressed like cooks stood frozen doing various cooking chores. Studying them helped me forget we were underground. Tables held make-believe food. "Jack."

"Hmm?"

"You didn't answer me. Who in your family still lives in Aberdeen? Or near Aberdeen?"

He studied the kitchen. "My mother passed away a couple of years ago from heart failure, but my father lives on his fishing boat there."

No wonder he understood the importance of Sumsion needing his medication. His mother had had heart trouble. This tidbit made Jack more normal to me instead of some spy devoid of feelings. And his father was still living. How fortunate for him. I missed my dad every day.

"Does your father know you work for Scotland Yard?" There. I'd inched closer to the meat of what I wanted to discuss.

A group of tourists joined us.

Jack glanced at his watch. "It's time we meet the professor and Raphael."

"Speaking of Raphael."

Jack stopped, waiting for me to go on.

"You must trust him a lot to let him come with us." I waited for him to answer.

Another tourist group entered as well, crowding the area.

Jack looked them over closely and stared at a couple who hung back. He grimaced like he had in the restaurant in Paris when he'd spotted the guy coming after us. It was time to leave.

Without looking again at the people who had caught his attention, I hustled up the stairs. He was either highly suspicious of the couple, or he just plain didn't want to discuss his friend with me.

Jack took my arm, guiding me near the north gate wall. "That couple . . . I've seen them somewhere before. And for the record, I'm not happy Raphael is with us. But we're in a tough spot. He's learned too much to let him go. I figured it would be better tae have him with us. If he didn't come, he'd send his goons tae tail us, which would add yet another group tae contend with."

"What about the concierge at Hotel Merci? He may have sent his men to follow." I hated to think so, but it was possible.

"You're right. He could have, but most small thievery groups stay within their country."

His comment made me chuckle out loud. "Are you forgetting the Frenchmen who tried to kill me at my friend's house in Salt Lake?"

"Point well taken."

I heard steps on the stone stairs. We were being chased. Jack must have heard them as well. He grabbed my hand and pulled me along. We rushed through the tunnel, coming out at the north gate.

I checked behind us. A nice-looking couple, both the same height, both brunettes, and both with normal, cheerful faces that turned sour at the same time as they set their sights on us. They headed our way, and I was pretty certain they didn't want to discuss the architecture of the castle.

Some unassuming tourists walked up the tunnel between us and the couple.

We raced through to the outer wall. Jack peered over as if wanting to jump but then stopped short. "We can't go that way."

I double-checked.

A drop-off that appeared to be a good hundred feet of sharp rocks lay in our path. No, we couldn't escape this way.

We were trapped, and I couldn't see a way out.

CHAPTER EIGHTEEN

JACK GRABBED MY ARM, AND we fled toward a line of several stone structures protected with a wall of rock in front. At least we wouldn't be seen there. We dodged behind the wall and fled past several buildings. All too quickly, we came to the end. A groundskeeper with a cart behind a four-wheeler parked between us and the couple.

Jack motioned for me to follow him. We exited from behind the wall, sprinting past what we thought was the last stone building and dodged into a structure that housed a tapestry exhibition.

Several tourists read the displays explaining how the unicorn was symbolic of Christ. We skirted around them to the far end of the building.

The entrance door opened. Jack discreetly checked. "It's them," he said softly, barely moving his lips. "Keep your head down." He took my hand, and we pretended to read the display.

The picture before us was of a tapestry of the unicorn in a corral. I wondered where the couple stood now. Out of the corner of my eye, I saw they had moved to the other side of the displays. Though they might recognize our clothes, if we stayed here with our heads down, as though reading, they might not see us, and we could double back and escape.

Jack pressed his hand against the small of my back, his signal that it was time to go. We hustled outside. The man on the four-wheeler drove toward us, now pulling an empty cart.

Jack flagged him down. "*Inntinn a 'toirt dhuinn turas?*"

A smile crossed his face. "Good to hear the native tongue, but I speak English. You can ride, but I'm goin' the back way." He said it like he didn't think we'd want to go there.

"That's fine." Jack looked to me.

I shrugged. "Why not?"

The man nodded for us to hop on the cart. We did, and as we pulled away, the couple chasing us came out of the tapestry exhibition. I wasn't sure if they saw us or not.

We rode completely around Stirling Castle, ending up at Queen Anne's Garden, where the groundskeeper stopped. "Ya, okay?"

Jack nodded thanks as we got off.

"Good day to ya." The groundskeeper went to work loading the cart with branches that had been trimmed from huge trees giving shade to the castle.

We walked away.

"We've missed the professor and Raphael. Think that couple will come upon them?" I didn't believe Sumsion could run very fast, but his endurance had surprised me so far.

"I doubt they'd pay him and Raphael much attention. It's you they want. Why do you think I paired up with you? You're the target. You have the pages." Jack scanned the area, ever on guard, and walked toward the main entrance.

I slowly followed, worry for the others still on my mind.

"Wait." Jack stopped, turned, and looked at me. "You didn't think I paired up with you just tae be alone with you, did you?"

"The thought never crossed my mind. But I wanted to talk with you alone." I'd said it without thinking and walked past him.

He caught up. The corners of his thick lips rose slightly. "Alone, huh?"

I was not amused. "I don't even want to be teased about you and me."

"So, on the tapestry regarding the unicorn we stood before back there, you're not the maiden who was caught?" His smile grew even more.

"You read that, too?" I was surprised. We hadn't stood there very long.

"It wasn't a five-hundred-page novel; plus, I was trying tae sell that I was a tourist. And I saw you reading it." He stopped, looking down at me.

I might as well admit it. "Yes, I read it. But I was also keenly aware of the danger we were in."

"As was I." His gaze changed. It was no longer playful but more serious.

"What is it?" I asked, concerned.

"Please know that I've lied tae you about who I work for only tae protect you." He looked to the ground and then back to me, and I had the definite feeling I was getting a glimpse of the real man. I felt closer to him than I ever had. Was he going to level with me? I wanted him to continue down this path.

"Jack, shielding me from the truth only makes what I'm going through more difficult. Don't you see that?" I hoped I was making him understand.

He hung his head. "If only I could tell you." He drew a deep breath, took hold of both of my arms, and peered deep into my eyes. "I—"

"There you two are." Sumsion and Raphael exited the main entrance and hurried toward us.

Jack let go of my arms and stepped away.

Sumsion's cheeks were flushed, and he seemed out of breath. "When there was no sign of you at the north gate, Raphael and I started toward here and came upon the castle exhibition. I thought it best we check it out and was richly rewarded."

Glad and also sad at the same time that the subject had changed and Jack was no longer close to me or gazing into my eyes, I asked, "What did you find?"

"I think I know where the next page could be." Sumsion appeared proud of himself. He looked around. "Ah, a restaurant." The aroma of freshly baked bread wafted through the air, and he pointed to a sign reading Unicorn Café. "I say we purchase lunch and talk it over."

Jack shook his head. "We don't have time. Skye and I ran into a bit of a problem." His guardian mode had returned. He peered behind us, on duty once again.

"What ez it?" Raphael followed Jack's gaze.

"We were being chased. That's why we weren't at the north gate. We need tae get Skye out of here." Jack hustled us down the path toward the exit. I spied our BMW in the parking lot. With any luck, we might be able to drive away without being spotted again.

The thought had bloomed too soon. The couple who had chased us was at that same moment crossing through the main entrance.

Jack handed Raphael the keys to the car. "Get them out of here."

"But where are you going?" Faced with the reality that we would leave Jack behind, I suddenly didn't want to. I may have argued with the man and didn't trust him, but he'd looked out for us. We were a team.

"I'll find you. Don't worry." He looked to the Frenchman. "Take the road heading south."

Raphael nodded, sprinting for the car.

Sumsion tugged me along. Jack was right. He had to stay behind and distract the couple. We had to go. I wished we'd bought burner phones so we could keep in touch. As much as I didn't want to, I turned my back on Jack and hurried toward the car.

Raphael drove right at us. I thought he'd run us down, but he slammed on the brakes; the car skidded to a stop. Tires burned and smoked. I opened the back door, letting Sumsion in first, then I got in.

"Let's go," I said, slamming the door.

Raphael stomped on the gas and tore out of the parking lot. The man at the gate yelled as we careened around a hairpin turn leading to the twisty road that headed away from the castle.

Sumsion held his hand to his heart.

"Are you okay?" I studied his face. His cheeks were flushed again.

"Fine. Who was that couple?" He craned his head, trying to see out the rear window, but the parking area no longer remained in our view.

Raphael braked and yelled in French at a car he narrowly missed. Then he floored the gas pedal again.

I held on to the armrest and tried not to look where we were going, leaning close to Sumsion. In an attempt to take my mind off of Raphael's driving, I asked, "What did you find in the exhibit?"

Sumsion's eyes grew wide, and at the same time, I could see him bite his lips together. He didn't care for Raphael's driving either but didn't say anything, just looked to me, and then the question I'd asked him about the exhibit registered. "Oh, there was a time line in there showing the various kings of Scotland, with a small biography."

"How does that help?" Raphael careened around another corner, throwing me against the car door.

Sumsion fell against me but quickly righted himself. In our haste to get away, we'd both forgotten to buckle up. We grabbed our seat belts and strapped in.

Sumsion cleared his throat. "I read that Robert the Bruce was buried at Dunfermline Abbey."

"And you think the page could be buried with him there?" In all the madness, something good.

"No."

My short-lived relief vanished.

"That couldn't be possible. In 1818, workmen breaking ground on the new parish accidentally uncovered a vault. Within the vault waited the remnants of a decayed oak coffin. Inside, there lay a body entirely enclosed in lead, with a decayed shroud of gold cloth over it. The lead formed the shape of a crown on the head."

"You don't mean they dug up Robert the Bruce?"

Sumsion nodded. "Indeed, they did. They also discovered fragments of marble and alabaster. Robert the Bruce had purchased a marble and alabaster tomb made in Paris. Of course, an investigation of the vault and the remains took place. Professors of anatomy studied them. The sternum was found to have been sawn open from the top to bottom, permitting removal of the king's heart after his death."

"How barbaric." I couldn't imagine.

"No, my dear. That was often the custom. Anyway, they determined that they had indeed unearthed the dead king's remains. His skeleton was placed on a wooden coffin board, and the curious were allowed to file past the vault to view the remains." He tisked. "The sad thing is, when it came time to bury him once again, they found some of his finger bones missing. But the rest of him was ceremonially reinterred in the vault. Before the lead coffin was sealed, they poured 1500 pounds of molten pitch in to preserve him. No jar was found with him. It is very unlikely that the page could have been buried with his remains."

I thought for a moment. "So, what happened to his heart?"

Sumsion smiled. "That, my dear, is the million-dollar question."

All at once, Raphael braked hard, throwing us against the restraint of our seat belts. The passenger door opened and Jack got in.

I almost reached over the seat to touch him to make sure he was real. I didn't know I'd been so worried about him, what with Raphael's wild driving and Sumsion's telling me more history facts. But with Jack's return to us, we were a team once more.

Leaves and twigs clung in his black hair, his jacket had been torn, and smudges of dirt smeared his face. His lip looked cut.

"Tumbling down the backside of the castle wall isn't as easy as it looks," he said.

Finding a clean tissue in my jacket pocket, I handed it to him. I'd looked down the wall and seen the jagged rocks and tangles of brush. The steep and dangerous terrain had appeared impossible to traverse. I could hardly believe that was what he'd done. But he must have.

"Let's get out of here," he said as he fastened his seat belt.

Raphael sped off once again.

"Everybody all right?" Jack peered in the back seat at Sumsion and me.

"We're fine. The professor was telling me about Robert the Bruce's heart."

"Aye." Jack nodded like he knew the story.

"You tell it, son." Sumsion motioned for him to go ahead.

Jack grimaced as though he didn't want to intrude on Sumsion's story, but the older man nodded at him.

"The version I grew up with had tae do with the king's good friends taking his heart tae be buried in Jerusalem." Jack looked to Sumsion as if asking if he had the information right.

Sumsion nodded.

Jack took a breath, still a bit winded from being chased, but then said, "His friend Sir James Douglas, along with an entire list of admirers and devoted followers, set off on a crusade tae deliver the heart tae Jerusalem. However, along the way, they were met with King Alfonso of Spain. For some reason, they joined the Castilian army besieging the frontier castle of Teba. Unfortunately, Sir Douglas and many of his friends were killed during the fight. Sir Simon Locard survived and recovered Douglas's body, together with the casket containing Robert the Bruce's heart. He brought them both back tae Scotland."

"Well, then, where is the heart now?" Why couldn't people just get to the point?

Sumsion looked to Jack.

Jack rubbed his brow, then winced like he'd pressed against a bruise. "Melrose Abbey."

"The abbey is no longer functioning and is mainly ruins with a few walls still standing, but that's where I believe the jar with the last page will be found." Sumsion nearly beamed. "It has to be there. Jeanne d'Évreux didn't die until 1371. She would have wanted the third and final page buried with her ally country's king's heart. Those loyal to her would have made sure it happened."

"I hope you're right. I don't know how much longer we can outrun the bad guys." Jack brushed dirt off his ragged jacket.

Hope welled up within my chest. This might be the break we'd been hoping for.

CHAPTER NINETEEN

When we reached the small town of Melrose, we were pretty tired and hungry. Raphael drove past several coffee shops and a bakery and then came to a stop in the parking lot of the abbey.

"We tour abbey first, no?" Raphael asked as he shut off the car.

"Not a bad idea." Jack gazed at the ruins.

They were right. The sooner we located where the heart was buried, the sooner we could form a plan. I felt my back, making certain the envelope was still there and then got out. The smell of freshly baked pastries hung in the air.

Sumsion's stomach growled.

I looped my arm with his and looked at Jack. "Why don't you and Raphael take the tour. Professor Sumsion and I will get us a booth at the coffee house down the street. Come find us when you're through, and we'll discuss what we need to do next."

A tour bus filled with tourists pulled up.

Seeing them, Jack nodded, and he and Raphael hurried on their way, as if wanting to get at the head of the line.

As much as I didn't want to separate from the others, I needed to sit, eat, and try to sort out my thoughts. A lot had happened. A lot more lay ahead of us.

When Sumsion opened the café's door, a bell rang. A table back against the wall with a perfect view of the abbey sat vacant. Sumsion seemed to read my mind and went straight for it.

The waiter came over, eyeing first Sumsion and then me. "Guid efternuin." He handed us two menus.

I wasn't sure what he'd said, but Sumsion knew. "Good afternoon to you as well, my good fellow. Give us a minute to look over your menu. But in the meantime, could I have a cup of Earl Grey?"

The waiter stood there for a while, then said, "Takin' a bit tae kin yer accent. Och aye, I'll gie ye a cuppa. Some for you, lass?"

I shook my head, and he left.

I leaned over the table. "What did he say?"

Sumsion chuckled. "He said it took him awhile to understand my accent and that he'll get my tea."

"I understood the tea part. We don't have accents." I looked over the menu and decided the safe bet was a hamburger. Like the view was a magnet, I turned my gaze out the window and down the street toward the ruins that made up Melrose Abbey.

Sumsion pulled his pipe from his jacket pocket, tapped it a couple of times, but then noticed the no smoking sign. A scowl captured his face, and he put it back. "That's not the original abbey." He nodded in the direction I had been looking.

"It isn't?"

"No. The original church was built in the 1100s. In 1322, Edward II's army sacked the abbey. Robert the Bruce helped the monks rebuild it. I think the king developed a soft spot for the monks and their way of life. Some say a month before the king died, he instructed that his heart be buried there."

"Wait, I thought he wanted his heart buried in Jerusalem."

Sumsion shrugged. "There are many accounts and legends. Let's just hope my hunch is right, and Jeanne was able to bury the page with the king's heart here."

The waiter brought the tea to Sumsion. "Thank you, my good man."

"Ur ye ready tae order?"

We talked slowly, giving him each of our orders: me the hamburger, Sumsion a shepherd's pie. The waiter left.

I peered down the street again, hoping to see Jack and Raphael walking toward the cafe. They weren't. "If Robert the Bruce helped the monks rebuild, why is it in ruins?"

He took a sip of tea, shaking his head. "The army of another English king, Richard II's, army destroyed the church in 1385. But then rebuilding began a year or two after that. Perhaps Richard felt guilty for sacking a church. Construction continued through the 1400s and even into the 1500s."

"Too bad they weren't able to maintain it."

"Yes, such a shame."

I spied Jack and Raphael walking down the street. Jack stood a good half a foot taller than his French friend. Such an odd friendship. Jack didn't trust him, and from what I could tell, Raphael didn't trust Jack either, except when it came to them fighting together against another foe. It made me wonder about the story of their friendship. Jack had made light of it, saying he'd helped Raphael out of a tight spot once long ago, but there had to be something more.

They entered the café and saw us right off. Jack took the chair next to me, Raphael the one next to Sumsion.

"What did you find?" Sumsion asked.

Jack surveyed the café. A couple sat at the far end. No one else was near. Still, Jack spoke quietly. "There's a marker showing where they buried the heart, which makes our job pretty easy. Getting over the fence won't be a problem. Raphael said he could take care of the security lights. What we need tae do is purchase some shovels. Notice any hardware stores as we rode through town?" Jack looked first at Sumsion, then me.

"Sorry." I hated not being more helpful.

"Not tae worry. There's a petrol station down the street. I'll ask them." Jack noticed the waiter coming over and quit talking.

The Scottish man carried a tray loaded with my hamburger and Sumsion's shepherd pie. He set them down in front of us and studied Jack and Raphael. "Dae they want tae eat?"

"Yes, we do. We discussed what we wanted on our way here." Jack placed an order for two plates of fish and chips. The waiter scribbled on his pad and left. Looking at me, Jack said, "You haven't had proper fish and chips until you've had them in Scotland."

Raphael nodded like he agreed and trusted his friend.

"I'm surprised you didn't order Irn-Bru to drink," I said.

He snapped his fingers at his lost opportunity. "I'll ask the waiter when he returns. Thanks. And please, you and the professor go ahead and eat. I know you're famished."

I cut my hamburger in half, picked up a piece, and took a bite. Sumsion ate as well. I listened while the guys talked. I hadn't realized how pleasant-sounding Jack's deep-toned voice was.

But still, Auntie had told me many times to never trust a liar.

And Jack had lied at least twice.

However, as we'd stood on the grounds of Stirling Castle waiting for Sumsion and Raphael, Jack had been about to level with me. In my heart, I felt he'd lied to keep me safe. He'd tumbled down the castle walls to keep the rest of us from harm. Jack had honorable intentions. As I watched him converse in this relaxed setting, I noticed he had a noble forehead, a straight nose, and a square jaw covered with stubble, which only enhanced his royal-blue eyes. Little lines creased the sides of his face as he smiled at something Sumsion said.

He turned, looking straight at me. "What do you think?"

"About . . . ?" I scrambled, trying to not appear as though he'd caught me appraising him.

"What time should we go to the abbey tonight?" His head tilted. "Are you all right?"

"Of course I am. I'm just worried about Auntie." Everything I did was to help find and rescue her . . . even assessing a very attractive man. I cleared my throat. "Midnight would probably be best."

"Midnight ez what I say as well." Raphael folded his arms, leaning back in his chair.

The waiter arrived with the fish and chips. The fish didn't look soggy with oil, and the small chips seemed crispy. Jack thanked the waiter.

"Can Ah gie ye anythin' else?" The waiter looked at Sumsion and me.

I was about to say no when Sumsion held up his hand. "If I remember correctly, the menu said you have Cranachan?"

The waiter nodded. "'Tis so."

Sumsion looked at me. "My dear, trust me on this, you're going to want one. We'll have two."

I nodded.

"Oui. Me too." Raphael wiped ketchup from his lips.

"Make that four." Jack added as he took a bite of his fish. "And add some Irn-Bru."

The waiter chuckled and left.

Sumsion rubbed his palms together. "I haven't had Scottish Cranachan in decades."

"What is it?" I loved desserts but rarely indulged.

Jack put his hand up, signaling Sumsion that he'd answer once he swallowed what was in this mouth. He wiped his lips with his napkin. "Whisky, oats, heather honey, and raspberries, but the main ingredient is cream."

"Oh, and it's not like the cream we have in the States," Sumsion jumped in. "Scottish cows produce the best cream, and the raspberries—well, think of Bear Lake's raspberries and how good they are and times that by ten." Sumsion finished his shepherd's pie and laid his knife and fork to the side of his empty plate.

"Really?" Auntie and I would make a special trip to Bear Lake every summer just to buy a raspberry shake. I found it hard to imagine any berries tasting better than those. Oh, Auntie.

She would have loved to be here with us. Sumsion seemed deep in thought, his forehead wrinkled with concern as his teeth worried his bottom lip. Perhaps he was thinking of Auntie too. They belonged together. She would have loved to try the dessert we were about to consume.

Auntie, please hang on.

* * *

Sumsion's little snores filled the car. We had been sitting in the BMW for several hours, parked down the street from the abbey, shivering from the cold, and Sumsion had dozed off, which was a good thing. He needed his rest.

Jack had already purchased a backpack, two shovels, a couple of flashlights, and much-needed burner phones for each of us.

The clock in the beamer's dashboard read midnight. Time to go. I nudged Sumsion. He coughed and cleared his throat but seemed to understand we were about to set out on our mission.

Without anyone saying a word, we all got out. The crisp, early spring air showed our breath as we padded down the street. The main entrance to the abbey was through a small building on the border of the property. Fencing around the ruins started and ended at that building. When we reached the fence, Raphael effortlessly crawled over, as if he did it all the time. Actually, he probably did. His shadow rushed across to the building. He must have had a set of lock picks because not long after he disappeared, he opened the door and went inside.

A shiver caught me. Jack seemed to notice and stepped closer, as if to shield me from the cold. With Sumsion on my other side, I felt well protected. My hand went to my back, pressing against the envelope under my clothes. Still safe. Before too long, we'd have the last page and I'd be with Auntie.

Raphael exited the building and ran toward us. "The lights and alarm are no more."

As he opened the outside gate for us to go through, I wondered how he'd learned his burglary skills but didn't dwell on it as we quickly ran across the lush lawn, dodging the ruins of the ancient structure that had first been destroyed by Richard II. The haunting walls of the abbey that had taken the first structure's place loomed over us, casting ghostly images. I could imagine the monks who had lived here pleading with us to leave and not disturb the heart buried in the sacred ground.

A couple of stone steps led to another grassy area. And then the light of my burner phone's flashlight came to a square of small gravel, and in the center rested the round grave marker with an x through a hollow heart. A saying had been etched around the edge. On top of the circle it read, A NOBLE HART MAY HAE NANE EASE. GIF FREEDOM FAILYE adorned the bottom.

"What does that mean?" I stared at the intricate carvings, admiring the craftsmanship.

"A noble heart can have no rest if freedom is lacking." Jack said the words in hushed, even reverent tones. In the moonlight, he bowed his head. Disrupting the king's burial plot had to be hard for Jack.

He unzipped the backpack and pulled out some extra-large Hefty garbage bags. "I thought we could put the marker and gravel on one and the soil on another so we can put it all back and leave the grounds looking like nothing happened."

He and Raphael quickly got to work. Sumsion stood beside me, watching the younger men labor.

I peered at our surroundings several times, worried that we might get caught, but all seemed quiet, except for the sound of shovel blades cutting through soil.

They dug and dug and dug.

"Are you sure it's here? I mean, why would they leave a marker where the actual heart was buried? That seems to be asking for trouble." My words mocked me, and guilt brought up the rear.

"Aye." Jack stopped, resting his arm on top of the shovel handle. "They made quite a ceremony of placing the heart in its rightful place. The Scottish Secretary of State even said a few words over it."

They dug for what seemed hours until Raphael stood chin-deep in the hole. "Ez not here."

Sumsion paced. "I was certain it would be. Perhaps—"

The sound of a car driving down the street made us all lie flat on the ground. I clicked off my burner phone. So did Sumsion.

A small hatchback cruised under a street light. It had large squares of blue and yellow above the blue word *Police*. A searchlight panned the ticket building and the cathedral ruins but fortunately missed us. The car rolled to a stop.

A policeman wearing a yellow jacket and flat cap got out.

Great. I held my breath and prayed he wouldn't come on the grounds or shine his searchlight toward us.

Jack took hold of my hand. He knew I was scared. "He's probably doing his rounds."

I hoped he was right.

The officer walked up the steps to the entrance of the building. Raphael had used the other door that opened out on the abbey.

The officer jiggled the door handle. He rattled it some more, as if double-checking, then grabbed the radio attached to the shoulder of his jacket. "False alarm. Everything looks fine here." He walked back toward his car, got in, and drove away.

Jack and Raphael leaped up and started shoveling dirt back into the hole as fast as they could.

"Professor, what were you going tae say before we were interrupted?" Jack said between shovelfuls.

I helped Sumsion stand up, offering an arm to steady him. "I need to look once again at both pages."

"Why don't you and Skye go tae the car and do that? Raphael and I will finish up here." Jack dropped more soil into the hole.

Not wanting to draw attention, we kept our flashlights off. Using moonlight as our guide, Sumsion and I skirted around the foundation ruins of the old monastery.

"I don't understand, my dear. I was certain we'd find the heart and page here."

I could tell by the shakiness in his voice he was still tired and very disappointed.

"It's okay. Look at it this way: we can cross this off the list of possibilities."

We'd reached the gate. About to step out on the sidewalk, I glanced toward the BMW. Someone stood beside it. I held Sumsion back.

Another person rummaged inside the car.

Despite all our precautions, we'd been followed.

CHAPTER TWENTY

I POINTED THROUGH THE DARKNESS at the BMW so Sumsion could see why I'd stopped him. He squinted, peering into the night, and then stopped cold.

We couldn't just stand there. They'd see us.

"Come on." I pulled on Sumsion's arm. "Let's go back and tell Jack."

In my haste to cross the grass, I banged my shin on a jagged stone poking up from the ancient foundation. Sumsion helped me around it, and then he tripped on another. Holding on to each other, we made it through the minefield of ruins. Amazingly, when we reached Jack and Raphael, they had finished filling the hole and were putting the gravel and grave marker in place.

"What are you doing back here?" Jack stopped, wiping his brow with his jacket sleeve.

"A couple of men are at the car." I huffed, trying to catch my breath.

Jack stood there as if dumbfounded.

"They're on to us, Jack. We've got to do something." I didn't know what, and seeing him standing there like a sail without wind kind of scared me. He was the seasoned spy who knew how to think on the run. He had to guide us through this.

As if coming to his senses, he grabbed his shovel and scooped up the garbage bags. "There's a shed on the other side of the cathedral. Let's go!"

We hurried as fast as we could through the shadowy night, afraid to turn on the flashlights on our phones, not wanting to draw attention. We skirted the looming cathedral walls. On the other side, we came upon tombstones, big and small, some with crosses on the top, some without. An eerie breeze picked up, swirling stray hairs that had escaped my ponytail into my face. I stopped to right my hair, but the elastic band broke, and my hair tumbled forward, obstructing my vision. I'd fallen behind. Someone grabbed my arm, and I nearly screamed.

"Watch your step." Sumsion guided me around a grave marker as tall as I was.

"Thanks," I muttered, embarrassed I hadn't seen it.

Tucked in the corner, away from the cemetery, stood the garden shed. Raphael reached it first and quickly worked his magic on the lock to open the door. Jack motioned us inside. The smell of freshly mowed grass and upturned soil welcomed us.

Once the door was closed, Jack clicked on his light, keeping it low and away from the windows. He leaned his shovel against the wall next to several others and shoved the garbage bags into a corner. Raphael did too.

Unable to contain myself, I said, "How did they find us?" In Paris, I thought Jack had tipped off our enemies, but not anymore. He was in this to help Auntie and me, so he wanted the pages just as badly as I did.

"The only thing I can think of is rental cars have tracking devices. They could have hacked into the car's computer and found us. But there's still the question of who they are." Jack paced within the small confines.

"The Black Prince wants the pages and is happy to let us do the legwork, so it's doubtful it's his men." I could almost hear his voice from the last phone call. He was a manipulator and cruel person. But he didn't seem the type to do grunt work.

I thought of my pursuers in Salt Lake and in Paris. "Raphael's men?"

Raphael placed his hand over his heart and seemed offended. "Non."

"Okay, maybe the other French group."

"Though it was dark, they didn't seem French to me. Too tall," Sumsion piped up.

"Too tall? Zee French are tall as well, monsieur." Raphael sniffed.

"I didn't mean to upset you, my good man; it's just that the French are generally shorter than others."

"Charles de Gaulle stood 195.58 centimeters tall." Raphael was not letting this go.

"It doesn't matter," Jack hissed.

Raphael recoiled.

Jack ignored him. "If we hide out here until morning, maybe they'll be gone. Skye, why don't you and the professor look at the pages again while I think about what tae do if they're still there by the time we need tae leave."

Sumsion guided me to a potting table. He wiped small bits of soil off of it with his hand, then spied a roll of paper towels and tore off several sections, placing them on the surface of the table. I pulled the envelope from my waistband, took out the cardboard, and opened it for Sumsion. He carefully pinched a corner of the protective sheeting between his fingers and set the pages on a paper towel.

I found a stool beneath the potting table and pulled it out for him to sit on.

"Thank you, my dear." He drew out the magnifying glass he'd used in Paris. "Could you please hold the light so I can read them?"

I looked to Jack to see if that would be all right. I didn't want to do anything that might draw the attention of anyone outside the shed.

He nodded.

I carefully aimed the beam away from the window and where it would help Sumsion. He studied both pages for a while before sucking in a deep breath. "Hmm. I guess instead of it saying *occultatum*, it could say *celantur*."

"It's all Greek to me." I smiled at him.

"*Occultatum* means 'hidden.' *Celantur* means 'concealed.' Very different meanings. And instead of saying 'with,' it might say 'within.' The line would now read, 'But concealed away within the heart of an allied land.'"

"What does that mean?" I hoped he knew.

"Many things. *Within the heart* could mean 'in the center of Scotland.' But that doesn't feel right. The line that really misled me was, 'A new hope lies buried, waiting to be free.'"

I couldn't let Sumsion blame himself. "It's confusing, to say the least."

He drummed his arthritic fingers on the table.

"I assumed *buried* meant 'in a grave,' but what if it doesn't?" Sumsion's teeth worried his bottom lip.

"Most likely means 'in the ground' though." I didn't know if I was helping or not but felt I needed to keep pushing him, make him think of possibilities.

"You're right. But there are other ways of being in the ground. Remember, I told you Robert the Bruce hid in a cave." He stared at me, waiting.

"Yes, that's where he watched the spider." I shivered at the thought. I hated spiders.

"A cave is buried in the ground." Professor Sumsion's gray brows rose on his forehead.

Jack had heard us. "No one knows where that cave is. It could be in Scotland, Ireland, maybe the Shetlands."

Sumsion nodded. "Could also be in the Hebrides. Wish I had a map."

Jack motioned for Raphael to leave the window and take his position by the door. He pulled out his burner phone. "Let's see if I can connect tae

Wi-Fi." He came to stand beside us, tapping the screen on his phone. "We're in luck." He handed the phone to Sumsion.

"You can't honestly see that?" Sumsion asked as he brought the magnifying glass in front of the screen, placing it close, then far, then found the sweet spot.

"There are hundreds of islands off the coast of Scotland. It could be any one of them." Sumsion studied the screen, slid a finger across, making the picture larger, then abruptly stopped and stared at me.

"What?" I tried to see what he'd been looking at on the phone but couldn't.

"The Isle of Skye." Sumsion's brows rose high on his forehead as he stared at me like all of a sudden everything made sense.

"Skye! Of course!" Jack focused on me as well.

"What's with you two? So what if there's an island named Skye. I'm sure it wasn't called that during Robert the Bruce's time. What does that have to do with me?"

"Not sure." Sumsion folded his arms. "But it could have everything to do with you, my dear."

CHAPTER TWENTY-ONE

I'D NEVER FELT MORE UNCOMFORTABLE, standing there in the garden shed at Melrose Abbey, in the dark of night, with three men staring at me as if I should know something I didn't. "It's just a coincidence that my name is Skye."

Sumsion pulled his pipe out of his jacket pocket as though tempted to use it but thought better of doing so. Still, he held it in his hand like it gave him great comfort, his thumb rubbing over the highly polished wood of the pipe's bowl. "I don't believe in coincidences."

"Neither do I." Jack stared at me now as if I'd been lying to him, like I had been keeping some deep, dark secret from everyone.

"It's not like I know why my father named me Skye. And I can't exactly ask him." I paced.

"Both your first name and surname are Scottish. Skye Armstrong." Sumsion tapped the mouthpiece of his pipe to his chin. "Perhaps you should have looked at those DNA reports you said you received."

Frustration welled up in me like a geyser ready to explode. I placed my hands on my head as if I could contain my thoughts and the hammering in my brain. "None of this has to do with the pages or the fact that my aunt has been kidnapped and could be dying."

"Are you sure?" Jack leaned over, staring at me with empathy I didn't deserve. Not after the way I had doubted him.

My stomach felt queasy. Light-headed, I leaned against the potting table. "My father named me Skye because he liked to fly. That's all."

All three men stood stone still, watching me, making me even more self-conscious.

"And Auntie never told me about the page she'd kept hidden in the safety-deposit box. I had no idea it even existed until the kidnapper emailed, telling me to retrieve something from the bank. When I saw it, I didn't know what it was. You've got to believe me." I took a deep breath, trying to clear my head.

"My dear, we believe you. You may not know or understand how you're connected to all this, but you are. And so is my Marjorie." Sumsion shook his head as if he wished he could fit the pieces together that lay before him, like he had everything that would make sense but didn't understand how to assemble them.

Raphael turned back to the door, keeping watch.

"It will be light in a few hours. We might as well get some rest if we can." Jack placed the protective sheeting holding the pages back in the envelope and handed it to me for safe keeping. I slid it beneath my waistband. Maybe I was more like Frodo than I thought. I, Skye Armstrong, was carrying ancient pages commissioned by a French queen regarding a mystery that now felt like it centered on me.

And I had no idea why.

* * *

Falling asleep in the garden shed proved difficult. We sat on the floor with our backs against the wall. Raphael insisted on keeping watch while Jack got some shut-eye.

I thought I'd closed my eyes for only a minute when I felt Jack touch my shoulder. "It's getting light."

I guess once I had fallen asleep, it hadn't been hard to stay asleep. In the metal-gray shadows of dawn, I saw concern line Jack's face. Of course he was worried about our situation, but I also felt he was more anxious about my well-being. A warmth settled in my heart.

Sumsion was already on his feet. Raphael stood next to the door. Jack held out his hand to help me up. "We've got to go."

The four of us rushed to the BMW, with no sign of the men who had been going over it last night. They could have been burglars that had had nothing to do with the nightmare I was living, but if so, it didn't appear as though they'd taken anything. Besides, that would have been too coincidental.

I stopped at the car and said to Jack, "Why are we taking the BMW if you think the bad guys are using the rental company's tracker to find us?"

"Because I have a plan." He opened the door for Sumsion and me to get in the back seat. Raphael hopped in the front. Jack settled behind the wheel.

"Want to fill us in on your plan?" I asked as he started the engine.

"They don't know we're on tae them, so why not use that tae our advantage?" He pulled out, driving down the winding road to the main highway.

"Want to fill us in as to how, son?" Sumsion appeared alarmed.

"We've got a long way tae go if we're heading tae the Isle of Skye. It will take most of the day, especially since we need tae ditch this car." He checked his rearview mirror.

"We can't very well rent another one. They'll just hack the tracker in it." I didn't want to state the obvious, but someone had to.

"I have a friend in Edinburgh who owes me a favor." Jack looked at me in the rearview mirror.

"Does that mean that another 'friend' of yours is going to join us?" How many more people could we afford to add to our group?

Sumsion had tilted his head back against the headrest and closed his eyes; still, he said, "Let him finish."

"No, he's not joining us." Jack sounded defensive. "I'll see if he'd mind switching cars with me. He'd like nothing better than tae get his hands on the wheel of a BMW. We'll take his car tae the island. Meanwhile, those guys who tracked us tae Melrose will be following him around Edinburgh." Jack raised his brows as if to say, "Does that work for you?"

"Will he be safe? I mean, what if they attack him?" While I didn't relish having another one of his friends in on our plan, I certainly didn't want him harmed either.

"Believe me, he can take care of himself. He's not skinny like Raphael here."

Raphael glared at Jack.

Jack continued. "McDonough has taken first place in Scotland's strongest man contest five years and counting. If those men pull him over, they'll take one look at him and leave."

We sat in silence as the miles flew by. Raphael and Sumsion seemed to have fallen asleep.

My mind returned to my name. Had my father named me Skye as some type of clue? Did my father know the entire story and the secret the pages told? Did he know Auntie had one of the pages in a safety deposit box? What if someone thought he had the page with him and his plane crash was no accident? Questions swirled around in my mind, gathering steam and multiplying with every second.

I looked at the rearview mirror, meeting Jack's gaze. He smiled slightly, like he wished he could answer my questions. I turned my head. His empathy did me no good, especially since he knew more than what he was saying. For some reason, he couldn't tell me, which didn't make sense. Why would Scotland Yard want to keep me in the dark?

Again, I wondered if he truly worked for Scotland Yard. If he didn't, why was he here helping me? There must be something in it for him. Maybe he was a fortune hunter who had stumbled on the tale of the missing pages. Maybe he was the leader of another group who wanted the pages for another reason other than money. I thought of the conversation Sumsion and I had had on the plane regarding people in Scotland who wanted their independence.

Scotland was Jack's native home. And it must mean a lot to him.

"Jack," I said.

"Yes." He glanced at me briefly in the mirror as he drove.

How could I put this? "A couple of years ago, when Scotland had a vote to leave the United Kingdom and become independent, what did you vote for?"

He said nothing for a while. I'd made him think, which was a good thing. Was he trying to come up with yet another lie? Or was he afraid to give me an honest answer? I wanted to jump in and say something else but held back. He needed to reply in his own way, in his own time.

"I have deep roots in Scotland," he said, keeping his eyes on the road. He bit his lips together like he wanted to say more but couldn't.

"But does that mean you're for independence or against it?"

He looked at me in the mirror again. "A noble hart may hae nane ease gif freedom failye."

I tried to remember what that meant. "A noble heart can have no rest if freedom is lacking."

He nodded.

"Then you want Scotland to have independence?" I needed him to say it and quit this odd riddle game he cunningly played. A simple yes or no. That was what I was looking for.

"Many people seek freedom." Raphael turned in his seat to see me.

Obviously, he was no longer dozing and had heard our conversation. I didn't know what to say to him.

"Zee French had revolution. Did not end well. But we become independent. We have a country." Sincerity glowed in his dark eyes. He raised his head a little higher with pride.

I looked from Raphael to Jack.

A Frenchman and a Scot.

Brothers.

An alliance.

Was that why they were friends? It made sense, yet the picture of them still appeared fuzzy. The facts were out of my reach.

I was about to say something when Sumsion cleared his throat. He sat up, blinked his eyes a few times, and said, "Are we there yet?"

"Yes." Jack quickly answered him as if glad the subject had changed.

I checked out the window. Without my notice, we'd arrived in the busy city of Edinburgh. A large park sprawled out on the right side of the street. Groups of young people walked together, with books loaded in their arms.

"This is the university." Jack turned at the corner. "McDonough lives just up the street here."

We passed several townhouses and stopped at the last one on the block. Jack pulled into a parking spot next to the curb. "Give me a minute." He got out and quickly covered the distance between the car and the building. He took the steps two at a time to the front door and rang the doorbell. I couldn't see who answered and let him in.

I sat back, frustrated that just when I'd made some progress in finding answers, we'd been interrupted.

Raphael remained in the front, scanning the area as if still on guard duty.

Sumsion took my hand. "Have patience, Skye. We'll find the answers together."

So he had heard the earlier conversation. Once again, I was grateful to have him with us, grateful that he loved Auntie, and grateful we had only one more page to find.

CHAPTER TWENTY-TWO

THE GARAGE DOOR BENEATH MCDONOUGH'S townhouse opened, and a white van pulled out. Jack sat behind the wheel. He stopped before the sidewalk and motioned for us to get in.

Jack hadn't slept for a while, so I went over to his window first and knocked on it. He rolled it down.

"Why don't you let me drive?" I smiled, trying to convince him.

He thought for a moment.

"I do know how." I tried to appear reassuring.

"Not in Scotland, you don't. Different side of the road and steering wheel on a different side of the vehicle."

"I've driven here on layovers before. Besides, you should get some sleep. And so should Raphael." I stood there, waiting.

He tapped his fingers on the steering wheel and then reluctantly said, "Okay."

As he got out to let me behind the wheel, Raphael and Sumsion slid open the side door.

"Seems we are not alone." Sumsion gazed into the back of the van.

Raphael checked that way too as he took his seat next to Sumsion. "There ez many, how you say, *équipement?*"

Jack got in the passenger side. "All McDonough's Strongman gear is in here. He didn't want to haul it out. I assured him it would be fine to leave it."

"Exactly what's back there?" I adjusted the rearview mirror.

Sumsion studied what rested behind his seat. "All sorts of weightlifting belts. Several boxes are stacked against the back door; one contains wraps and guards, the other weightlifting shoes. There's also a huge sandbag and an apparatus that says 'Sled' on it."

Leave it to Sumsion to give a detailed list.

"Now you know why he wanted tae leave it in here." Jack clicked together his seat belt. "I promised him we'd return the van within the week. He doesn't have an event until the end of the month, so it's fine."

With everyone buckled up, I pulled onto the street. Jack stayed awake and alert, guiding me out of the city. Once we were on the M90, his eyes became droopy. "We're heading tae Glencoe. Get off M90 and take the A9 when you see it. We should stay on that for a few hours. Wake me if you get confused and definitely if you find we're being tailed."

Before too long, I heard little snores from not only the passenger seat but the bench seat behind me as well. The men had conked out, which was fine with me.

I checked my mirrors regularly, ever on the alert. No car seemed to follow, so I relaxed a little. I wondered if McDonough had had any surprise visitors yet, driving the BMW around town. With any luck, he'd be safe. And with a little more, so would we.

Driving gave me time to think. So much was on my mind, I didn't know where to start.

We'd had a major setback in not finding the other page buried with Robert the Bruce's heart. I tried to remember if Auntie had mentioned anything out of the ordinary about our extended family. She rarely spoke of our ancestors, always sidetracking me away from the subject by discussing the day-to-day things, like her flower garden, what new movies were being released, and cooking.

The image of her with her Wonder Woman apron on, busy in the kitchen, made me smile. Auntie loved to cook. She made a fuss whenever I had time off. She'd have cooking themes for each week.

For Chinese week, she made Chinese noodles, Peking roast duck, or lion's head with crab. During Mexican week, she served chile rellenos, arroz con pollo, taquitos, and chimichangas. Italian week was spaghetti and meatballs, shrimp portofino, and fig marsala. Most of the time, the food tasted delicious. But she'd had some disasters, like the time she'd forgotten to turn on the oven or the time she'd added too much brandy to her flaming crepes and had nearly caught the kitchen on fire. Whenever the unexpected happened, she'd say, "Not to worry. I'll conjure up something else."

She loved baking too: cookies, cakes, and breads, and she usually gave most of what she made away. I smiled. She liked to leave food on her friends' doorsteps without a note or anything.

Auntie was a force to be reckoned with, and everyone loved her. To think of her being kidnapped and incapacitated by a stroke made me sick inside. But that was what had happened. At least that was what the Black Prince had told me.

If this modern-day Black Prince had earned his nickname by mercilessly achieving his goal like the original, he may be torturing and doing unspeakable things to her. I didn't want to dwell on the possibilities. Poor Auntie.

We'd been living this nightmare going on five days now. Would it end with everyone still alive? I seriously wondered. The miles continued to roll by. Several hours did as well. And I became sleepy.

There was a CD in the player, so I turned it on, keeping it low. The tunes of Kenny G played. I couldn't imagine this friend of Jack's, who was the Strongman champ for five years straight, enjoying Kenny G, but to each his own.

However, soft lilting music wouldn't keep me awake. I needed something with a little more pep. I couldn't very well look for another CD in the console and drive, and I didn't want to stop the car. That would wake up everyone.

"What's the matter?" Jack yawned as he sat up in the passenger seat.

"Just trying to stay awake is all." As if on cue, I yawned too.

"This tune isn't going tae help. Let me have a look." He opened the glovebox. "Ah, he has Django Django's *Storm* CD. Let's give this a try." He ejected the Kenny G and replaced it with the CD he seemed to like.

The beat sounded quicker, livelier.

"Where are we?" He put the CD away and gazed out the windows at the vast landscapes that seemed ready to burst with spring buds of yellow and white and green. In the distance were mountains.

"I've been watching for road signs, but there aren't very many."

"Scotland isn't like America, with lots of billboards." He scrubbed his hand over his face. "The A9 is known as the spine of Scotland because it's the longest road in our country."

"How long is it?"

"Around 270 miles or close to 434 kilometers."

I couldn't help but think of the freeways back home and how they were much longer, but America was a bigger country, so it made sense. This seemed like a good time to ask Jack a little more about his Scottish background. "So, your father is a fisherman?"

"Aye, he is at that, though I think of late he regrets it." He looked at me out of the corner of his eye, and I could tell he wondered where this was going.

"Why?"

"Politics make it hard for a fisherman tae earn a living." He took a deep breath. "When the UK was part of the EU, we had tae share our waters with other countries, which cut into profits. Many fishermen were for Brexit and pulling away from the EU, thinking that would bring back business. But . . ."

"But what?"

Jack rubbed his brow. "Now they fear that once Brexit takes hold, the government will stab them in the back and give away more fishing rights tae the EU tae save the UK economy. Tae put it in a more American way, they'll throw the fishing industry under the bus."

"I had no idea there was such bad feelings between Scotland and Britain."

"It's not all of Scotland." Jack tilted his head. "But enough that some people are talking about independence again, at least fishermen like my father. They're tired of Parliament dictating what Scotland should do."

Not wanting to dwell on politics, I tried to steer him away. "Have you done your family history? I mean, how far back has your family lived in Scotland?" On the surface, the question wasn't unusual. However, after all we'd been through, he had to know I was digging into his background.

"I know a little about it, I suppose. I'm a bit peckish."

I'd heard *peckish* a few times in my travels. It meant he was hungry. But I was hungrier for information. Besides, I knew he wanted to sidestep my question. "Come on. Being from Scotland and with a name like Duncan, you have to know a little more than that."

He tilted his head. "There are so many Duncans in our family tree that it looks like an American tumbleweed. It's all jumbled up."

I thought of my own family tree, which I knew nothing about and which Auntie had always steered me away from. Once again, I wished this horrible nightmare were over and she were with me, where she belonged. "A family tumbleweed. Sounds complicated."

"Aye. It is. And there are many Duncan families in Scotland. During the Jacobite rebellions in 1745 the Duncans were split, with some fighting for the Jacobites and others fighting for the British." He gazed out at the scenery as if picturing a battle.

"So, which side did your Duncan clan fight on?"

"The Jacobites, or so my father says, but his brother says we were with King George."

"Tell me about both." I waited.

"Uncle said we are from the Duncan clan from the east of Scotland, the Duncans of Lundie. Admiral Adam Duncan. He fought for Britain and was in the Royal Navy. From what I understand, he made quite a name for himself. But then, my father says we're from James Duncan, who was a mere servant from Aberdeenshire. He was captured and put in prison after the Battle at Culloden."

"The Battle at Culloden? Sounds pretty ominous." I'd never heard of it.

"The battle was the last one ever fought on British soil. Have you never heard of the Jacobites?"

Though I didn't look at him, I sensed Jack studying me intently. "Not a lot. Why would I? It's not like I'm from Scotland. I have enough trouble remembering American history." I kept my eyes on the road.

"Crash course. The Jacobites wanted tae overthrow the House of Hanover and King George II and restore the House of Stuart and King James tae the British throne." He'd said it like that should clear up everything.

"Why would they want to trade one king for another?" I couldn't understand their reasoning. Jack stared at me as though measuring my words. I continued. "As long as you have a king, the people will be at their mercy. It's all fun and games as long as you have a benevolent king who puts his people and their well-being ahead of his own, but as history has shown over and over, good kings die and bad kings take their place, and then the people are stuck. Why not fight for freedom? Why not give the people a choice?"

"Spoken like a true American." He gave me a nod. "And believe me, after the Battle at Culloden, some Scotsmen were thinking the same thing. In fact, many fled for their lives, and guess where they went?" He folded his arms, waiting.

"Oh, this is tough." I playacted, taking the bait he dangled in front of me, and said, "America?"

"Yes. Some of the founders of America had learned some brutal lessons here and knew independence was the only way tae go." He seemed pretty proud of himself.

"Who do you believe? Your father or your uncle?"

He rubbed the back of his neck. "My father. But it really doesn't matter. It's in the past."

"Don't you know that saying?" I tried to think of it. I wanted to get it right. "Those who don't know history are doomed to repeat it."

"Aye. And here's another one: Every man dies, but not every man lives."

"Deep. I'm sure the professor would be proud of us."

Jack nodded and seemed content to let the conversation stop there.

I couldn't let that happen. I wanted to know more. "What about before the Jacobite rebellions? What did the Duncan clan do?"

"Some were fishermen, others raised sheep." He appeared uncomfortable talking about them.

"Any other famous Duncans in your family tumbleweed?" I smiled, hoping to keep him talking.

He chuckled a little. "The clan was quite widespread. Some say our name came from Donnachadh Reamhar, known as the Stout Duncan. He was a chief and"—he bit at his lip like he really didn't want to say what came next, but all at once, he did—"he led the clan into the Battle at Bannockburn in 1314."

"Isn't that the same era as Robert the Bruce?" Did I hear him right? I wasn't certain.

He nodded. "Aye."

"Did your great-great-great-whatever fight alongside Robert the Bruce?" I held my breath, waiting for his answer.

"My father believes so." He peered out the window as though he hadn't dropped an information bomb at my feet. "I could really use something to eat. Why don't you turn off when you see a café?"

My grip on the steering wheel tightened. "I find this very coincidental that your ancestor helped Robert the Bruce, especially since, somehow, Robert the Bruce is involved with these pages and especially because my name is Skye, so we're going to the Isle of Skye because that's where you guys think he hid in that cave, and the page might be there." I didn't know if my words made any sense, but I was so full of angst and frustration, I didn't care.

"You said it. It's just a coincidence." Jack peered out the window again.

Sumsion cleared his throat. "There are no coincidences, son."

Ah, so Sumsion was awake.

"Ordinarily, I'd agree with you. But in this case, there are." Jack let out an exasperated sigh. "If you were tae throw a Scotsman into a crowd in Edinburgh, you're bound tae hit someone whose ancestors helped Robert the Bruce or someone whose kin nobly fought in the Jacobite rebellions. That's part of our history. It has nothing tae do with Skye or the pages."

"You really don't expect me to believe that, do you?" I glared at him.

"I don't care what you believe. My being with you has everything tae do with my job and not my ancestors. My family has no grudge. We've made our peace with the fate that history dealt us. I wish my family had emigrated with the others who went tae America. For some reason, they didn't. I guess one of them was a stubborn son of a Scotsman."

Sumsion chuckled. And I thought I heard a chuckle from Raphael as well.

Jack turned in his seat to look back at them. "What happened in my family's past doesn't affect me. Besides, clans and titles mean nothing today. It's all about earning money. My family turned tae fishing tae make ends meet. You want me tae tell you a fishing story? I've got plenty of those."

I shook my head. "I've already heard about the one that got away."

A smile tugged at Jack's lips. Sumsion guffawed. But Raphael didn't. Obviously, the Frenchman hadn't been fishing.

"My father has a boat full of them." Jack turned serious. "Spending days on end out at sea didn't appeal tae me, so I chose some other way tae make a living."

"And that some other way includes keeping me and the pages safe?" I wasn't about to say Scotland Yard because even with everything we'd been through, I didn't buy that story.

"Yes, it does." He peered out the window again. "I could have sworn there was a small restaurant along the A9 somewhere around here."

Delving into Jack's history had brought more to light but had also dug up more questions than I'd bargained for. He might think the subject was closed, but I had news for him; I'd just begun this round of interrogation.

CHAPTER TWENTY-THREE

I PULLED OFF THE ROAD when we reached the next town and parked in front of McKenzie's Pub. We needed to stretch our legs and get something to eat. All through lunch, we were strangely quiet. I kept thinking about what Jack had said regarding his family history. His claim that every Scotsman had an ancestor who had helped Robert the Bruce or who had fought in the Jacobite rebellions played over in my mind. But I still wasn't convinced there wasn't more to Jack's story.

When Jack and the professor finished eating, Sumsion pulled his pipe and tobacco out of his coat pocket. "Think I'll have a smoke, if that's all right." He looked at me.

"Of course." I smiled.

Jack stood with Sumsion. "I'd like tae stretch my legs too. I'll go with you."

I hoped Sumsion would continue to question Jack. Maybe Jack would be more willing to tell another guy his secrets. They exited the cafe, leaving me alone with Raphael.

"Family history ez important, no?"

That surprised me. "Why do you think so?"

"A person must know his roots. Where he come from and where he go to." He set his knife and fork on his empty plate.

"I guess. Where does the Dubois family come from?" I was mildly curious and wanted to be friendly.

"France."

"You got me there." I must have sounded like an idiot. "But what part?"

"Here and there. They help build French Empire and served with Napoleon Bonaparte." He nodded, and his dark complexion flushed with pride.

"That's impressive." I wondered what he thought about kings and queens. He had heard the conversation in the van. "Are you glad your French Revolution overthrew the monarchy?"

He thought for a moment, and I wondered if he'd understood what I'd said. But instead of jumping in and rephrasing my sentence, I waited.

"Zee revolution necessary. Sad, no?"

"Very sad, yes." From what I remembered, the French Revolution hadn't turned out as well as the American Revolution had.

"We have our own Lady Liberty, like you, but ours lives in painting at zee Louvre."

I knew the painting he spoke of. "I've seen it. I may not go to cathedrals while I have a layover in Paris, but I do go to the Louvre. That painting of *Liberty Leading the People* is striking and full of emotion."

"Oui. French artists, bon!"

I thought of the artist Sumsion said illustrated the pages. If Raphael was a fan of art, maybe he knew more about the man. "Do you know Jean Pucelle's work?"

"Oui. Zee *Book of Hours.*"

"Is there any other work he may have done?" I didn't know why I'd asked, but I was curious about the artist who had helped Queen Jeanne by supplying the pages for her.

"Non. Zee *Book of Hours* ez only provable art he make."

"I see."

"He no live long. His work very valuable." He looked directly at me, as if wondering if I understood that the pages I concealed beneath the waistband of my pants were priceless.

Suddenly, I felt very uncomfortable. I nodded, not knowing what to say.

Jack came back inside the restaurant. "I think we'd better go if we want to get there while it's still light and we can ask about caves."

I wiped my mouth with the napkin and went out with him, keenly aware that Raphael trailed behind us. For some reason, our conversation didn't set well with me. He wanted me to know how significant his history was, that he felt the French Revolution was necessary, and that the pages Jean Pucelle had created were very important. Yet, there was an underlying tension in his words and tone, as if he were measuring me.

* * *

Jack took the driver's seat, and I was only too happy to let him. I didn't want Raphael sitting behind me. I wanted to keep him where I could see him. I got in the back with Professor Sumsion. He smelled of pipe tobacco, a sugarberry scent I could easily get used to. He patted the seat next to him, and I gladly took it.

As Jack pulled onto the main highway, it started raining, and the wind picked up. Just what we needed. Bad weather.

"I called and made reservations at a hotel in Portree. Hope you don't mind." Jack kept his eyes on the road, but I knew he spoke mainly to me.

"Sounds good." I wanted to lay in a bed with clean, crisp sheets, blankets, and a soft pillow. We hadn't had a good night's rest since this had started. And while I found the thought of not plowing ahead and doing everything I could to help Auntie revolting, I also knew I needed rest. But could I truly rest when I didn't trust those I traveled with? Sumsion patted my arm as if he'd heard my thoughts and wanted to reassure me.

Listening to the rhythm of the wiper blades made my eyelids droopy. Before drifting off, I wanted to know more about our destination. I turned to Sumsion. "What do you know about the Isle of Skye?"

"Not much, my dear. I'm afraid Jack's the man to ask."

"When I was a boy, I spent many summers there staying with my aunt, who lived on the island." His face gentled as he reflected. "She passed away in my teens, but I have fond memories of the place."

"What's the island like? Are there lots of trees, or is it mainly open terrain?" Thinking of the spider story of Robert the Bruce, I added, "How many caves could an island have?"

"The Isle of Skye has a bit of everything," Jack said, keeping his eyes on the wet-slick roads. "Mountains, valleys, fishing villages, and medieval castles. As tae how many caves are on the island, I know there are quite a few, but I think if we concentrate on three main ones, we might have more luck. They aren't easy tae get tae, and we'll have tae keep track of the tide for some. For instance, Prince William's Cave's entrance is only exposed during low tide, and it's a good hike tae reach it. The Gold Cave is very secluded and hard tae find. It's about five miles north of Uig. I understand it can be tricky getting down tae the mouth of the cave, but if luck is with us and it doesn't rain tomorrow, we might be able tae explore it."

"Why is it called Gold Cave?" Sumsion asked.

"Not sure. Maybe we'll find out."

"What's the third cave?" I asked.

"Spar Cave near Elgol. It shouldn't take too long tae reach it. I've heard rumors about this cave all my life."

"What kind?" I didn't like the sounds of that.

"Oh, that clan chiefs' daughters hid their bairns in the cave, that mermaids live there, and there's also a pirate tale or two."

A gust of wind slapped against the van, catching Jack's attention as he adjusted to keep us on the road.

The mere thought of going inside a cave gave me gooseflesh, but I couldn't very well tell the others I wasn't going. I looked in the mirror and met Jack's eyes.

Did he remember our conversation when I'd told him about my fear? Doubtful since we'd been running for our lives, yet he held a sympathetic gleam in his eyes. Maybe he was just concerned about me. I hated being vulnerable. I hated that we were being chased. And I mostly hated that Auntie was somewhere sick. But there was little I could do about it except find the third and final page.

Once I did that, then what? Somehow, the Black Prince would know. And how he would know, I didn't have a clue. Worry was like a steady IV dripping caffeine into my veins. Too wired to sleep and too sleepy to keep up casual conversation, I turned my attention outside. Rain slid down the van windows.

"I've heard the sun only shines one day in nine in Scotland." Sumsion peered out at the gray day turning bleaker by the moment. "Perhaps tomorrow will be the one."

"We can only hope."

At that moment, a car's headlights sliced through the van as it started to pass.

"What the devil?" Jack added a few cuss words as he slowed down.

The passing silver sedan swerved, slamming into the van. Jack laid on the horn as the van fishtailed. Weight belts that had been hanging in the back of the van flew into the air. Most slapped against the opposite wall, but the buckle of one hit me in the forehead. At the same time, the weights on the floor slid forward, ramming into the backs of my feet and legs. The sandbag collided with the bench seat and threw both Sumsion and me forward into the back of the two front seats.

Jack managed to stop the van. We all froze where we were, as though to take a collective breath. The only sound echoing through the van was the wiper blades swishing back and forth, fighting the rain.

Jack turned and peered at me smashed against the back of Raphael's seat. "Are you all right?"

"I think so." My legs throbbed, and my head ached, but I was in one piece. "How about you, Professor?"

Crammed against Jack's seat, Sumsion pushed the back on the bench seat that pinned him and me in our current awkward positions. "A bit shaken, but I'll rally."

"You're bleeding." Jack pointed to my forehead where the belt buckle had hit me. He motioned to Raphael. "Look in the glovebox for a tissue."

I heard Raphael rustling around as Sumsion and I stumbled over weights, trying to move the sandbag and sled out of the way.

"Wait." Jack shut off the van, opened his door, and got out. The smell of falling rain leaked in. Then the back doors opened. With hardly any effort, Jack leaped inside and pulled the sandbag and sled back where they belonged.

While Jack and Sumsion secured the bench seat, Raphael handed me a tissue. I dabbed the spot where I thought the blood was.

Jack noticed and stopped what he was doing. He took the tissue from me. Holding my chin with one hand, he wiped my forehead with the other. His tender touch and caring look as he gazed into my eyes told me he felt something more than concern. For a second, I forgot everything and everyone around us and wanted to lean into him.

Sumsion cleared his throat, drawing our attention. He sat in his seat, a curious yet knowing look on his face. "To answer your earlier question, my man, we're just fine." He then patted Jack's shoulder. "Expert driving, I must say. We could have been killed."

"I think that was the goal," Jack said, the moment over. "Somehow, they've found us. Why they didn't stop, steal the pages, and make sure we were dead makes me wonder if they have something more in store." He jumped out of the back and slammed the doors shut.

Guilt fell on me for not trusting Jack and for doubting Raphael. Stress and worry loved playing with my mind. This was a crazy roller coaster of emotions. Whoever had tried to run us off the road had tried to kill all of us, not just me.

I was back to square one and trying to figure out who wanted the pages so desperately that they would kill several people to get their hands on them.

CHAPTER TWENTY-FOUR

JACK RETURNED TO THE DRIVER'S seat. "Did anyone see what kind of car that was?"

"It happened so fast," I said. "All I know is it was a silver sedan." I looked to Sumsion and Raphael to see if they had anything else to add.

They shook their heads.

"Neither did I." Jack gave an exasperated sigh. "Stay alert, and let me know if you see anything unusual. I need tae drive over Skye Bridge, and I don't relish having an encounter on it like we just experienced." He adjusted the rearview mirror, and he looked at me again. "You sure you're okay?"

"Yes." I'd forgotten to buckle my seat belt and did so right away.

Jack turned the steering wheel, righting the van, and slowly pulled onto the wet road to continue our journey to Portree on the Isle of Skye.

The van fell quiet, except for the swooshing sound of wiper blades, and we drove on until the winding road came to the great bridge. In my travels, I'd been on and seen bigger bridges, but right here, right now, I felt Jack's worry. Bright headlights from another oncoming car in the other lane nearly blinded me, but somehow, Jack managed to drive past.

Just when I thought we'd reached the end of the bridge and were on the island, we were once again on the bridge. A two-parter. The wind picked up and gave an eerie whistle. The narrow, two-lane road disappeared into the rain as the bridge arched over the ocean. I clung to the bench seat. Lights from an oncoming car reflected on the wet road and had me on edge. Was this the car that had run us down and was now returning to finish the job? I held my breath as the vehicle approached and drove by.

Grateful the car passed without a problem, I breathed a little easier and checked my watch: 5:00 p.m. It seemed later. Peering out the windows,

I could barely see the lights of buildings along the bay. The road shortly left the bridge, and street lights fought to give us guidance on the island's winding highway.

"How much farther to Portree?" I hoped it was close.

"Another forty-five minutes." Jack looked at me in the rearview mirror. "Raphael and the professor can keep watch while you take a nap."

I really wanted to. The droning hum of the van's wheels on the highway and the gentle sway of the vehicle made me drowsy. I gave in and closed my eyes. Flashes of Paris's city lights, of being in the alleyway standing next to Jack, and of running with the threat of being killed taunted me. Images of Auntie tied and gagged made me jerk awake.

We had arrived in Portree, which reminded me of a seaside Park City, Utah, with buildings on hillsides. Below was not a valley but the ocean. Several boats were anchored in the bay and bobbed up and down. Jack pulled up in front of the Sea Eagle Hotel and stopped in a temporary parking space.

"Let me dash in and make sure everything is taken care of." Jack got out, and Raphael did too. Fighting the lashing rain, the two men crossed to the hotel entrance.

I wondered about Sumsion. He seemed contemplative and tired. "How are you holding up?"

"I'll be better once we have our Marjorie with us again." His eyes misted with emotion.

"You really love her, don't you?"

He nodded. "Once she's in my arms, I'm not letting her go until she agrees to marry me. My heart is true as steel. We're getting up in years and don't have time for all this flirting and dating nonsense."

I smiled. "I agree."

"Are you sure?" He stared intently at me.

"Yes. Why?"

"You're the reason Marjorie keeps saying no." He rubbed the stubble on his chin.

"What? I worry about her while I have to fly. I don't like her being alone. She knows that." I was puzzled.

"Don't you see, my dear?" He placed his age-spotted hand on mine. "She feels a strong bond with you. She told me how awful it was for both of you after your parents died, how you struggled with nightmares, and the only way she could calm you down enough to sleep was to give you warm milk and then cuddle up to you on the bed and sing."

Those blessed moments of having her comforting arms around me had made me feel like nothing could ever hurt me. I knew she loved and treasured me and that even though my parents were gone, she would always be there. "But I was a child then. I'm a grown woman now. I don't want her to put her life on hold for me. I've told her that many times."

"I'm glad to hear it. However, with the revelation that she stored one of the pages of Jeanne's *Book of Hours* in a safety deposit box, we both know there was more to her reluctance. She bore the burden of an ancient secret on her shoulders. I wonder if she knew the repercussions of shielding you from the truth." He fell quiet, as if he wished he knew the entire story.

I too would love to have Auntie tell us. After what we'd been through, we both deserved to know.

The front doors of the van opened. Jack and Raphael climbed in. "Turns out the hotel is family owned. They combined several fishermen's houses together, so the rooms aren't cookie-cutter but are various sizes and shapes. I reserved a single room for Professor Sumsion on the main floor." He handed him a key. "Didn't think you'd want tae climb up and down the stairs. There's no elevator."

Sumsion nodded. I was impressed with how thoughtful Jack had been of the elderly man.

"Raphael and I will bunk together on the second floor. And, Skye, I'm afraid your room is in the attic." He reached over the seats, giving me my key. "You have quite a climb, but you have your own bath and shower and a good view of the bay."

Again, I was impressed with Jack's thoughtfulness.

"I need tae leave the van a block away. The hotel doesn't have its own parking spaces. So unless you want tae walk back with me, I suggest you get out here." Jack craned his neck, looking at Sumsion and me.

"After all the excitement we've had today, I'm good with getting out here. How about you, Professor?" I asked.

He moved like he agreed and wanted out.

Raphael opened the sliding door for us, and we made our way to the quaint hotel while Jack took care of the car.

We didn't have luggage, and the buxom woman with shortly cropped gray hair who was minding the caretaker's desk gave us a rather odd look but didn't question. Sumsion headed down the hallway and disappeared inside his room. That left Raphael and me to climb the stairs, but I hung back.

"I just remembered something. Go ahead."

He shrugged and took the stairs two at a time.

Returning to the woman who eyed me as if I were prey, I said, "Is there a clothing store close by that might still be open?"

"Sorry, lass. They close at five, and 'tis half past." She still studied me closely.

I didn't blame her. I hadn't had a shower in three days, my makeup had to be gone, my long pale-blonde hair was in desperate need of a comb, and I really wanted some clean underwear.

A smile slowly crossed her round face. "Ah might have somethin' ye can buy in the gift shop." She placed a Back in a Minute sign on the counter and guided me down the hall and to the right. The selection was limited, mainly T-shirts and sweatshirts with the Sea Eagle logo sprawled over the front. The tapered jeans were two sizes too big for me, which made me wonder how I could keep the envelope in my waistband, but then I found a belt that had a large buckle with a Sea Eagle on it.

She waited by the door as I searched for underwear but couldn't find any. I didn't want to ask, but she seemed to know what I needed and guided me to a counter where there were two kinds of underwear: ladies thongs and men's briefs. And, of course, they had the logo with the Sea Eagle on them.

I grabbed the men's briefs.

"Canna blame ye for choosing them. A woman has to be knockered to wear those thong things. But they are one of me best sellers."

"Thanks. Where do I pay?"

"Up front at the till." She led the way, took down the sign she'd left on the desk, and rang up my purchases.

I pulled out my passport and realized I had only credit cards. I couldn't use those. They'd lead the bad guys right to us. Jack had been footing the bill for everything.

She watched as I stuffed my passport in my hip pocket.

"I'm sorry. I can't pay for it," I said.

She came around the register. Biting her lips together as if wondering how to say what she wanted to, she suddenly blurted, "Lassie, ah noticed ye don't have luggage. Have ye been kidnapped?"

I reared back. "No! I just had to leave home in a hurry and neglected to pack and get travel money."

"Nor yer panties?" Her brows raised, but a smile tugged at her mouth.

I chuckled. "Yeah. But I'm fine. Really." I didn't want her thinking badly of the men I traveled with.

The door opened, and Jack stepped in. His black hair was matted to his head from the rain. He zeroed in on the woman and me and seemed to know something was up. "Are you okay?"

"The lass has no Bunsens for her purchases." The stout woman now focused on Jack, assessing him as though he might be a criminal.

I put my hand to my mouth, hiding a smile.

He pulled out his wallet and handed her some bills. "Give her whatever she needs." He spied the boxers, which made him glance at me, a question in his eyes.

I didn't want to explain, so I merely stood there.

He shrugged.

I stepped closer to him. "They didn't have regular women's undergarments. Well, they did, but not the kind I'm comfortable wearing."

He thought for a moment, and I had the definite feeling he was trying to envision what underwear I liked, but then shook his head as if to erase the images. "Bring me the change when we meet for dinner, say in about an hour? Does that give you enough time?"

I nodded. Even though I yearned to crawl into bed, I could at least take a shower in that time. I wanted to meet and decide which cave we would search first thing in the morning.

He disappeared up the stairs.

The woman completed the transaction and added a complimentary hygiene kit. "Ah thought ye might need other necessities." While handing me the bag, she leaned close. "Ah don't know what he's on about." She nodded in the direction Jack had gone. "But if you need help, me room is in the back here. Come straight away. Me name's Fiona. Me guidman will help ya as well if he's here." The stern look in her glassy blue eyes told me she was dead serious.

If only she knew how much help I really needed, she wouldn't give such a tremendous and heartfelt offer. I wanted to hug her but knew it might make her even more suspicious, so instead, I said, "I'm fine. Really. But thank you, Fiona."

She gave me change, and I hurried up the steps, feeling her eyes on me until I reached the second floor. A sign taped to the wall with an arrow and the words *attic room* pointed to another set of stairs.

Taking a deep breath, I trudged up them as well. I inserted the old-fashioned key and opened the door to a small room with white walls. Against one side stood a twin bed. A pretty bed cover with wide purple trim and the print of purple thistles waited at the foot. Stark white pillows sat at the head with a purple one in the mix. The ceiling slanted, as it would with this being the attic, but a huge window opened out onto a quaint bay.

I put the change on the nightstand, pulled the envelope from my waist, and set it next to the change, then dumped the bag with my purchases on the bed. My teeny-tiny private bathroom filled one corner. I turned on the shower, grabbed the complimentary vials of shampoo and conditioner, along with the square bit of soap, and hurried in to take my shower. As I stood in the warm, inviting water, letting it cover me, I worried someone might slip in and steal the envelope. I shifted gears and hurried as fast as I could.

Toweling off, I scanned the room. The envelope lay where I'd put it. Relieved, I slipped on my new clothes and shoved the change in my pocket. The underwear felt a bit odd, but at least it was clean. I didn't know what to do with my dirty clothes, so I folded them and placed them on the rack near the door. Using the small comb from the bag Fiona had given me, I untangled my fine hair. I grabbed the complimentary blow-dryer and crunched curls into the long strands.

A knock came at my door. It had to be Jack.

I rushed over and opened it only to find no one there. Odd. Closing the door, I noticed a white business envelope on the floor, my name scrawled across it. I hadn't told Fiona my name. There was no reason for Jack or Sumsion or Raphael to leave me a note. That meant only one thing.

The kidnapper knew I was here.

CHAPTER TWENTY-FIVE

THE SEA EAGLE WASN'T A huge hotel like we'd stayed at in Paris, with lots of people coming and going in the hallways. With any luck, Fiona might have seen who had left the message. Desperate to find out who had left it, I slid the manila envelope with the pages into the waistband of my pants and made sure the belt kept it cinched in place.

Then I clutched the white business envelope and shot down the stairs, taking them two at a time. I rushed to the caretaker's desk, but Fiona wasn't there, just her Back in a Minute sign. There was a chance that whoever had left me the message had come and gone and no one had seen them. Maybe I could catch a glimpse of them on the street.

I raced to the door. Rain poured down. A cold wind rushed through me as I stepped outside. Only a few people were about. A family bunched together, headed to the fish and chips place. A couple of elderly ladies sharing an umbrella scurried to the corner and turned. No one else. No one who fit the description I had for a sneaky kidnapper like the Black Prince.

Feeling utterly defeated, I returned inside.

"Skye, my dear." Sumsion had stepped out of his room and was shutting the door. "You look refreshed . . . and also upset. What's happened?"

I held out the business envelope with my name on it.

"Where did you get this?" Worry lined his face.

"Outside my door. Someone knocked, and when I answered, this lay on the floor."

He shook his head. "And so the plot thickens. Have you told Jack?"

I shook my head. "I came straight downstairs, thinking I might be able to catch whoever had left it. Plus, I hoped Fiona might have seen who it could have been, but she's not at the till."

"Fiona?" Sumsion's head gave a curious tilt.

"She's the woman who was at the desk when we first arrived."

"Ah, yes. Why don't you open the envelope?" His eyes were fixed on it.

"Might as well wait until we're all together." Though I wanted to tear it apart and read the message, I felt reluctant to do so.

Sumsion pulled his watch from his jacket pocket. "Jack said to meet in the hotel restaurant at seven. We're a tad early, but why don't we go in, get a table, and maybe have a whisky while we wait. Scotland has the best." He held his arm out.

I took it. Unexpectedly, I felt very tired and wanted to sit down. Receiving the message was the topper of another long, dreadful day. "Think Jack will do the honors and read it?" I stared down at it, then looked up at Sumsion.

"I'm sure he would, should you ask."

A young woman who had Fiona's kind eyes met us as we entered the restaurant, reminding me that this was a family-run business. Made me wonder who did the cooking.

"Two?" she asked.

"No, four. There are two others in our party who will join us shortly, but we thought perhaps we could get a table and have some of your best whisky, if that's okay." Sumsion gave her a kind, old-man smile that would warm any stranger's misgivings toward him.

She took us to a booth against the wall. Jack would appreciate that. Once we were settled, she set the menus in front of us and disappeared.

I placed the mysterious envelope on the table. Sumsion and I didn't say anything, just sat there with the elephant in the room staring up at us. A knot twisted my stomach. Had something happened to Auntie?

The young woman returned with our drinks, then left again.

Sumsion took a sip. "Mighty fine." He motioned for me to have some of mine.

"I shouldn't have ordered one. My stomach is a little queasy. I don't think alcohol would be a good idea."

Voices came from the threshold between the hotel and the restaurant. Jack and Raphael had arrived. Jack's black hair shone with moisture from a shower, his face freshly shaved. He searched the restaurant and spied us, offering a broad smile that creased his angular face.

I couldn't believe it, but a warmth flashed through me as if I had feelings for him, which seemed ridiculous. If only he weren't so darn good-looking, with a smile that could curl a woman's toes. They both wore sweatshirts with the Sea Eagle logo on the front. Obviously, they had visited the gift shop too.

Raphael spotted us as they walked over. Jack said nothing and slid into the booth next to me. Raphael sat beside Sumsion.

"Care for a whisky?" I offered mine to either one of them.

Raphael quickly grabbed the glass. "Even zee French appreciate Scottish whisky." He took a swallow, wiped his lips with the back of his hand, and sighed like it had hit the spot.

Jack's eyes went to the envelope. "What's this?" He picked it up.

I explained what had happened, then said, "Would you mind reading it?"

"Not at all." He tore it open, blew inside, and tugged out a note.

He read it first to himself.

"Come on." Though I had been reluctant to read it, I was also very anxious to know if it said something about Auntie.

"'She grows worse. Please hurry.'" He showed me the message with the two measly sentences.

"I don't believe this." I leaned my elbows on the table, holding my head.

Jack stroked my back. "We're very close tae finding the page. Once we do, he'll release her. If we're lucky, it might happen as early as tomorrow."

I leaned back, taking solace in his encouraging words. "So . . . where are those caves?"

Jack turned the menu over. The backside displayed a map of the island. "Gold Cave is north of here, up by Uig. It's a short hike, but we have tae climb down some steep cliffs so I think we should do that early in the morning when the tide is at the lowest. I'm thinking we should leave around five. It will take an hour tae drive there."

"Where ez other caves?" Raphael studied the map.

Jack pointed to the bottom of the island. "They're both near Elgol, a good two-hour drive from Gold Cave. But from what I understand, neither of these caves is the climb that Gold Cave is. We should be able to check them out in the afternoon."

"Now the only problem is the weather." Sumsion took another sip of whisky.

The young woman came back to take our orders. I wanted something light, something that wouldn't keep my stomach turning and would let me rest because, whether I liked it or not, tomorrow I would be spelunking.

* * *

I had a hard time sleeping, knowing the Black Prince knew exactly where we were staying and even my room number. I tossed and turned and seemed to finally drift off just before the burner-phone alarm rang. I tumbled out of bed, got dressed, secured the pages to my person, then opened the door to leave my room but stopped. Jack sat on the floor next to my door, sleeping.

He must have been worried about me. Touched by his kindness, I squatted beside him. His head was bent to his chest. Whisker stubble shadowed his chin and cheeks and upper lip. His long sideburns framed his manly shaped ears. With each passing day, he was earning more of my trust, especially when he did things like camping out in the hallway of the Sea Eagle to make sure I was safe.

Deciding to tease him, I reached over and barely touched his ear.

With his eyes still closed, he grabbed my wrist, dropped me to the floor, and pinned me with his body. His blood-shot eyes stared at me as if he didn't see me, didn't register who I was.

"Jack! It's me, Skye."

He blinked and stared at me again. The warmth of his breath fanned my cheeks, his nose but an inch from mine. "Sorry." He let go of my wrist and leaned up on his elbow. "You took me by surprise."

"I got that. Has no one ever tickled your ear?" I gave him a gentle smile, something that might make him relax a little.

"No. You all right?" He studied my face, not as if worried but more like he liked what he saw.

I had no makeup on and had only finger-combed my hair when I'd rolled out of bed and dressed. He couldn't be attracted to me, could he? Professor Sumsion's claim that Jack had feelings for me came to mind. Maybe he was right.

Jack reached up and smoothed away that irritating lock that taunted me. "Your hair looks like rays of sunshine." He paused, and his thumb traced my jaw. "Your eyes are blue as a bonnie Scottish harebell."

I didn't know what a harebell was, but I understood bonnie. I gulped. My gaze went to his thick lips. All he had to do was lean just a little, and our lips would touch. I didn't dare move, not because I wanted him to kiss me but because I didn't know what I'd do if he did. What would it be like to have this virile man press his lips to mine?

And then I thought of the reason we were here. This was not the time or place for romance. "Jack."

"Yes."

"We need to go. Professor Sumsion and Raphael will be waiting."

He didn't move immediately, just gazed into my eyes as if promising me that before our time together was through, he would kiss me and kiss me well.

He took a deep breath and rose to his feet. He held his hand out to help me. At first, I didn't want to take it. I needed to be strong on my own if I was going to get through this unscathed. But then I found my legs wouldn't support me, so I yielded and took hold of his hand. He pulled me to my feet.

We stood there a moment too long, waiting for one of us to go down the stairs first. Of course, he was being the gentleman, wanting to follow me, the lady. I let go of his hand and started down the stairs, very aware that he trailed close behind.

Reaching the ground floor, I found I was right. Sumsion and Raphael were waiting in the lobby.

Fiona stood at the front desk. "Off to go explorin', are ye?"

I stopped. "Yes, a few caves."

"Might Ah ask which ones?" She looked at me like Auntie would when I'd tell her I was leaving for a flight.

Jack got my attention and shook his head to say I'd already said too much.

"Just those we come upon." I tried to be as vague as possible.

"A word of warnin'," she said, leaning near to both Jack and me. "To reach some caves, ye have to cross private property. There's bad blood atween some landholders and toorists trompin' over their pastures. Tak' caur. Dornt litter. And be quick." She nodded like she'd done her good deed for the day.

I couldn't help it; I liked Fiona. I thanked her as we left the Sea Eagle, hoping that the true danger following us would leave this good woman and her family alone.

CHAPTER TWENTY-SIX

ON THE ROAD TO UIG, we drove by the ruins of a church and came to a good place to park the car.

"Last night, I bought some headlamps," Jack said before getting out. "That way we'll have our hands free as we explore the cave. And, Professor, I know this isn't your style, but"—he pulled out a hoodie sweatshirt like the ones he and Raphael wore—"I thought you might appreciate one of these."

"Thank you, my good man. I'll wear it with pride." Sumsion pulled it over his leather jacket, giving the older man another layer of protection against the elements. I zipped up my fleece jacket, grateful for its softness, and hoped the weather would be warmer than it had been in Paris.

Jack gave each of us a headlamp. Once we had them secured on our heads, the four of us started the hike, with Jack in the lead, then me, Sumsion, and Raphael bringing up the rear. The air felt crisp and clean. A misty fog rolled from the ocean, making us take special care as the path came near a cliff's edge. The trail dropped down a steep, grassy slope to the rocky shoreline.

Jack went down first and found good footing before reaching up for me. With a shaky hand, I took his.

"You know, there are several legends about Gold Cave," he said as I stepped down beside him.

"Do tell." Sumsion came next. "I'm always up for a good folktale, except when I'm trying not to make a fool of myself by falling into the ocean."

"No worries." Raphael encouraged him from behind, and Jack did the same from the front. Sumsion made it safely down, and Raphael jumped to us with hardly any effort.

A spark lit Jack's eyes as he passed me, walking carefully on the slippery rocks leading to the cave's opening. "In this very cave, legend says Scotland's best piper met the Fairy Queen."

"Fairy Queen? Yeah right." I couldn't help but scoff.

"'Tis true." Jack's pretense of looking hurt lasted only a second as he continued to talk and walk at the same time. "As a young man, the piper was drawn tae explore the cave paved with gold. Finding his way in, he met the Fairy Queen, pretty as you please, just sitting there as if waiting for him. They talked for a while, and when it came time for the lad tae go home, she asked what parting gift she could give him."

"A pot of gold." Sumsion fed into the story.

"No, something a wee more important tae him. She gave him the gift tae play his bagpipes like no other. However, on a certain day and time, he would have tae return tae her and the cave." Jack helped me over a pool of water.

"So he became a good piper?" I asked as Jack let go of my hand and helped Sumsion.

"No, he became the best piper in the world. He enjoyed his fame and fortune for many years, and then the time came when he'd have tae return tae see the Fairy Queen." Jack guided us to the mouth of the cave. Columns of basalt rock on both sides gave the cave a tall, narrow opening, and down the middle of the bottom, the rocks looked like gold.

"Some say you can still hear him playing." Jack motioned for us to turn on our headlamps, then he started in, stepping from one rock to another.

"Did he die?" I walked on, feeling the dread of being in close spaces creep over me.

"No one knows." Jack's deep voice echoed off the walls. "'I am woe, woe, under the spells to go. I'll be for aye in the Cave of Gold.'"

"That's an old Scottish chant, is it not?" Sumsion asked.

"'Tis so." Jack took us farther and farther, and though the cave had good height, the walls seemed to close in tighter and tighter. Before too long, it came to an abrupt end.

"There ez no place here to conceal a page." Raphael stated the obvious, a sharp edge in his voice.

The wind outside picked up, blowing into the cave.

"Do you hear it?" Jack stood still.

"What?" I paused, listening.

"The callin' of the pipes." He smiled.

I couldn't help myself. I chuckled and pushed him out of the way. "No, that's common sense telling us to leave." Yesterday, I would have bitten his head off, but a good night's sleep and finding him guarding my door had mellowed me.

By the time we returned to the car, it was close to eleven. During the two-hour drive to the next cave at the southern tip of the island, Sumsion regaled us with tales of his travels to India and other parts of the world. I, however, felt the urgency to find Auntie swell within my chest once again. Fortunately, the drive didn't take too long.

Sumsion nudged my shoulder. "We're here."

I yawned and peered out the window. Jack had parked the van at the harbor at Elgol, and we piled out. A storm had arrived, but it was light. Still, after putting on our headlamps, we pulled our hoods over our heads to protect us from the steady, light drizzle. With the wind blowing in our faces, we headed south, following the scary cliffs.

It seemed to take forever before we arrived at the boulder-strewn beach. The tide was out, but the rain made the rocks wet and slippery. We slowly picked our way around the shore.

"What is the story about this cave?" Sumsion asked as Jack helped the older man maneuver around a large rock.

"As you may be aware, Bonnie Prince Charles led the Jacobites in their rebellion. They did quite well for a while, but when the French ship carrying supplies and more money tae fund their cause became lost at sea, the Jacobites were doomed."

"What happened?" I picked my way over slippery green rocks to reach the men, who had stopped for this little history lesson.

"The Battle of Culloden is what happened. 'Twas a bloody fight and lasted less than an hour. In the end, nearly 2,000 Jacobites lost their lives. Prince Charles fled tae the Hebrides tae hide from the British. He fled from island tae island, always ahead of the soldiers looking for him. One close call had Flora Macdonald dressing him up as her maid and crossing tae Skye. It is said that she hid him in this cave."

The misty fog had lifted. Jack pointed to impressive craggy cliffs. "There are several caves hidden, but the main one that would have kept Prince Charles safe is the second one." He led the way, climbing over rocks to get to the cave, which couldn't be seen from the beach.

I could understand why the prince would have been safe hiding there.

We came to a small triangular opening of brownish-red rocks. With the quickening of my heart, my fear of caves sprang to life once again. I sucked in deep drafts of air. Everyone flipped on their headlamps as they readied to crawl inside. Jack went first. He climbed into the small opening over the rocks.

"Okay, come on."

I hung back. I needed a moment, so I motioned for Sumsion and Raphael to go ahead.

Gold Cave hadn't been as bad as this. At least we could just walk inside, no bending over. This one was a different story. I felt nauseated and wanted to run away. But I had to do this.

My turn came, and I knew I couldn't put it off any longer. Keeping my eyes on the ground, I scrambled over the rocks. The strong scent of mold and mud had me covering my nose with my hand. The constant drip of water echoed in the cave.

Someone took hold of my arm. I looked up, and my light shone into Jack's face.

He smiled. "I've got you."

Here he stood, watching over me again. I didn't want him to think I was some delicate flower, so I gently pulled away. "Thanks, but I'm all right." Eager to show him and the others I could do this, I stepped forward and immediately bumped my head on a low-hanging rock, knocking my head-lamp askew.

Jack chuckled from behind. I tried to act like it was nothing and reached to right the light. A good-sized goose egg had already formed on my forehead. I pressed on, extremely aware that Jack was there to catch me should I fall. I hated to admit it, but his presence comforted me.

The cave grew large with giant slabs of rock trimmed with moss. Smaller rocks were covered with moss as well. And then the cavern became smaller and smaller. Sumsion and Raphael stood hunched over ahead.

"I can't imagine the good prince staying here very long." Sumsion scanned our surroundings. "And a page would not last in this moisture."

"He ez right, no?" Even Raphael appeared uncomfortable and convinced we would not find our treasure here.

"Okay, let's head to Spar Cave." Jack turned around and led us out.

I couldn't leave the cavern fast enough. When I crawled to my feet without a ledge of rock overhead, I took a cleansing breath, glad to be outside and away from the stench. The rain had let up some. I helped Sumsion out, and Raphael joined us.

Instead of going back the way we had come, Jack cut through a gully. It smelled almost as bad as the cave, and debris had washed ashore, but I was grateful to be away from the rocks.

We crawled up to the cliffs. With the wind at our backs, we started toward the parking lot until Jack put his arm out, stopping us.

He turned around. "I recognize the car parked next tae the van."

I strained to see. A silver sedan was parked next to our vehicle but appeared empty.

"Looks like the car that attempted to run us off the highway." Though Sumsion squinted to see into the distance, he seemed pretty certain.

Jack quickly checked again just as a couple of men walked around from the other side of the van. "Gavan Macgregor and Aleck Balmoral." Jack turned his back to them as though afraid they might recognize him.

"Who are they?" I turned around as well. A biting burst of wind and rain lashed at my face.

Without answering, Jack started back down the path to the beach. For him to be this worried wasn't good. I followed and knew without looking that Sumsion and Raphael were with us. Jack led us to a bend in the path, taking us out of sight of the parking lot before he stopped. We huddled around him.

He took a deep lungful of air. "Remember the Jacobites?"

"What does something that happened over three hundred years ago have to do with those men?" I pulled my fleece hood more tightly over my head as I struggled to understand.

"In recent years, there's been a revival of sorts, a new Jacobite cause." Jack bit at his bottom lip.

"Yes." Sumsion nodded. "Skye and I talked about this before. A group of Scots still want independence from Great Britain. The people voted on it, but it failed."

Jack rubbed his chin. "There are still some trying tae rally support for independence. They feel that Great Britain's economy depends on keeping Scotland in line. Without Scotland, the pound might fail, and the UK would go under. There are forces in Britain earnestly trying tae squash any uprising."

"Are those men checking out the van part of this new Jacobite cause?" I wanted to take another look at them but didn't want to risk being spotted.

"They are." Jack rubbed his chin with the back of his hand.

"It's a long story." He stared at me. "But now that I see who they are, I'm fairly certain they don't want to kill us. Driving us off the road was just to rattle our cage. They're on a mission, and that mission is to capture *you*."

CHAPTER TWENTY-SEVEN

THE RAIN MAGNIFIED WHAT JACK had said. I reeled from his words and blinked several times, trying to take it in. Why would people who sought Scotland's independence want to capture me? "That doesn't make sense. It's not like I have a lot of money."

"I said that wrong." Jack stole a deep breath. "But the fact that they didn't return and gun us down at the side of the road adds tae my theory that they want tae capture you tae get their hands on the pages. That's what I meant tae say. They are probably following us, wanting us tae do all the legwork so they can swoop in and steal them when we have all three. If they could prove the pages exist, it might rally people tae their cause, remind them of Robert the Bruce and all he stood for." Rain drizzled in rivulets down Jack's serious face.

"Son, what should we do?" Sumsion didn't miss a beat, didn't seem taken aback by the want-to-steal-the-pages scenario.

"We can't go back tae the van, but we can't go on tae Spar Cave without it." Jack ignored me and popped his knuckles as his eyes scanned the beach below.

"Zee French will come to rescue again. Allow moi to fetch zee vehicle." Raphael held out his hand, wanting Jack to give him the keys.

"Wait a minute!" I was still trying to make sense of what Jack had said. Something seemed lacking in his explanation. I was hung up on what he'd first said, that they wanted to capture me. Jack had told me over and over that he was here to keep me safe. "Why did you say they wanted to capture me?"

"I misspoke. I need tae get you tae safety right now. I'll explain later." Jack dropped the keys onto Raphael's palm. "Be careful and don't take any additional risks."

Raphael nodded and started away.

"Wait." Jack stopped him. "If you manage tae get in the van, turn south when you leave the parking area. The highway will switch back and forth. We'll meet you about a mile down the road."

"Oui." Raphael took off.

Jack looked at both Sumsion and me. "Come on." He took my arm and tried to hustle me back down to the rocky shoreline.

I pulled away. "How can you just let him go like that? They might kill him."

Jack clenched his teeth as though any patience he'd had was about to come to an end. "He chose. And, I might add, we have no other choice."

"Yes, we do. We could have walked. I'd rather walk all the way back to Scotland than have one of us die because of those stupid pages." I swiped rain from my face.

Jack glared at me like he didn't know what to do or say.

Sumsion passed us, going in the direction Jack wanted to go like he didn't want to hear the argument.

With Sumsion out of earshot, I tried again. "Why? Why do they want to capture me?" I glowered at him, demanding an answer.

"I told you I misspoke. But chew on this. What if those pages say something that might defeat their cause? What do you think they'll do then?" Jack took hold of my arm, forcing me to walk.

I pulled away from his grasp but kept walking. "Destroy them?"

"Okay, what do you think they would do tae people who knew about the pages?" He waited, and a serious, steely-type look claimed his face.

"Kill them . . ." I uttered, hoping I was wrong.

"You're a smart girl." He walked past me. "Come on," he said over his shoulder. "The professor might become a target on the beach alone."

Just as things started to become clearer, they muddied up again with the threat of death. So Jack had told us a good possibility all the while shielding us from the reality of a worst-case scenario. How did he walk on the knife edge of hope and total despair? What other horrible possibilities lurked behind us that he'd never told us about? I thought of Auntie. Did he know something more had probably happened to her but didn't want to tell me? Probably, but I didn't really want to know. What my own mind conjured up was bad enough. Why had all this befallen us?

Answers weren't going to find me here in the rain. As I walked, I listened for the sound of gunfire and prayed Raphael would be safe.

We made our way to the rocky shore where Sumsion waited patiently. Jack walked ahead, guiding us toward another gully away from the rocky cliffs.

Sumsion slipped and nearly fell. I grabbed hold of his arm, righting him. "Thank you, my dear," he said. "Did you and Jack make up?"

I held on to him as we picked our way over the beach. I could tell him the ugly truth Jack had just shared with me. But maybe it was better to let him think we had been arguing and things were better. "I guess. I just wish I had answers to so many questions."

"Well, I have one answer for you." He sidestepped a puddle of water.

"What is that?" I wanted to humor him.

"Jack has strong feelings for you."

"Back to that, are we? Well, he has told me several times that keeping me alive and safe is his job. I still can't figure out why."

Sumsion nodded. "It is a puzzle, but one we will find the answer to together." His reassuring look made me feel much better.

Jack disappeared up the new gully. We continued to slip and slide over the bogs and rocks. As we reached the mouth of the gully, he returned. "The pastureland above should take us straight tae the road. But there's a farmhouse close by. Not sure how the owner will feel about our trespassing."

"We don't have a choice, do we?" Sumsion asked as he climbed his way to Jack.

"No, sir, we don't." Jack squatted down and offered a hand to Sumsion. He took hold and, with great effort, scrambled to the lip of the gully.

That left me. Jack offered me his hand. I looked into his eyes that were so dark-blue they appeared black. I couldn't get sidetracked with romance now. Without saying another word, I shoved my feelings aside and took hold as he helped me.

He held my hand a little too long. I awkwardly pulled away.

Sumsion had walked ahead and was stopped by a gate in the fencing that framed in the pasture.

As I neared him, I saw a sign with bold red and black lettering that read, "Absolutely no trespassing. This means you!"

Would our challenges never stop?

Jack ignored the sign and opened the gate, letting us through.

I wanted to state the obvious but knew better. This pasture was the quickest way to the road where we could meet with Raphael. And we didn't have the luxury of time on our side.

Arm in arm, Sumsion and I hurried through.

"Keep going," Jack said. "I'll catch up. I want tae make sure the gate is secure."

I could tell Professor Sumsion's energy was leaving him. He'd done very well with everything we'd had to do today, but the stress of not being able to take a break between climbing down to Prince Charlie's cave and back up and then back down and dashing across this field had taken a toll on him.

Jack caught up and got on the other side of Sumsion, taking his arm as well.

"Now look, you two." Sumsion gazed at both of us. "I might be able to help Skye, but I don't have the strength to help Jack too." The older man feigned seriousness, but he suppressed a grin.

"I just don't want you taking off with my lass," Jack said.

Sumsion gave me the see-I-told-you-so look, which I quickly ignored.

In the distance, we heard the slamming of a door. A man came out of the farmhouse waving his arms and shouting, "Gie it!"

"What did he say?" Sumsion asked.

"He wants us tae get off his property." Jack waved to the man. "Mah mukker needs help."

"Nae mah problem. Gie it."

Jack hurried us along. "We will. Uir ride is comin.'"

The man folded his arms but stayed on his porch, keeping a close eye on us. Fortunately, our exit from the pasture wasn't close to the farmhouse. Jack sprinted ahead and opened the gate.

Sumsion breathed heavily. I worried he might have a heart attack but didn't voice my concern. It would only add to everyone's stress level, especially Sumsion's. As we exited the field, he leaned even more heavily on me. He'd held it together long enough for us to get out of the limelight, and now . . . Well, now, we were still in trouble, but at least the farmer had gone back inside his house.

"Do you think that guy sits at his window all day, just waiting for people to traipse across his pasture so he can yell at them?" I asked as Jack joined us.

We started up the hill, heading for the highway.

"Can't blame him if he does." Jack took his post on the other side of Sumsion again.

As we reached the crest of the hill at the road, we found it empty.

"Raphael should be here any minute." A bend in the road made it impossible for us to see if he was coming or not. Jack jogged ahead to take a look while Sumsion and I stayed put.

"At least the rain has stopped." Sumsion held out his hand as if to test what he'd said.

I hadn't noticed until then, but it had. The wind wasn't blowing as much either. I wished there was a stump or something Sumsion could sit on while we waited.

The elderly man looked at me. "A week ago, I never dreamed I'd be here with you."

I nodded, agreeing.

His forehead wrinkled. "Plus, I never thought our Marjorie would be fighting for her life."

I patted his arm I held next to me. "We're going to find her." I said it not only to assure him but myself as well.

Jack raced toward us. "Get behind the wooly willows!"

I saw silver-leafed bushes not far from us. As fast as I could, I guided Sumsion to the other side of the bush, away from the road. I pushed him down to sit on the wet gravel-mixed soil. Jack must not have thought he'd reach us in time and dove off the side of the road, lying flat as he could against the hillside.

The roar of a car engine raced past. Tires squealed as though they banked around a corner. I took a chance and peered out from behind the willow bush, catching a glimpse of the silver sedan's taillights as it disappeared around another bend.

"Do you think Jack is all right? He's not moving," Sumsion asked, a note of concern in his voice.

I looked where Jack lay. I expected him to jump to his feet, but he didn't. Fear grew inside me. I sprang up and dashed over the fifty yards that lay between us.

He'd managed to roll onto his back by the time I reached him. Pain ricocheted across his face. I pulled my hood off my head and knelt on the wet ground. I touched him to see if he was all right, but he inhaled a deep shock of breath and moaned.

"What is it?" I studied his arm, which didn't look bent or awkward.

"I've dislocated my shoulder," he uttered. His face turned red. Pain lined his chiseled face.

"What can I do?" I felt helpless.

Sumsion had made his way over and stood on the other side of Jack. "Has this happened before?" He peered down on him.

He nodded, biting his lips together, probably in too much pain to answer verbally.

"Skye." Sumsion motioned to me. "Reach across his body and take hold of his side. When I tell you to, pull him toward you while I tug on his arm."

I quickly did as asked. My long hair fell across my face. I tried to brush it aside with my shoulder. That was when I saw Jack staring up at me, worry in his eyes. I tried to reassure him. "It's going to be all right."

"Ready?" Sumsion asked.

"Yes." I glanced at Sumsion, who had taken a firm hold of Jack's arm. He slowly pulled while I gently tugged in the opposite direction.

I peered down at Jack. He stared at me, discomfort slanting his brows. He looked like he wanted to tell me something, but the agony from his shoulder stopped him.

"Okay, keep holding him steady, my dear."

I felt the tension in Jack's body as Sumsion applied steady pressure in the opposite direction. I continued to hold Jack.

He slid a little.

"Hold him steady, Skye," Sumsion said.

I reinforced my hold. Once again, my eyes were drawn to Jack's. We stared at each other. So many thoughts raced through my mind. I hated seeing him in pain. This was not the Jack I'd come to know. This Jack was vulnerable. This Jack needed me. And I was here for him, like he'd been for me. Yet, distrust stood between us. More than anything, I wanted to trust him. I wanted to not have this barrier between us. I wanted him to just tell me the truth.

His breathing became labored as his pain seemed to heighten.

"Hang on, my boy. Should be any time now." The elderly man steadily pulled on his arm.

Jack's eyelids closed tightly as he fought against excruciating pain.

Something popped. The stress lines that had creased Jack's face immediately disappeared.

"There we go," Sumsion said.

I released my hold and sat on my heels. Sumsion carefully laid Jack's arm across his chest. "I would feel better if we had a sling for you to use."

Jack eased up to a sitting position, hugging his arm to his body. Small bits of damp weeds and grass clung to his hair and the back of his sweatshirt. "Thanks, Professor." He looked at me. "Thanks tae you too. I couldn't have gotten through without having your pretty face tae look at."

My cheeks grew warm. I rose to my feet. Wanting to put distance between me and the situation, I peered down the road. "Where do you suppose Raphael is?"

Using only his legs, Jack stood. He still hugged his arm to his chest. "That looked like Macgregor and Balmoral who drove by, so either they beat Raphael and know where we're going, or worse, Raphael's driving around lost. That Frenchman has no sense of direction. It's amazing he gets around Paris as easily as he does."

"His sense of direction helped us get out of the Sainte-Chapelle." I surprised myself by sticking up for Raphael.

"True enough. But if they captured him, they will torture him." Jack looked to Sumsion. They exchanged a knowing glance. Like they both agreed that if the bad guys had captured Raphael, he would have given us up.

"What?"

Sumsion took a deep breath. "It's just that if he told them we were going tae Spar Cave, we can't search it. They'll be there waiting for us." The rally of energy that had seen him through doctoring Jack had been short-lived. And now, with the added burden that Raphael could have told where we were going and put our search in jeopardy, he seemed heavily weighed down.

I tried to think of what I could do. We couldn't stay here, standing on the side of the road. There was a chance the bad guys could return, and we were sitting ducks. With Jack nursing a bum arm and Sumsion needing a rest, it was up to me to find help. "Do you think that farmer who yelled at us would give us a lift?"

"No." Jack started walking down the road. "You don't understand how stubborn a Scot can be. If you tried tae get his pity, he'd probably say it served us right tae be afoot."

"At least let me try." I turned around, ready to go back and face the fire of the farmer when the sound of another vehicle coming around the bend took us all by surprise. We were too far away to hide behind the willows again.

Then the white van came into view, a smiling Raphael at the wheel. Relieved to see him, I clapped with joy. He pulled off to the side of the road, and we crowded around the driver's side as he climbed out.

"What took you so long?" Jack asked, anger threading his words.

"Zee men no bother me."

"That doesn't make sense." Jack glared at him.

"Ez true. I hide and wait till they go in their automobile. Then I leave." He held the keys out to Jack.

Sumsion patted Raphael's back. "Good job!"

"With our van there, why would they leave?" Jack rubbed his chin and stared at Raphael like he didn't know whether to believe what he'd said or not. "You go ahead and drive."

Raphael studied Jack as he stood there holding his arm to his body. As though realizing Jack had been hurt and that was why he wanted him to continue driving, Raphael kept the keys. He raced around the van and opened the sliding door, disappearing inside. Before we caught up to him, he was out again, holding one of the Strongman belts in his hands. He fashioned a sling around Jack's neck and arm, then helped him get in and settle on the bench seat.

Sumsion motioned for me to follow. I hesitated, uncomfortable with the thought of sitting that close to Jack. We might argue, or worse, I might feel more attracted to him than I already did.

Good grief. I was a grown woman. I could handle sitting next to the man. And why not ply him with questions? It might be best if everyone heard the raw truth of what might befall us.

I slowly did as Sumsion wanted.

Raphael slid the door shut behind me and raced around to the driver's side while Sumsion got in the passenger seat.

"We go to Spar Cave, no?" Raphael asked as he fastened his seat belt.

Jack leaned against the armrest. "Yes. Even though they might be there waiting, we have tae. Follow the road, but take your time."

Raphael checked both ways before pulling out.

I took a breath, ready to interrogate Jack, but he leaned his head against the back of the seat and closed his eyes. His shoulder must throb. I decided to hold off.

If Jack was right, the worst of our adventure may lay ahead. If we found the third page and what it said didn't cast Scotland in a good light that Macgregor and Balmoral liked, all of our lives could be in danger.

But we didn't have the page yet. We still needed to check Spar Cave without the bad guys finding us. On top of that, we had the tide to consider.

Time was not on our side.

CHAPTER TWENTY-EIGHT

THE SLIM ROAD BECAME EVEN narrower as Raphael drove over the wind-swept moor to Glasnakille. Fortunately, on the way, there were no signs of a silver sedan or the men Jack called Macgregor and Balmoral.

When we came into a quaint village, Jack rallied and sat up. We'd come to a T-intersection. "Make a right."

Raphael did as told.

Jack winced as we rode over a bump. I almost reached out to comfort him but thought better of it. He'd focused his attention on the road and where Raphael was driving.

We came to an old, roofless house.

"There." Jack pointed to a spot to park on the other side of the road. "We can leave the van here while we check out the cave. I hear it's a short walk down tae the beach."

"Are you sure you want to go?" I knew the walk would be tough on him, let alone going inside the cave. "You could stay here in the van and keep an eye out for those men."

"I'm fine. I've worked with two broken ribs. This is nothing. Thanks tae you and the professor, I'm almost good as new." He moved his arm to show me but gritted his teeth when he didn't think I would notice.

Raphael and Sumsion exited the van. I slid open the side door. As I climbed out, a burst of wind flipped my hair into my face. I pulled my hood over my head.

Raphael had come around and reached to assist Jack, but Jack ignored the offer.

"I've got it." Jack crawled out and took off the makeshift sling, setting it inside the vehicle before closing the door. "Everyone check your headlamps; make sure they're working."

We stood in a row, hoods over our heads, clicking our headlamps on, then off. I noticed Sumsion patting his sweatshirt hoodie. He must be checking on his pipe and magnifying glass.

I thought of the manila envelope. I didn't feel it on my back. I double-checked. Yes, still there.

We'd walked a good five minutes to the stair-shaped cliffs at the shore. Jack found the path down to the sea inlet. We pressed on, going over the zigzaggy trail, dodging low-hanging branches crisscrossing our path. We reached the bottom only to find boulders and angular rocks we had to walk on, around, and over, plus a muddy beach.

"In the early 1800s, visitors would come by boat tae the cave. Of course, they came during high tide. The tide is coming in, so we can't be long," Jack said as we walked.

Sumsion offered me his arm. I took it, thinking we could help each other over the rocky terrain. Jack and Raphael were fine on their own and headed down the shore.

"This is it," Jack called to us. He stood by what appeared to be a rock wall, but the middle of it had been knocked down. Plants and moss grew along the ridge and spilled over the sides. "About a century ago, they built this wall tae keep people from going inside the cave. Vandals were knocking down ancient stalagmites. But the wall didn't work. They say in 1814, even Sir Walter Scott scaled over it with a rope."

Turning toward the inlet, I found sheer walls rising on both sides. The muddy beach turned sandier. Picking our way around seaweed, we reached Spar Cave's opening.

"Turn on your headlamps." Jack flipped his on, then stopped as if making sure we all did what he said before leading the way inside.

Raphael stepped back, allowing Sumsion and me to enter before him. I hesitated only a moment, fighting a twinge of claustrophobia. If I concentrated on the ground, I'd be okay. I pushed forward, with Raphael behind me.

Leaving the distant sound of waves, we stepped around the worst of the entrance's mud. Right away, I heard the dripping, splashing, and even running of water. To the right, the base flooring turned into a massive cream-colored flowstone that looked like a ramp rising a good eighty feet before disappearing into darkness.

Sumsion reached down and touched it. "It appears that calcium carbonate coats the surface."

A fine sheen of clear water coated the marble-like slope. "Do you think it's slippery?" I asked, realizing if we were going to continue, we'd have to climb the ramp.

Jack tested it out. "It feels grippy. Not slick at all."

As I stepped on the flowstone that looked like marble, it felt oddly spongy and even "grippy," like Jack had said. We made our way to the top of the ramp and found spectacular columns of other flowstones, giving the cave a cathedral feeling. I marveled at the strange but natural creations of this underground world, where layers of calcium dripped down in alabaster spirals. Other rocks reminded me of the gargoyles we'd seen at Notre Dame, except the rocks had tentacles. Small pools on the floor had more calcium that had solidified around the edges in thin sheets of ice. This was a type of plateau where I thought someone might be able to hide for a while.

My eyes went to the rear of the cave. Another flowstone ramp, but steeper than the one we'd climbed up, ran down about thirty feet. Jack led the way yet again. Despite his injury, he seemed set on being the leader. "This is Scott's 'sunless well.'"

Sumsion hung back. "I'll wait here. You go ahead."

I didn't blame him, though this ramp seemed even more grippy than the other one. A crystal-clear pool, the water bright-blue, filled the bottom.

"Didn't Sir Walter Scott write about a mermaid who lived here?" Sumsion called to us. "Something along the lines of 'She bathes her limbs in sunless well . . . where dazzling spars gleam like a firmament of stars.'"

Jack nodded and seemed impressed.

Raphael ventured down a narrow, gloomy part of the cave. "Ez wet here." He returned to us, wiping water from his face.

"I don't think Robert the Bruce could have hidden the page in this cave." Jack's voice sounded more discouraged than I felt. He'd said what I'd been thinking.

"Unless . . ." Sumsion called to us. "Unless he put it in some type of stone box that would keep the moisture out."

We climbed back up to Sumsion.

"Wish you would have thought of that before." Jack seemed a little out of breath, and he held his injured arm close to his body. "If the page was placed in a stone box that would keep moisture out, we need tae go back and check the other caves once again."

"Maybe so. The Bruce might have hidden it in this plateau." Sumsion looked around. "He was rumored to be here for several months. Look up at the ceiling." He pointed at it. "That blackness could be from campfire smoke."

"I can't imagine staying in here that long." I shivered at the thought. Again, claustrophobia tried to rear its ugly head, but I fought it back.

"The cave dates back tae the ninth century." Jack said it like he'd thought out loud. "Its true Gaelic title is *Slochd Altrimen*."

"What does that mean?" I asked.

"Nursing cave. Legend has it that a local princess fell in love with the son of the chief of Colonsay, who was shipwrecked on the Strathaird coast. But the parents of the young lovers were sworn enemies. When the princess gave birth tae a child, she hid the bairn in this cave tae ensure it would survive until the feud ended." Jack rubbed his sore shoulder.

"If a baby could live here, Robert the Bruce could tolerate a few months." Sumsion studied the limestone formations around us.

We checked every nook and cranny but could find no place where a stone box could have been hidden. We were so focused on searching for the treasure, time slipped away.

"The tide!" Jack looked like he'd been sucker punched.

He and Raphael raced down the flowstone and disappeared.

As much as I wanted to leave this cave, I stayed behind and helped Sumsion down the gradient.

Before we reached the bottom, Jack met us. "No sense in hurrying. We'll be here for the night. The tide's come in, cutting us off from the shore."

The thought of spending the night in the cold, water-dripping cave was too much. "Are you kidding me?" I wanted to scream and yell and have a complete tizzy fit but knew I couldn't. As calmly as I could, I said, "Not only did we not find the page, but we're stuck here?"

"Yup." Jack nodded.

I had to block out the heavy rocks above us and not think that they could easily smash us all or that the walls seemed to move closer. I had to make the best out of our situation. I scanned the cavern. Only a few bare patches of ground were without water. How could we keep warm? What would we eat?

We stood there staring at each other with nothing to say. We were all guilty of not checking on the tide. And to be fair, Jack had warned us before coming in. But the need to find the page had been uppermost in our minds.

Raphael found a dry ledge and leaped onto it. Against a narrow strip of limestone, I saw another dry place. "Professor, why don't you sit over there?" I motioned toward the spot.

"Oh, I couldn't. You should take it. Or Jack—he's the one who was injured. How is the arm, son?" Sumsion mined beneath his sweatshirt and pulled out his pipe, pouch of tobacco, and lighter.

"Stiff and sore, but I'll live. I've had worse." Jack looked around the cavern. "Professor and Raphael, come sit with us. The temperature of this cave is going tae get close tae freezing. We need tae huddle together and stay warm. There's a place here for all of us next tae that huge slab of stone."

What place was he talking about? He motioned for me to follow. Not ten feet away waited a dry area. How had I missed it?

Sumsion and Raphael migrated to us.

Jack rubbed his hands together. "Your body temperature only needs tae drop tae 95 degrees for hypothermia tae set in, and then your body will start shutting down. At 94 degrees, you're dead."

"Thanks for the pleasant thought." I wanted to throttle him. Didn't we have enough to worry about?

"I said it because we're going tae need tae snuggle up and hold each other. But first, because we're stuck in here for at least eight hours, we need tae conserve our headlamps. Turn off your lights, and I'll keep mine on for the first hour or so. Then someone else can turn theirs on."

We did as asked. The cave grew dimmer. Grateful we'd already explored so I knew there were no animals inside, my fear level rose only mildly.

"I'll sit." Jack eased down, careful of his arm, his back to the huge stone. "Now, Raphael, you sit next tae me." He did as told. "The professor can sit in front of me, and I'll put my arms around him. Skye, you sit in front of Raphael, and he'll put his arms around you."

I didn't like the setup. Sumsion must have sensed my reluctance and crossed over to Raphael. "Jack, I think it best for your arm if you hold Skye. She's not as big as I am."

Relieved and yet reluctant, I stayed where I stood. "Jack, let me be the one to hold you. Your shoulder doesn't need the extra strain."

He shrugged and scooted forward so I could take my place behind him. Once I had settled on the ground, I sat spread-eagle so I could cozy up to Jack's back. Careful of his sore shoulder, I gently slipped my arms beneath his and hugged him to me. His warmth quickly calmed my shivers. He folded his arms over my hands.

Raphael had done the same to Sumsion.

"Don't mind if I smoke, do you?" Sumsion prepared to light his pipe.

"Might help." Jack voiced his approval.

The comforting aroma filled the cavern, making it not seem so cold.

"Could we use the professor's lighter and start a campfire?" I asked, wondering why I hadn't thought to ask before.

"No fuel," Jack said into his chest. "And we're cut off from the beach, so we can't look for any either."

Sumsion's eyelids were puffy, and I could tell he wanted to sleep.

"One good thing about being in the cave." Jack's voice echoed off the walls.

"What's that?" I couldn't imagine anything good about being stuck in here.

"At least we're safe from Macgregor and Balmoral." Jack yawned.

"True enough. If only we could have found the page. How could we have been so wrong?" I felt totally beaten and frustrated.

"There's another cave on the island." Jack rubbed his shoulder. He must be miserable.

I was tempted to massage it for him, but I didn't, afraid I might hurt him even more. "For a small island, Skye has a lot of caves. What's the other cave called?"

"Cave of Knives."

I shuddered. "I don't think I want to go there. Maybe the professor should look at the two pages again."

Sumsion had fallen asleep, pipe in his hand. Raphael's head rested on Sumsion's back, and his eyes were closed too. They made an oddly comforting sight.

"You're probably right. But let him rest a few hours first." Jack ran his fingers through his black hair, then folded his arms over mine again. "I thought for certain Spar Cave would be the one. It's the oldest on the island. Robert the Bruce had tae have known about it."

"Still, we have to face the fact that maybe he didn't come here." I yawned, exhaustion taking its toll.

"You might be right." He shivered and pulled me closer.

With the ice around the pools of water, I had to ask, "Do you really think we could freeze to death?"

"Not as long as one of us stays awake and can periodically wake the others and make us move around a bit before sitting again." He rubbed his hand over my arm. "You want the first shift?"

Jack had been fighting pain for several hours. He needed sleep more than I did. "Sure."

"Good. Turn on your headlamp, and I'll shut mine off."

I clicked mine on about the same time he turned his off.

I scanned the cavern. If Robert the Bruce had watched a spider in here, it must have been one hardy creepy crawler to survive the cold. Again, I was certain this couldn't be the right cave.

Jack had told about the girl who had hidden her child in here. How had she kept the baby warm? The mother and father had probably gathered wood when the tide was low so they would have a fuel supply. And there was plenty of water. Food might have been a challenge. What I'd give to have something to eat. Even airplane food.

My thoughts turned to Elizabeth and her husband. I felt bad that Jack and I had left those thugs in their house—one dead and the other knocked out. Before Jack had shot the guy who'd died, the man had spoken in French, like Raphael. Had Raphael himself sent them to Salt Lake? I looked at him beside me, still asleep. I wondered again, Was Raphael's finding us in Paris planned?

Three different groups of people were after me: Macgregor and Balmarol, who were Scottish; the Black Prince, who was English; and the Frenchmen from Salt Lake and Paris, who could either be Raphael's men or the concierge's at the Hotel Merci. I lumped the French together. But Jack thought the concierge's group were small-time conmen and wouldn't follow us. Raphael's men wouldn't have come since he was with us, but then again his being with us was perfect cover. His men could still be after us, and he could be guiding them to our locations. What was Raphael about anyway? He didn't seem to have even known about the pages as he'd helped us at Sainte-Chapelle. But then he knew all about Jean Pucelle. Raphael was a puzzle. I thought about the others.

Most wanted the pages, some wanted the pages and me dead, and the Scottish group wanted the pages and to capture me.

Jack had said if the pages didn't say what the Scots wanted, they would destroy the pages and kill us all. But what if the pages said something the Scots liked? Did that mean they would still want to capture me? And if so, why? If Jack had been awake, I would have questioned him more. We had plenty of time.

But my thoughts kept returning to the roadblock of why.

CHAPTER TWENTY-NINE

THE NIGHT SEEMED ENDLESS, AND the questions plaguing me about the Scottish group became lost in wanting to just survive the night. After an hour, whoever had stayed awake would wake the others, and we'd get up, walk around, realize how very cold the cave was when we were apart, and cozy up again on the dry area next to the slab of rock.

As we gathered for what we hoped would be the last time, Jack insisted on sitting in back of me. "My shoulder needs tae stretch a little."

I didn't know if he was putting on an act or really meant it, but my back was cold so I didn't argue. Sumsion and Raphael had changed positions many times during the night.

As Sumsion prepared to sit behind the Frenchman, he said, "I've been thinking about that second page."

We paused, waiting for him to complete his thought.

"Where it said, 'A new hope lies buried, waiting to be free,' I know I said that could mean placed in a cave. But as I've thought about it, I believe it has to be buried, especially if the page is hidden in a cave such as this one." His eyes scanned the darkness.

"Why?" Jack said before I could.

"Because the moisture would destroy it otherwise. The Dead Sea Scrolls were preserved in a cave because of the arid climate of the Mediterranean. But here, an artifact such as the page would have to have been kept dry. Like the second page we found at Sainte-Chapelle, it would need to be preserved inside something."

"There ez no place to bury something in this cavern." Raphael stated the obvious.

"Should we double-check before we abandon the cave?" Sumsion leaned against the rock. The ordeal of spending the night here had taken a toll on his elderly body. His face had deep creases; his shoulders drooped.

Jack turned to Raphael. "What do you say you and I take another look?"

The Frenchman shrugged like he agreed.

"Skye, you and the professor can sit this one out." Jack tilted his head and looked at Sumsion like he wanted me to stay behind to watch over him.

"Not a problem." I sat on the dry spot and patted the space beside me, looking up at Sumsion.

As Jack and Raphael climbed up the flowstone, Sumsion eased down beside me. I snuggled up to his side. He held his pipe. Having smoked all the tobacco in his pouch, he now played with it in his hand. "I keep thinking of my sweet Marjorie, wondering how she is faring."

"Me too."

"She's my beautiful swan." His voice broke.

I rubbed his arm.

"Swans can bond to their mates for a lifetime. I wish I'd met Marjorie when I was younger. I'd so like to have more time with her." His fingers quit fondling his pipe. His tired, blood-shot eyes teared up.

I leaned my head to his. "We're going to find her. And then you two can spend the rest of your lives together."

He chuckled. "What we have left."

"Some couples can be together for decades and not appreciate each other as much as you two do. Besides, you can do a lifetime of living filled with love and joy in the space of a few years." I couldn't bear for him to think he wouldn't have a future with Auntie.

Actually, I couldn't bear to think of my life without her either. We sat in silence for a while, with only the sounds of Jack and Raphael in the distance.

An interesting thought came to me. "Do you think Robert the Bruce could have sat right where we are?"

"Possibly. See that rather large arthropod?" He pointed to an eight-legged spider heading straight for us.

I made a muffled shriek and shot to my feet.

The critter scrambled across the dry area where I'd been sitting and disappeared inside a crack. Sumsion just sat there watching it, studying it.

"Think that thing has been crawling on us all night?" I flinched and brushed my arms, staring at the crack.

"Follow it." The voice.

I hadn't heard it since Paris. The instructions were clear. I needed to follow the spider. A warmth spread through my limbs as if to confirm my thoughts. "Professor, you don't suppose the page could be behind there, do you?" I motioned to the rock.

He thought a moment, looked from me to the rock and back again. He shrugged like "Why not," and tapped his pipe on the stone. It sounded hollow. We both looked at each other.

"Are you kidding me?" Forgetting my fear of the spider, I ran my hand over the smooth surface, eager to find another crack. "Could it really be possible?"

Sumsion rose to his knees and tapped the rock again and again. "Very possible and highly likely."

Jack and Raphael climbed down the flowstone just then.

"No luck," Jack said, then saw that we were anxiously searching the rock. "What's up?"

"A spider crawled into that crack." I pointed to it.

Jack looked at me like I was crazy.

"Remember the story of Robert the Bruce." I waited for him to catch on. When he didn't, I continued. "And while he was stuck in that cave, he watched a spider building its web?"

"It couldn't be the same spider." He stared at my face as if looking for signs of cave sickness.

I rolled my eyes. "Of course not, but if a spider crawled in back of the rock, that means there's space behind it."

"*Ō, sacrebleu!*" Raphael crowded in between the slab and me.

Sumsion got out of Jack's way, allowing him a look at the crack.

Jack pried his fingers inside. "Raphael." He motioned with his head for him to do the same.

Higher up from Jack, Raphael managed to squeeze his fingers into the crack, and together, they pulled.

Jack winced as he visibly fought pain in his shoulder. But he continued to keep the pressure on the stone until the slab moved a little.

This made it so the two men were able to stick both hands inside and tug even harder. The slab slowly inched away, then moved more until it gave and fell to the ground with a thud.

A spider web filled a trunk-sized hole, but beneath the webbing rested a stone box.

Hope bubbled within me.

The large black spider that had led us to this find scampered out, abandoning its lair. Though tempted to step on it, I couldn't. Neither could anyone else as we watched it crawl across the cave.

Jack stuck his hands into the webbing and retrieved the box. He teetered a little, favoring his sore shoulder. Raphael immediately grabbed the other side to help him. They set it on the spot where we'd spent the night.

Sumsion knelt beside it as Raphael pried off the lid.

Inside was another jar like the one that had contained the page in Paris. Sumsion reverently took it out. He flipped on his headlamp and stopped a moment as if realizing the significance. He smiled, then twisted the lid and pulled. It seemed to pop as though it had been hermetically sealed.

Sumsion peered inside. "The page!"

"Do you believe we were sitting right next to it all night long?" I could hardly comprehend our good fortune.

"If it weren't for getting stuck here at high tide, we may never have found it." Jack shook his head. Amazement lightened his face, brightened his deep-blue eyes.

"Even then, we would never have thought to look behind the rock without Skye." Sumsion squeezed my hand.

"Give zee jar to me." Raphael held a pistol aimed at the elderly man.

Our joyous mood over the discovery evaporated. How did he get his hands on a gun?

Sadness slanted Sumsion's wise eyes. "You don't want to do this."

"Oui. Zee pages belong to me and my family." A coldness darkened his eyes; his entire demeanor had shifted from friendly to hostile.

I thought of the Frenchman Jack had killed in Elizabeth's house. "You've known about the pages long before you met us in Paris."

Raphael grabbed the jar from Professor Sumsion, who begrudgingly let him have it.

"Zee family Pucelle have long searched for these pages." He motioned for me to hand over the folder I carried in my waistband.

I thought of Auntie. I couldn't do it. I couldn't give away the only things that would save her life. I shook my head.

"Skye, give the pages tae him." Though he spoke to me, Jack kept his eyes on Raphael.

I looked at Professor Sumsion. He would understand. He wouldn't want me to give in.

He gave a nod, an okay to do the unthinkable. As much as it broke my heart, I pulled out the envelope.

Raphael reached to grab it, and Jack lunged at him. Raphael must have caught him moving out of the corner of his eye and sidestepped the attack. Jack fell to the ground on his sore shoulder and groaned in pain.

Raphael glared down on him, aiming the pistol at Jack's head. "After all we been through, *mon amie*, ez time to say *au revoir*." He tightened his grip on the gun. His index finger moved to press the trigger.

I dove for the weapon, grabbing hold as a blast reverberated through the cave. Pain stabbed my upper-left arm before I hit the ground. I couldn't move, couldn't talk.

Commotion sounded all around me. Another shot rang out. I tried to rise up to see what was happening but couldn't. The action was out of my periphery.

All I could do was lie there, staring up at the ceiling above.

A web looped from ceiling to wall, and on it crawled the spider.

CHAPTER THIRTY

SOMEONE PULLED AT ME, REMOVING my fleece jacket, then ripped the sleeve of my Sea Eagle T-shirt and worked on my injury. Pain knifed through my arm like a white-hot dagger. I gasped and opened my eyes. Jack's face came into view.

"Hey there," he said. "You're going tae be just fine. The bullet nicked your shoulder. I wrapped my undershirt around it tae stop the bleeding."

A little blood had seeped through the white material.

"You were lucky." He quickly pulled his sweatshirt over his naked chest to cover it. He stared at me for a moment, concern knitting his forehead, then spat out, "Why did you do that? You could have been killed."

I swallowed and ran my tongue over my lips, trying to think of what to say. "When someone you care a great deal about has a gun pointed at them, you just act."

Jack leaned over and pressed his lips to my forehead. With great care, he checked the crude compress he'd fashioned on my arm, his hand lingering.

Sumsion peered over Jack. "You gave us quite a fright."

"Sorry."

"No need to be. We survived." Sumsion adjusted his headlamp.

I realized there was no sign of Raphael. He'd held a gun on Jack, threatening to kill him. "Raphael. Where is he?"

"Don't concern yourself." Sumsion caressed my cheek. "Jack took care of him." A slight smile warmed the old man's face.

"And the pages? Where are they?"

Sumsion held up the jar we'd recovered in the cave and the envelope that protected the other two pages so I could see them. "We have them all, my dear."

"We don't have time for the professor tae read them right now." Jack scooped me up in his arms.

Pain needled my shoulder, making me grit my teeth. Behind us, I saw Raphael's lifeless body on the ground.

Sumsion led the way. "Come on; let's get out of Dodge."

I chuckled at his remark, something I never expected him to say, but after the shoot-out in here, it seemed appropriate. I glanced up at Jack as he walked, remembering his sore shoulder. He must be running on adrenaline because no sign of pain creased his brow. He peered down at me. "Don't ever do that again."

"What?" I thought I knew, but I wanted to hear him say it.

"Take a bullet for me."

"Why?" I played innocence.

"Because when a guy watches the woman he cares a great deal about get shot saving him, it's like dying a thousand deaths." He cradled me to his chest.

Both of us had avoided saying the *L* word. We weren't there yet. We'd known each other less than a week, but still, with everything we'd been through, a growing attraction for each other ran deep. Tears threatened. I snuggled my cheek to his chest and heard the pounding of his heart. Things could have gone so wrong, and Jack would have been the one lying dead on the cave floor. I wanted to wrap my arms around him and forget everything else but knew I couldn't.

"I need tae tell you something." He hesitated, looking ahead. About twenty feet from us, Sumsion seemed to have found new energy. Jack looked down at me as though having an internal debate about whether to say what he wanted to. "I don't exactly work for Scotland Yard."

I couldn't help it. Despite the ache in my arm, I smiled and then uttered, "I know."

"Really?" He seemed surprised, but he shook it off and added, "Did you also know I was an MI6 agent for Scotland Yard and was in deep cover, spying on the rise of the new Jacobite cause in Edinburgh until recently when I was reassigned?"

"No." But something inside affirmed to me that here it finally was—Jack's true story was floating to the surface. He started walking again. Sidestepping a boulder at the entrance of the cave, he walked out into the early-morning rays of the sun. We basked in the warmth and light, glad to leave the dark, damp cavern behind.

Seagulls cawed overhead. The smell of seaweed and wet sand filled my senses. A slight breeze blew a wisp of my hair into my face. I swiped it aside with my good arm.

I hoped Jack would continue to trust me and reveal more. I now understood why he knew about the Scots who wanted to fight for independence. A strength rekindled inside me as questions I'd bottled up broke free. "Is MI6 like the American Special Forces?"

He nodded.

"Why did MI6 reassign you to keep me safe? How are Auntie and I involved in whatever is going on? And why do you think if the pages put Scotland in a positive light that Macgregor and Balmoral would want to capture me, or if the pages put Scotland in a negative light, they'd kill us? I don't understand."

He paused a moment as if summoning more courage. "I'll try tae answer all your questions. My boss is, or rather was, the Black Prince."

"What?" I stared at him, trying to comprehend.

"Calm down. I'm telling you this tae help you, not upset you."

I didn't know if I could handle more truth after that, but if Jack was willing to tell me, I needed to hear it.

All of it.

He plowed through the mud, avoiding seaweed as he spoke. "We were both on your plane from Heathrow."

My mind tripped back to that flight. I had a vague recollection of an Englishman who had resembled Hugh Grant. It had to have been him.

I'd actually seen the Black Prince, had waited on him. A chill rippled through me. And he is—or was—Jack's boss? "The Black Prince is part of MI6? I don't understand. Why would the British government kidnap Auntie? Why would they want the pages? And if you work for him, why are you telling me this?"

"The UK would never admit that the Black Prince worked for them. In fact, they would deny his division was part of MI6. But make no mistake; he works for them, and they don't want France or Scotland tae know about the pages because it would jeopardize their power. And the reason I'm telling you this is that I quit by saving your life at the airport. I was there to make sure you died, but instead, well, you know." He huffed like that had been hard to admit.

I remembered the entire scene like it had just happened. More bare truth. I had to keep digging. "Why did you save my life?"

"Because if my job is to covertly save the world, killing you went against everything I believe. In that split second when I pulled you out of harm's way, I knew I was on my own. I had tae help you find the pages so we could learn the truth and keep you alive."

My admiration for him soared. But while I felt extremely grateful that he'd saved me, something again didn't add up. I hated to sound like I didn't trust him when he was finally baring all, yet I still had to risk alienating him. "But if the Black Prince and you were both on the plane, who kidnapped Auntie?"

"He had a team already in place. The original plan was tae kill you and make your aunt give us the page. She was less than cooperative and held out until your plane landed. They told her you were dead, and that's when she had a stroke. So the plan changed. That young flight attendant who flirted with you—"

"Ian Murphy?" My mouth gaped open.

"Yes, his job was to distract you so the car would run over you. But he must have had deeper feelings for you than we knew. He chickened out, and for that, the Black Prince killed him. So the hit on you fell tae me."

Ian was dead.

Because of me.

I could hardly breath.

"The Black Prince has undercover agents everywhere. I don't even know where they all are. Some have been working on this mystery for years. When you sent your DNA tae be tested, our spies alerted us about you. See, you set things in motion that have been stifled for hundreds of years."

"Wait." He wasn't making sense. "What does my DNA test have to do with your boss wanting me dead?"

"Everything." Jack stood still.

"The tide's well out." Sumsion called back to us. "Hurry. We need to get Skye to a doctor." He seemed puzzled that Jack kept stopping.

Jack held me tighter as he quickened his pace.

"Jack, please tell me more." I knew he literally had his hands full trying to traverse the rocks on the beach and talk at the same time, but I had to know.

"There's a legend that an heir has Robert the Bruce's and Jeanne d'Évreux's DNA." He slipped and jostled me against his chest. He clenched his jaw as if in pain.

"Jack, the bullet hit my arm, not my leg. I can walk."

He reluctantly set me on my feet. Leaning into each other, we continued to follow Sumsion.

Wondering about what Jack had been telling me, I said, "The professor told me about Robert the Bruce and Jeanne, but he said nothing about their children who married."

"That's because it was a secret. It's a long story, and you're really in no shape tae hear it. Like the professor said, I've got tae get you medical help." He quickened his pace.

"Please, I need to know."

Jack paused a moment. "Robert the Bruce was good friends with King Charles IV. When Charles died, leaving his pregnant wife a widow, France held a collective breath, hoping her unborn child would be a son. Instead, she was blessed with yet another daughter."

He looked at Sumsion, who walked a good twenty yards ahead of us. "Great Britain claimed their king should rule over both countries. France didn't agree. Turmoil broke out between the two nations. Behind the scenes, Jeanne felt the throne had been stolen from her daughters. Legend tells that Jeanne begged Robert the Bruce to take her oldest living daughter, Marie, to wed his son, David. At the time, the Bruce was king of Scotland. They hoped the marriage would make an alliance that would never be broken. Plus, if a grandson should be born from the union, he would someday reign as king of both countries, which might have helped them break free of Great Britain's hold."

"Tell me more."

"I told you the Black Prince has spies all over the world. But so does Scotland's underground Jacobites and the French. They have known of the legend and have tried to find proof for years, following one lead after another. Your DNA rang bells that the legend was true. People in all three countries wanted desperately to find you and either find the pages too or kill you and let the legend die or capture you." Jack stared at me and appeared to be holding his breath.

I quickly pieced together the information he'd told me, and then I knew what all the secrecy, what all the espionage had been for. "They think I'm the heir?"

He slowly nodded.

CHAPTER THIRTY-ONE

THE CRAZY THOUGHT THAT I was the heir of Robert the Bruce and Jeanne d'Évreux made me light-headed. If, in fact, this was true, what then? "Are you saying I'm the rightful heir and possibly the queen of Scotland and France?" The idea hit me square in the chest, like a bullet.

Jack stared at me as if weighing his options of how to answer but then nodded.

"What does that even mean? I'm an American citizen. Have been all my life. It's not like I can do anything. It's not like my father was king."

The memory of my father whispering in my ear before he got on the plane came to me. "Watch over Auntie while we're gone." Had he known about our lineage? And if he had, had he been scared for his life and mine? "Did they kill him because of this?"

"When your father died, what DNA testing could prove was just coming about, so there was no solid proof of his ancestry, but I think it was highly likely that they suspected he was heir and may have gone after him, afraid that he might unite two countries against the UK."

"So that's what the Black Prince is worried I will do?"

Jack took a moment, staring at me as if still reluctant to answer. "Not exactly. France has their independence, but you could become a force for Scotland."

The tsunami of information crashed down on me, leaving me dizzy.

Jack must have sensed I needed to sit down and guided me to a rock to lean against.

"What's the holdup?" Sumsion walked back to us. "Are you worse, my dear?"

He needed to know what Jack had just told me, but I was still absorbing it and had no idea how to put it into words.

Sumsion's worried face reinforced part of the reason he thought we were here. Auntie. And even though I had learned so much, still, a hole of information had not been filled in. The thought of being an heir to royalty was more than mind-numbing and far too big for me to wrap my head around right now. I had no idea what I was supposed to do, not when so many people were after me and the pages. What was most important at this moment was rescuing Auntie.

I knew Professor Sumsion's surge of energy had to be because he was anxious to read the page that would lead us to her. I couldn't blame him. So was I. The rest would have to come later. I hugged my throbbing arm to me.

Jack put his hand on Professor Sumsion's back. "Would you mind going ahead and getting the van ready? Skye should lie down in the back."

"Of course." He held the jar and envelope containing all our hopes and dreams. But he'd have a devil of a time climbing up the gully with both of them in hand.

"Professor, let me take care of the envelope." I motioned for him to give it to me.

He complied. I tried to stuff it in the back waistband of my pants but had trouble doing so since I had the use of only one arm.

"Here, let me help." Jack lifted my fleece jacket, giving me easy access. I quickly stored it.

Sumsion set off to tackle the climb up the ravine by himself.

"Why did the plan change when Auntie had a stroke?" I asked once he was out of hearing range. "And you've known all along about the history of the page. Why didn't you tell me?"

"The plan changed for two reasons: when your aunt had the stroke, she could no longer get the page for them, and also, I went against my boss and saved your life. Once I did that, I was cut off from what they planned next, so I stayed as close tae you as I could. The Black Prince obviously decided tae use you tae get the other pages."

"Why didn't they kill Auntie?" A shudder flashed over my skin as the horrible notion settled on me. "I mean, why keep her alive and take her out of the country?"

"Keeping her alive gave you motivation tae find the other pages. With his special diplomatic clearance, the Black Prince moved her out of the U.S., which made it possible for him tae do what he wanted with her." Jack rubbed his chin. "And I didn't tell you everything so you would have plausible deniability. But I've been winging it. Despite all the odds against us, I hoped we could find the pages and turn them over tae a news source that would get the word out and bring justice down on the Black Prince and his secret operations."

"But what about Auntie?" How could he have forgotten?

"Of course we'll save her." He said it like an afterthought, like he knew something but didn't want to say.

I didn't want him to voice it either.

"How can they be sure I'm the heir? I mean, labs get it wrong all the time," I said, wanting to reason away his earlier claim.

Jack shook his head. "The direct lines of Robert the Bruce and Jeanne d'Évreux have certain DNA markers that make it impossible for a mistake to happen. You're the one. Plus, with the help of professional genealogists, the Black Prince and his team have been watching your family for quite some time. But they didn't have conclusive data tae do anything until the results of your DNA came out."

Other answers clicked into place. "Is this why Auntie had the page?"

He nodded. "Though, I believe it was in your father's care until his death. Your aunt did the best she could to keep you safe and the page a secret."

"So there are three groups of people after me, right?" I took hold of his arm, and he helped me to my feet.

"Aye. The underground Jacobites; Raphael's group, who were descendants of Jean Pucelle—they wanted the pages merely for profit; and the Black Prince, my old boss, whose job it is to procure the pages and kill you so Britain can keep the status quo." He guided me around another boulder.

"And MI6 is okay with that?"

"MI6 will never admit that he works for them. The powers that be have given him carte blanche. They don't want tae know the details of how he accomplishes his work, and they will deny he was ever part of their division. They just want possible threats tae the United Kingdom done away with. The underground Jacobites are a threat. You are a threat."

We'd reached the gully where we needed to climb up the grassy slopes. We quit talking for a while and leaned on each other like wounded soldiers coming away from battle as we pulled ourselves over the rise.

Sumsion met us, motioning for us to go back. He was out of breath. His face had turned blotchy red, and his hands shook as he held the jar.

"What is it?" Jack asked, trying to calm the elderly man.

"Those goons from before. The ones who waited for us at Prince William's cave."

Jack gave a disgusted huff.

Sumsion gulped. "I saw them from across the field, waiting for us at the van. I don't think they saw me."

Jack slipped by Sumsion to take a look for himself.

"Are you okay?" I wondered if Sumsion had brought his medication. But if I asked and he hadn't, it might upset him even more.

"Fine, my dear. Don't worry over me. It's you who has me concerned." He studied my shoulder.

Jack returned a bit winded. "He's right."

"Are those two men part of the underground Jacobites?" I asked, trying to think of what we could do.

Sumsion turned to me like I'd just told him the world was flat.

"Yes." Jack paused, avoiding Sumsion's gaze.

"Can you talk with them? Tell them the two pages we have put Scotland in a positive light and offer them the third page? If we're sincere enough, it might make them understand what's going on with Auntie." If he could just do that, maybe we would turn them to our side and have one less group after us.

"Not an option." He clenched his jaw. "Just before I was reassigned tae you, MI6 nabbed a couple of their most powerful leaders. Because I disappeared at the same time, these men believe I had something tae do with it."

"Did you?" Sumsion asked. He hadn't been privy to the bulk of our conversation but seemed to understand our getting away depended on this.

"Yes." Jack looked at me. "It was my job. Maybe we should let them take you two. At least you'd be safe."

"No." I knew that wasn't possible. "Without me, the Black Prince would kill Auntie."

"We can't stand here and go over ancient history." Jack guided us toward the trail.

"What should we do?" I held my throbbing arm close to my body.

"I know this isn't what you want tae hear, but if you don't want them tae capture you, our only option is tae work our way down the shoreline." He looked at Sumsion and then me. "With the tide still low, we should be able tae reach Glasnakille without too much trouble."

"Let's go, then." Sumsion started for the village.

I wondered if I should tell Sumsion what I'd learned. I held back. The news was too fresh, and I was still coming to terms with it. Once we were out of danger, I'd tell him everything.

Jack kept us going as fast as we could while sidestepping rocks and ruts.

The little village we were headed toward wasn't exactly a hub of activity, so I had to ask, "What are we going to do once we get there?"

"Find a boat that will take us tae the main land." Jack pulled my good arm over his shoulder and quickened our pace.

Retracing our steps took no time at all. Instead of turning toward the cave, we went in the opposite direction. Strewn with driftwood, rocks, and tidepools, the shoreline became an obstacle course. We plowed through the best we could. Jack kept looking behind us as if worried we were being chased.

"There they are." He had us huddled up behind an enormous boulder. My heart pounded against my ribs; my arm throbbed.

Jack eased up to check where they were. "Don't see them anymore. They must have seen me when I went tae double-check. Hopefully, they'll think we're in the cave and go there. Once inside, they'll find Raphael and know we're near. Come on."

Jack bent over, so Sumsion and I did too. We trailed him down the beach. Jack raised up to check where the bad guys were. "They've gone to the cave. We don't have long."

He studied the small village. In the bay, a pier had several launches bobbing in the water. "You two head for the boats. I'll see if I can find a boat owner on the shore." Jack didn't look back but ran toward the village.

A few wooden row boats appeared abandoned on the beach where the tide had gone out. Sumsion and I sidestepped seaweed that tried to block our path on all sides as we kept our main focus on getting to our destination. As we reached the pier where the larger boats docked, water lapped at the concrete steps green with moss. No handrail.

Using each other for security, Sumsion and I climbed up.

"Who are the underground Jacobites you and Jack were talking about?" Sumsion asked as we walked down the pier toward the vessels.

"Jack says it's a group of Scottish people who want to become independent of the United Kingdom." I wondered if I should have deferred the question to Jack. He hadn't told me the information he'd shared was top secret. Besides, after what Sumsion had gone through, he deserved to know.

"I see. From what I gleaned from your conversation, Jack works for MI6?" He seemed concerned.

"Not anymore. Jack will tell you all about it once we're safe." I turned my attention to the bobbing boats. They appeared to be sightseeing launches. One had the name *Skye Dolphin* painted on the side and looked to be about forty feet long. It had a cabin and benches for people to sit on.

Jack raced down the shoreline and leaped up the stairs. "No one was about. I think the owners are eating breakfast at the main café on the hill. We're going tae have tae borrow a boat." He hopped on the *Skye Dolphin* and reached over to help me onboard.

"Do you think this is wise?" Sumsion asked as Jack helped him board.

"Probably not, but we've got tae get out of here. Don't worry. I'll make things right with the boat's owner after we're safe." Jack made certain we were both onboard before he hurried to the steering wheel.

I found seats for us just inside the cabin, out of the sun. I knew nothing about how boats worked, but I did know that once Jack turned on the engine, we'd need to be untied from the pier. I returned to the rope and tried to untie it, but the knot held firm. I'd have to use both hands.

Forcing the pain to the back of my mind, I raised my injured arm, and with both hands, I worked the knot. It loosened enough that I was able to slip it off the hook. My task accomplished, I went back to the cabin and found Jack on his hands and knees.

He'd reached under what looked like a dashboard and had pulled down some wires. He tapped two together, and the engine turned over.

"That's promising," he said.

He tapped them again, then did something with what I assumed was the throttle, and the engine came to life. He backed the boat away from other vessels tied to the pier, and when we were free and clear, he pushed down on the gas.

I heard yelling and turned to see men running toward the pier.

"Looks like the owner might take exception to us using his vessel," Sumsion said loud enough for Jack to hear over the engine's roar.

Jack shrugged as if it was out of his hands. "We could have stayed there and talked with the owner and explained our situation, but by then, Macgregor and Balmoral could have left the cave and tracked us."

"And our mission to find Auntie would have been over," I added.

Sumsion nodded, yet I caught worry on his face as he looked back at the shore and the small crowd gathering there.

The bow of the boat beat against the waves as it sped over the water. Fine sea sprays sprinkled us.

Sumsion spoke loudly. "I imagine Her Majesty's Coastguard will be notified. We may soon have even more people after us."

"I'm going out tae sea a bit in hopes of throwing them off," Jack yelled over the roar of the engine.

I hoped he was right. I hugged my aching arm to my side and thought about all Jack had told me. I was an heir of Robert the Bruce and Jeanne d'Évreux. Talk about crazy. I could see why the Black Prince wanted me out of the way and the pages to never see the light of day. If news were to leak out to the public that pages from Jeanne d'Évreux's *Book of Hours* had been found and they told of a new heir and it pointed to me, that might stir up the entire country of Scotland to want me to guide them to independence. Britain wouldn't want to contend with such an issue, not when their own monarchy was closely scrutinized on their worthiness of such titles. If the pages spoke positively about the Scottish people, they might start banging the drum for their own royal family, and chaos could break out.

I was a definite threat to Britain, Scotland, and who knows who else. But so was Auntie because she knew of the pages. And Jack and Sumsion. They were in as much danger as I was. But maybe if I came face-to-face with the Black Prince, I could ease his mind, tell him I had no desire to move to Scotland or become involved with their politics. Then maybe he'd let Auntie and I leave. Even as I thought it, wished it, I knew it was highly unlikely.

I had to somehow think of a way I could deal with the man who had been given a carte blanche deal by his government to make me go away. Of course, the easiest thing for the Black Prince to do would be to kill me. How could I talk him out of doing that? The man was on a secret mission to protect his country from foreign agents. That Auntie and I were considered foreign agents boggled my mind.

I was so wrapped up in trying to solve this unsolvable problem that I jumped when Sumsion nudged my leg. He pointed behind us.

A speedboat headed in our direction.

I reached over and tugged on Jack. "We're being followed," I yelled.

He looked over his shoulder and cussed under his breath. "We won't be able tae outrun whoever it is."

"Have any idea who it could be?" Sumsion asked.

"It's not HM Coastguard. They have bigger boats." He thought for a moment. "And it can't be Raphael's men. They don't know he's dead yet."

"Maybe it belongs to someone with the underground Jacobites?" I said.

"No." Jack stared at the boat. "It has tae be the Black Prince's men. Somehow, he's traced us. Somehow, he knows we've found the last page, but this was what you wanted, right?" He looked at me.

"Yes, but not so fast. How could he know we have all the pages?" I didn't understand. It was like the man had an all-seeing eye.

"Could have been the lady at the Sea Eagle Hotel, or maybe he picked up on a radio transmission tae HM Coastguard saying that a boat had been stolen, and he put two and two together." Jack checked over his shoulder again.

The boat was closing in fast.

"Do you trust me?" Jack stared at me.

If he'd asked a day ago, I would have said no. But so much had happened, so much had been said. A strange surety took root within me. "Yes, I do."

He looked to Sumsion. The older man, clutching the jar to his person, nodded.

"Okay, play along, and act like I've kidnapped you." He shut off the engine, and the boat glided in the water, slowly coming to a stop.

The speedboat came alongside. A man dressed like a tourist—jeans and windbreaker jacket—jumped from the boat onto ours. "Took you long enough. Boss said you'd come through in the long run, and here you are."

I stared at Jack. For a split second, I saw tender affection in his eyes. It quickly dissolved as he greeted the man. "He knows I always deliver the goods."

Sumsion squinted; his forehead wrinkled as if he questioned the trust he'd placed in Jack.

My heart sank to my toes, but I clung to Jack's words—Do you trust me ?—and prayed that we could.

CHAPTER THIRTY-TWO

ONCE THE THREE MEN HAD us on their speedboat, we were on our way, leaving the stolen launch bobbing in the water. Jack had us sit at the back of the boat while he talked with the men clustered around the driver.

My wounded arm ached with each bump as the speedboat cut across the ocean waves, but that was the least of my worries. I watched as Jack easily conversed with the men, like they were long-lost buddies. Of course they were. They had been colleagues and believed he worked with them, not against them. But how much was an act on Jack's part? I didn't know what to think. Plus, I felt a little woozy. Sumsion must have noticed.

"Skye, my dear, lean your head on my shoulder." He scooted closer, still holding the jar protectively in his hands.

I gave in and accepted his kind offer. The faint scent of pipe tobacco hung on his clothing. Sumsion had been my one constant in this ordeal. He'd become the grandfather I'd never had. As the boat skimmed over the ocean, taking us to who knew where, I thought of my father.

Even though I'd been only nine when he died, I'd adored him. He must have known the secret of his family, and that was why he'd named me Skye. All along, I had thought his motivation for my name had been that he loved to fly. He loved aviation. And to name his only child Skye had seemed natural. Did he really know all of the secret, that Robert the Bruce had hidden the third page on the island and that was why he'd named me Skye? He must have had some idea. Oh, how I wished I could talk with him.

And how I hoped that even though the Black Prince was determined to kill me, he'd give me time to see Auntie.

Jack was still talking with the others. Surely, he was working on a plan to save us. We'd come all this way, and for it to end bitterly, with Jack betraying not just me but Sumsion and Auntie as well, seemed unimaginable.

Sumsion leaned over and spoke close in my ear. "Believe in him."

"I do."

"What are you two doing?" The stern-looking man guarding us, who appeared lean and muscular as a Doberman, stepped closer.

"She's been wounded," Sumsion readily defended. "She needs medical attention before infection sets in."

Though he tried to appear tough and noncaring, when he gave another look at my bandaged arm and the tired, older man seated beside me, sympathy seemed to take hold. "Jack radioed ahead. A medical team will be waiting when we arrive. Would you like some water?"

"That would be most kind." Sumsion nodded.

The guard left to speak with the others. Soon, Jack walked toward us holding a bottle of water, with the guard dutifully by his side.

Jack opened the water and handed it to me. Our fingers touched for a moment. He stared into my eyes, pleading with me to hang on.

The guard opened another bottle and gave it to Sumsion.

"We should reach our destination shortly." Jack said it like this should make me feel better. I felt many things: wary, tired, and angry, to name a few, but mainly anxious. Anxiety had arisen in me like a blister ready to pop. Frustrated beyond belief, I stared up at him.

His emotion-filled gaze rested upon me, embracing me with a new-found comfort. In that moment, I trusted him. Not only because I had no other choice but because I really did believe in him too. I had no idea what awaited us at the end of this boat ride, but the only way out of this mess rested on Jack.

He gave me a nod and returned to the others.

An island appeared on the horizon and grew closer and closer. With each jolt of the boat cutting across the waves, seawater splashed into the vessel.

"There are over a hundred islands in the Hebrides." Sumsion also stared at the island we were speeding toward.

I didn't say anything. I didn't care how many islands the Hebrides had.

"In fact, in Cladh Hallan, they found mummies buried that dated back to 2000 BC." Sumsion still stared ahead.

"Mummies?"

He looked at me. "Yes." Though it sounded like he merely rattled off unimportant facts, I could tell he'd thought of what our fates might be. Would our bodies end up buried on one of the remote islands to be found hundreds of years later by people who wouldn't know of our trauma? That was a high possibility.

I had to give Sumsion hope, like he had me. I leaned close. "Remember, we need to believe in him."

"Of course, my dear." His words didn't match the consternation furrowing his forehead. He clutched the jar even tighter.

"They haven't noticed you have the jar yet." I wanted him to be careful and not draw attention to it.

"A rather fortunate development." Sumsion's fingers caressed the vessel.

"Are you going to translate the page for them?"

"If it means Marjorie will be returned to us, yes." His eyes teared up. The old man's emotions had been tattered through this experience, but one thing I knew for certain: he loved Auntie. If all went well and we got out of this alive, I would strongly encourage her to marry this man.

As we neared the island, I expected the boat to slow down so we could dock. It slowed a little but was still going too fast. And then I saw why. The driver, a burly man with a beard, headed toward a sea cave. Large jutting rocks sat at the mouth, but he expertly glided by.

Inside, the cave walls were vertical pillars of gray and black rocks.

Sumsion studied the high ceiling. "This reminds me of Fingal's Cave, but this is much wider. Looks like the same basalt rock though."

I wondered how he knew.

He must have read the expression on my face. "I watched a special on PBS about Fingal's Cave."

A dock rested near the end of the cavern. Several wave runners bobbed in the water alongside another speedboat.

Two men dressed in black suits awaited our arrival. To think, a week ago, I hadn't ever known of such a place. But, of course, a week ago, I had been happily living an ordinary life. I'd had a routine. Work for a couple of weeks, then home for a couple. And yes, I'd traveled the world, but I hadn't really seen it. And in my downtime at home with Auntie, we'd gone to movies, taken hikes, and enjoyed our lives together. But all along, she'd been keeping this secret from me. How could she have done that? And why? If I had known, I might have been more prepared, I might have thought of a way to quash the legend, and I surely wouldn't have sent my DNA in to be tested.

The boat docked. Jack hurried to assist us off. Our guard and another man left the boat as well. Only the burly skipper stayed behind, checking his vessel. When no one was looking, Jack winked at me. I didn't know if it was a don't-worry-I-got-this wink or a nervous tick. I had to believe it was the first.

We followed the suits up rusting metal stairs to a platform. To the left was a long white hallway, to the right a door. The two men who had been on the boat with us went through the door.

The suits escorted us down the hallway, the sound of our footsteps echoing off the flooring as we walked. I was amazed that such a place existed. How had they built it? How had they kept it a secret? This was something out of James Bond, not the real world. Yet, here it was.

They took us to a door and swiped a card over the lock. A little green light appeared, and they opened the door to a sleek, contemporary room that reminded me of a high-class apartment. One entire wall was a window that looked out on the ocean. The wall parallel was covered in gray floor-to-ceiling curtains. In the middle of the room was a conversation area with a large gray-toned rug. A contemporary sofa the color of deep-water-blue stood flanked by two gray side chairs. A glass coffee table rested between the sofa and chairs.

One of the suits motioned for us to have a seat. We stood there like statues. I didn't want to sit as if we were here on a friendly visit. We had been taken against our will and were here because some nefarious man had kidnapped my aunt and would very likely kill us all. No, I had no intention of sitting.

"We're fine standing," Jack told him.

"I'll let the boss know you're here." The suit who offered us a seat left. But his companion stood guard at the door.

"Have you been here before?" I asked Jack.

"No." Jack walked over to the picturesque window. "I've only heard about this place." By his tone, what he'd heard wasn't good.

Professor Sumsion's shoulders slumped, his cheeks appeared sallow, and his eyes were bloodshot.

"Professor, why don't you sit?" I said.

"I'm not the one with a bullet wound in my arm. I can stand right here beside you." He straightened his stance as if to show solidarity.

My arm ached but not as much as before, which was odd. Maybe the adrenaline coursing through my body was weakening the pain. The man on the boat had said that someone would look at my arm once we arrived. I really shouldn't be surprised that it hadn't happened.

Jack came over and took a peek beneath the T-shirt he'd wrapped around my wound. He winced. "Are you sure you don't want tae sit? You really need tae rest."

I shook my head, not giving in. "I want to see Auntie first."

The door opened, and in walked the Englishman I remembered from the plane ride. His gray hair matched the color of his tailor-made, thousand-dollar suit. The white Brooks Brothers shirt beneath appeared to be starched as rigidly as his back. He was a strikingly suave and debonair man, the type I would admire if I saw him on the street. He walked over to Jack and shook his hand. "Job well done. You had me worried for a while there, but you came through in the end."

The man turned, tilted his head to the side, and held out his hand to shake mine. "I'm Edward Prince." His king's English accent sounded prim and proper, much better than it had over the phone.

I didn't accept his offered hand. "Where's my aunt?"

He stepped back and smiled. Lines crinkled the skin at the sides of his cold, sea-green eyes. "I like a woman who speaks her mind and gets right to the point even though she is in pain." He motioned toward the sofa. "But please, before we get down to business, won't you have a seat. You must be tired. I understand you spent the night in a cave and you've been wounded." He studied the T-shirt wrapped around my upper arm.

Sumsion left my side and did as asked, sitting on the sofa. He patted the cushion for me to sit too. Though I'd rather suffer another bullet wound than sit, I did it, all the while keeping my eye on the Black Prince.

"Don't worry. When we verify the pages, I'll have my medical staff take a look at your arm." He sat on one of the side chairs.

Jack sat on the other.

The thought came to me that he had no intention of seeing to my arm because he was going to kill me. Why treat a dying woman?

"And you have the pages?" With his elbows resting on the arms of the chair, Edward steepled his fingertips together, waiting for a reply.

Sumsion carefully set the jar on the glass coffee table.

"Correct me if I'm wrong, but that appears to be a jar of some kind, not a page." He stared at Sumsion, disappointment shading his complexion.

"The page is inside." Sumsion leaned back.

Edward rose and went to the sidebar hutch. He lit a cigarette, slipped the lighter inside his jacket pocket, and opened a drawer. He pulled out the largest ashtray I'd ever seen and brought it over, setting it on the table.

Tapping ash from his cigarette into it, he said, "Professor, do what I've paid you for—pull the page out of that ugly jar you seem so fond of and read it."

At first, I didn't know if I'd heard him correctly. "You paid him?"

The lines in Edward's face deepened as he chuckled and grinned. "How else do you think I was able to keep track of your whereabouts?" He took a puff of his cigarette and blew it out. "Sumsion has been an agent of ours for what?" He paused, looking at the professor as if the older man would fill in the blank for him. But Sumsion didn't move, didn't say a word.

"Thirty years, isn't it?" Edward taunted him.

Sumsion rubbed his chin, not looking at his accuser but gazing down at the floor.

"Of course," Edward's face brightened as if he delighted in upsetting the older man, "his vast historical knowledge has been a great asset. See, I thought we'd put an end to this problem when your father's plane went down, killing everyone on board. But then we learned you and your aunt didn't go on the trip."

The stinging truth prickled my skin. Jack's theory about my father's death had been right.

Edward zeroed in on me. "Once we suspected your aunt of harboring the pages, we sent Sumsion to keep an eye on her. However, there have been times when he's allowed his personal feelings to cloud his better judgment and put our mission in jeopardy."

I stared at Sumsion, the man I had believed to be as kind as a grandfather, the man I had thought loved my aunt and even me. Had Auntie suspected that he was a spy? Is that why she hadn't married him, because she didn't trust him?

Shocked beyond knowing what to say, I sat there like a lump, unable to form words, unable to think. I didn't know what to believe anymore. Did Jack know Sumsion worked for Edward? I shot a glance at him.

He stood there slack-jawed, looking as though he'd been sucker punched. Obviously, he'd been broadsided too.

Sumsion's sorrowful eyes avoided my gaze as he turned his back on me and tugged off his sweatshirt. He dug in his jacket pocket, pulling out a cell phone I'd never seen before, like the one Jack had ditched in Salt Lake because it had had a GPS tracker on it. That was how he'd kept Edward informed. Sumsion also retrieved his magnifying glass and the small mirror.

"Old man, what are you doing now?" Edward's harsh words didn't rattle him.

"Edward." Sumsion sat on the edge of the sofa, the jar in front of him on the table. "Don't disrespect your elders. I know people higher up on the MI6 food chain than you. This vellum is very old. I'd prefer not to pull the artifact from the jar because I might destroy parts of it before we know what it says. And I need more light."

Jack covered his surprise better than I did and smoothly stood. He pulled out his burner phone, tapped the flashlight app, and knelt beside Sumsion, directing the beam where needed.

As Sumsion and Edward's attention focused on the jar, Jack stared at me. No guilt showed in his eyes. Only true compassion. Even though my world in the last few days had twisted and turned like a kaleidoscope, revealing one lie after another, Jack had finally told me the truth as we'd left the cave.

And right now, the truth was we were in trouble.

"A pen and paper would be most helpful." Sumsion stared into the jar.

Edward snapped his fingers to the suit guarding the door. He rushed over to the hutch, opened a drawer, and brought both pad and pen over, setting them on the table, then he returned dutifully to his post.

Still numb from the jolting news that Sumsion was a traitor to both Auntie and me, I feigned interest in what the vellum said but was more keenly aware of Edward sitting in the side chair, smoking his cigarette and patiently waiting. I felt his eyes on me, as though he was appraising my earthly value. What would this cold, calculating killer do once he knew what the page said? He'd definitely planned to kill me. Had tried several times. And he had killed my parents, even before my DNA had set off alarm bells.

He knew full well who I was, had sent Jack to take care of me, had killed Ian because he wouldn't. Funny, the Black Prince hadn't reprimanded Jack upon greeting him. Surely, he'd have punishment waiting for an agent who had gone rogue but seemed to have returned to the fold. Unless he planned to kill him too.

Jack seemed intent on helping Sumsion.

Sumsion worked the mirror and magnifying glass, then he took notes and read once again. It seemed to go on forever. Of course it would. The message in that bottle had been hidden from the world and had waited a long time to be found and read. It should take a while.

Sumsion drew a deep breath and set down the magnifying glass and mirror. He scrubbed his face with his palm and leaned back. "It is in Old Latin, as I'm sure you are well aware." He picked up the paper with the scribbles.

Edward set his cigarette on the ashtray and folded his arms. "And the translation says?"

Sumsion studied the words. "'The true heir, male or female, shall touch hearts and heal grateful nations yearning to be one against their adversary. The houses of Capetian and Bruce shall be one. God be with their people and the rightful heir.'" Sumsion looked at me.

Everyone in the room looked at me, the true heir. I wanted to hide, to dry up and disappear. If only the floor would open and swallow me whole. But wishful thinking couldn't help me. Suddenly, something clicked about Robert the Bruce and Queen Jeanne, something deep inside, and a calmness quieted my nerves.

Edward leaned forward, resting his elbows on his knees and stared directly at me. "You have the other two pages, I presume."

I had expected him to say something about my lineage and the crown. But, of course, he didn't. His job was to get rid of me and the evidence. I didn't want to merely hand the pages over to him. "Auntie. Where is she?"

He motioned to the guard at the door.

The man drew open the drapes, revealing a glass wall. Behind it rested a hospital bed, IV stands on both sides with tubing draped over them, no longer connected to the patient. My heart leaped within my chest. I rushed to the glass, straining to see.

Stark white sheets covered the person. Short wisps of white hair feathered across a bruised forehead, and short strands in a youthful bob drew to a curl beside each ear. Pink lips no longer smiled.

There she was—Auntie.

CHAPTER THIRTY-THREE

"MARJORIE!" SUMSION'S FACE PALED. HIS hand covered his heart.

Jack's concerned eyes looked from me to the woman behind the glass and then back.

I focused on Auntie lying so very still. A quivering deep inside erupted in my gut, yet somehow, my legs took me to the glass, the glass that kept me from helping her. I pounded on it. "Auntie! Wake up!"

She didn't move. I pounded harder.

Edward spoke beside me. "I warned you to hurry. She passed away last night."

While we'd been stuck in that horrible cave, fighting to stay warm and find the last page, Auntie had died. And it was all Edward's fault. This man had taken so much from me. Filled with wild rage, I leaped at him, wanting to scratch his eyes out, wanting to hurt him as much as I hurt.

He grabbed hold of my arm and wrenched it in back of me.

Pain shot through my shoulder, making me gasp. I sank onto my knees, and he let go.

"Must you torment her?" Sumsion's voice sounded as if he'd moved to stand behind me and that he cared. I wanted to lash out at him as well. He'd made me think he loved Auntie enough to marry her and that his love for her was why he'd trailed along with us. But it was all a lie.

I knelt there unable to move, unable to think.

"Leave her be!" Jack stood near too. I didn't look at him. What would be the point? We were beaten. The Black Prince had won.

Unable to hold them back, tears rolled down my cheeks. Auntie's voice had sounded so faint on the telephone as she'd spoken my name only two days ago. She'd died alone in that bed, with strangers surrounding her. My parents had died alone on a mountainside. And I was the cause of all their deaths, the rightful heir. I no longer cared if I lived or died. An ache for all I had lost filled my heart more painfully than the wound in my arm. I leaned my forehead against the glass.

That was when I saw it, a spider crawling across the floor. I thought of the spider in the cave, Robert the Bruce's inspiration to keep fighting.

A tremendous legacy weighed on me. Hundreds of years had passed, yet I'd found the pages, and the proof of my lineage rested in my DNA. So what was I supposed to do? I couldn't grasp the full meaning of the pages, but I had an important role in whatever was to come about, though the days when kings and queens ruled were mostly over. I had no desire to join their ranks, but for some reason, the pages had come to me, the rightful heir, and because of that, people in power felt threatened, so much so that they wanted me dead.

Edward's black, highly-polished oxford shoe rose and stepped on the spider, smashing it. The spider crunched beneath his sole.

"*Help them.*" Again, the voice. The voice had guided me throughout this horrendous ordeal, helping me find the pages. And now it fed me courage I lacked and prompted me to take action.

I too had to keep fighting. This Black Prince, Edward, could not win.

"My dear, come away." Sumsion took hold of my good arm, trying to help me up.

I recoiled from his touch, wiped tears from my cheeks, and, with dogged determination, rose to my feet by myself. Not looking at Sumsion or Jack, I turned to Edward. His sea-green eyes squinted as he studied me, as though looking for a weak spot in my mental armor. It took all the strength I possessed not to lunge at him again, but I had to play along and pretend that I was stronger than I felt. Following a sudden prompting, I said, "Perhaps we should look at all three pages."

He stepped back and seemed a bit surprised and wary at the same time. He held out his hand, waiting for me to deliver the other two.

I pulled the envelope from my waistband, and as much as I hated to, I gave it to him. Why? I didn't know. But I felt guided to do this.

He bowed slightly, as if accepting my defeat. "Thank you."

Our eyes met. Could he see the resolve in my soul? Did he have any idea the determination that pierced through me?

He turned away, brushing me aside as inconsequential, and returned to the glass coffee table where the jar holding the other page waited.

I followed, looking for any opportunity to get the jump on him. Jack and Sumsion joined us. We stood around the table, staring at Edward.

He slowly opened the manila envelope, tugged out the cardboard, and opened it. He took each page from the protective sheeting and laid them on the table. The illustrations and text so meticulously drawn by Jean Pucelle made me wonder what he had thought as he'd created them. Did he have any idea of the importance the pages would play in history? Or that they would be secreted away, never to be seen until hundreds of years later?

Edward reached over and picked up the jar holding the third page. He looked at me and then Sumsion. As if to offer a treaty, he held out the jar, then took a couple steps back off the area rug. Then he turned his hand and deliberately dropped the ancient jar on the marble floor.

The aged clay fractured and crumbled like an imploding building. Parts of the vellum poked out of the ruins. He plucked it up and blew away dust. Jagged holes had been torn in the artifact. He set it on the table with the others.

There lay all three. A frisson tingled my skin. I glanced at Jack. His eyes met mine. I'd mistrusted him, yet I'd clung to the hope that he'd turn out to be a good guy, never more so than now.

I looked at Sumsion. He stared at me like he expected me to do something, say something. But I couldn't. In this profound moment, words failed me.

Ignoring or not even comprehending the powerful occasion, Edward snatched up all three pages, pulled out his lighter, and flicked it.

Fire sprang to life. He lit the corner of the pages, and his eyes gleamed with delight.

I gasped as hungry flames ate the history that had so long been preserved. "No!" I yelled and reached to knock the pages from Edward's hand.

He merely stepped out of my way. I fell hard on the marble floor, biting my tongue and jolting more pain into my wound. I moaned and turned over, desperate to do something but came up short—the pages were nearly fully engulfed in flame. Edward dropped them into the large ashtray.

As if overcome by rage, Jack leaped on Edward, taking him down. They rolled over the area rug, bumping the table, and upturned the side chairs.

The guard at the door rushed over, gun in hand. He ignored me because I was still on the floor. I had to stop him. As he aimed at Jack, I kicked his legs out from under him.

He face-planted on the floor. His gun skidded across the marble, coming to a stop at Sumsion's feet. I had to get that gun. As I scrambled on hands and knees, the guard lunged past me, but the elderly man beat us both and snatched up the weapon.

The guard latched on to his arm, and the gun disappeared between them. A loud blast echoed through the room and mingled with smoke. I stared at the two men, holding my breath, praying Sumsion hadn't been shot. The guard grew slack and dropped to the floor, the gun still in Sumsion's shaking hand.

Jack and Edward ceased their fighting, and Jack warily stared at Sumsion as he carefully gained his feet.

Edward rose and kicked Jack in the shin. "Traitor," he spat out like a child. Straightening his suit jacket, he then turned to Sumsion. "This is going in my report. You'll be a hero." He started toward him, but Sumsion stepped away, aiming the gun at Edward.

"You said Marjorie would not be hurt." Sumsion's age-spotted, arthritic hands shook. He looked past Edward at me. "I truly loved her. It wasn't supposed to end like this, Skye. You have to believe me."

Numb, I didn't know what to say. Yet I felt he spoke the truth.

Edward stepped toward him, taking the older man's attention.

Sumsion stepped back again, glaring at Edward. "You promised I could drop the charade and be free to marry her." His sad eyes went to the bed behind the glass wall. "You lied."

Edward gave a deep sigh, shaking his head. "You know how unpredictable a job like this can be. Don't throw away years of service and your retirement." It was like he hadn't heard a word Sumsion had said and ignored the pure hatred glassing the older man's eyes.

The door opened, and the other guard who had greeted us when we'd first arrived rushed in. Gun raised, he fired at Sumsion. Sumsion grabbed his chest and melted to the ground. I wanted to run to him, but the guard turned his smoking gun on Jack and me as he warily awaited instructions from his boss.

Edward shook his head, staring at Sumsion as he walked over to him. "So many years wasted, and for what?" He glowered down on the old man.

Sumsion gasped for air and motioned for Edward to come closer, like he had something more to tell him. As Edward cautiously leaned over, Sumsion raised the weapon and squeezed the trigger.

The semiautomatic fired several times. As each shot hit Edward, he stepped back as if he couldn't believe what was happening.

The guard blinked like his eyes betrayed him. Jack lunged, tackling him to the ground. The gun was still in the guard's hand.

I carefully inched my way to them as they wrestled, ever aware of where the gun pointed. If I could get the weapon out of the man's hand, Jack would be able to overtake him. First, it was up, then down. The guard somehow raised the weapon and aimed at Jack. A prickling flashed over my skin as I focused. I lunged and grabbed hold of the guard's hand. The man's fingers had a death-grip on the cold metal. Not knowing what to do, I bit the guard's hand hard. He still didn't let go, so I bit even harder, drawing blood. A coppery taste assaulted my mouth. Moaning, he dropped the weapon.

I scooped it up and wiped my lips. Jack pounded his fist into the man's face, knocking his head against the floor. He went slack.

Jack slowly gained his feet. Shaking the hand he'd used to hit the guard with, he looked at me and said, "Remind me not tae get in a fight with you."

Knowing he was more experienced with a gun, I handed it to him and turned to see how Sumsion was doing.

He lay on the floor, a pool of blood beneath him. Jack and I rushed over. I took Sumsion's hand in mine. "Professor."

He opened his eyes. He reached up and stroked my cheek. "Make the Bruce proud." He sucked in a sudden breath, as though fighting back pain. He gasped. Fear filled his eyes.

I squeezed his hand, trying to give him comfort.

He squeezed back tightly and stared into my eyes. "I really did love her."

"I believe you." I kissed his knuckles.

His eyes froze as I felt his arm grow heavy with no life.

"No, no, no," I mumbled. Tears filled my vision. Even though he had betrayed me, he'd done it thinking he was helping Auntie.

Jack's hand stroked my back. "Skye, we've got tae get out of here."

I knew he was right. I laid Sumsion's hand over his chest and, with Jack's help, stood. He guided me toward the exit. Passing the huge window that forbade me from going to Auntie, I couldn't help but look at her. It broke my heart to leave her behind, but I had to if we were going to get away.

"She understands," he said as if he knew I didn't want to go without her.

"You really think so?"

"I do. Even though I never met her, I know she did everything in her power tae shield you from harm and keep you safe. She would want you tae survive and make a difference." Again, he was right.

I blew Auntie a kiss, and we fled out the door only to come face-to-face with the skipper of the boat who had brought us here.

"Is it done?" The tall burly man stared at Jack.

"Yes, and where in the world have you been?"

"I had my own problems." He pointed down the hall. A couple of the guys who had been on the boat with us lay on the floor, out cold.

Jack herded us down the long hallway. "This is Frazier. He's sympathetic tae the underground Jacobite cause too. But unlike some, he wanted the pages brought tae light no matter what was written on them."

The man who reminded me of a sea captain gave me a smile and nod.

Jack motioned for us to move along. "I'll explain more later. We don't have much time before Edward's men find the mess we've left behind."

The three of us raced to the platform leading to the metal stairs.

Our feet pounded on the steps as we bounded down them, and I worried that at any moment, we would be found. The wave runners and other boat I'd noticed when we'd arrived were still tied to the dock. Frazier's speedboat had been turned around and was ready to leave.

Jack motioned for me to get in. Frazier jumped in behind me, and Jack untied the ropes holding the boat to the dock.

Once Frazier started the engine, Jack pulled the boat bumpers in. Then he looked at the other speedboat.

"Wait a minute," he yelled to Frazier.

Jack leaped onto the deck and dashed to the other vessel. He disappeared inside the cabin for several moments.

A commotion came from the platform above. Several men took aim at us as others stormed down the stairs.

The pfft, pfft, pfft of bullets whizzing by pinged against the dock and sliced into the water.

Jack must have heard them too. He leaped out of the other boat, returned fire on the men shooting at us, then dodging bullets, he raced toward us. Our speedboat had drifted away from the dock. He wasn't going to make it.

"Run, Jack!" I held my breath as I watched him charge toward the end of the dock. With great effort, he leaped into the air. The men fired more shots as Jack's legs flailed. Bullets zinged by. One of Jack's feet hit the side of the boat as he missed and fell from my sight.

I screamed. Rushing over, I found he'd grabbed the boat railing. With what must have been adrenaline-enhanced strength, Jack pulled himself up. As I helped him crawl inside, he yelled, "Hit it!"

The engine roared to life, and the boat plowed through the water.

Several men had reached the dock and leaped onto the wave runners and into the other vessel. Men shouted as they tried to start their boat. Jack pulled wires from his pants pocket. "They won't follow us. And there's no way the wave runners can outrun us."

Frazier managed to keep our speedboat in the middle of the channel and shot out of the cave, clearing the pillars of jetting rocks on both sides.

The wind had picked up since we'd been on the island. A storm boiled the ocean and swirled the sky above.

Our speedboat left the wave runners far behind.

Jack pulled me close. "You done good, kid."

I snuggled up to him. "So did you."

Memories of what we'd lived through flew at me like startled bats from a cave.

Cave.

If I never went inside another cave, I would not regret the loss.

I thought of Auntie, Sumsion, and Raphael. All dead. Heavy grief settled on me as I thought of their sacrifices.

"What's going to happen to us now?" I peered at Jack.

"Nothing. Since Edward was over this deep cover division the world was never to know about, I'm sure everything that happened here will be swept under the rug. Believable lies will be written of his heroic death."

"But will the British government keep coming after me? I mean, if they truly believe I'm a threat, won't they still want me dead?"

He paused a moment. "It's possible. You're a challenge tae their power and the rightful heir of Scotland."

"But that means nothing now. Especially since the pages no longer exist." I tried to reason, more with myself than Jack.

"You forget I took a picture of the first page. And the second when you weren't looking." His eyes widened.

"But without the originals to back up the photos, who is going to believe us?"

"True." He grew quiet for a moment. "Remember the underground Jacobites?"

"Yes."

"With the picture I took, they'll know you're an asset to their cause. And they'll want you to join them."

"Why?"

"Your DNA. You've already met Tara, one of the dominant leaders. She's the woman who offered you a ride and then pulled a gun on you."

I couldn't believe it. Then I remembered seeing her again. "Was she the woman I saw you with in Paris?"

"Yes." He nodded. "She wanted tae kidnap you tae get the pages, but in Paris, I was able tae reason with her, convince her that you could help. I knew she'd have a fight on her hands convincing others, like Macgregor and Balmoral. But after they learn what's happened today, I'm fairly certain they'll want you tae lead their cause for independence." The wind tousled Jack's black hair. He squinted against the sea spray, staring at me, making me think.

"*Help them.*" The voice. Again. Guiding me. I thought of the spiders: the one in the cave and the one Edward had stepped on. Had Robert the Bruce sent me a message using the creatures that had inspired him to keep fighting? He'd thought breaking away from Britain so important that he'd taken Jeanne d'Évreux's daughter with him and had had his son marry her. Meanwhile, Jeanne had had pages written and hidden away so they would inspire those courageous enough to take on the burden of righting the wrongs of the past. But so much had changed in the world since their time.

France no longer needed to be liberated. And Scotland . . . they were still part of the UK. But the monarchy didn't call the shots anymore. Parliament led them. However, someone high up in their government thought I was a threat and had sent the Black Prince after me. And that person was still alive. Would they stop and leave me alone? I'd already lost so much.

Edward had killed my parents and Auntie trying to squash the legend that turned out to be true. I thought of the words on the grave marker for Robert the Bruce's heart: "A noble heart can have no rest if freedom is lacking." How very true.

And then I knew. I couldn't turn my back on my family and all those who had sacrificed so much. Freedom and the right to choose was important. I wanted to champion that cause, and in doing so, maybe I could make a difference.

I took Jack's hand in mine. "I'm going to need help, and we're not going to win independence with weapons."

"Okay."

"We're going to gain Scotland's freedom from the UK the right way, with persuasion. They will be an independent nation." A warmth came over me as if confirming I'd made the right decision, as if Robert the Bruce and Jeanne d'Évreux were smiling down on me, along with my parents and Auntie.

A smile pulled at Jack's lips.

In that moment, I realized something. "This is what you wanted all along. The underground Jacobites you were supposed to spy on actually converted you."

He shrugged. "It nagged at me, the way Edward's men dealt with the Jacobites I turned in. Didn't seem right. But it wasn't until I pulled you tae safety from that speeding car that I realized I couldn't just stand by. In that moment of pulling you tae safety, aye, they did convince me. You did. It won't be easy convincing some that we can help them. I mean, there are some who will see us as a threat."

"You mean Macgregor and Balmoral?"

"Tae name a few." He nodded. "But if anyone can do it, you can. I believe in you."

"I have to tell you, I'm scared out of my mind."

He pulled me into his arms. "I'm going tae be right by your side. It's my job tae keep you safe." Jack leaned over and kissed me soundly on the lips.

THE END

ACKNOWLEDGMENTS

DURING THE SUMMER OF 2017, I was diagnosed with breast cancer. After surgery, my daughter Trizia wanted to give me something to take my mind off of radiation therapy, as well as something to look forward to, so she booked a trip for us for March 2018 to London, Paris, and Edinburgh. She was right. Thinking of the trip did take my mind off my health troubles.

I struggled to think how I could combine all three locations into a story. I mentioned the trip to my good friend Amanda Sowards, and she suggested I look into the Hundred Years' War for inspiration. I found a gold mine of information and characters I have come to love.

As Trizia and I toured the cities, I was able to not only enjoy the sights but also picture my characters there and what they could and couldn't do. There's nothing like visiting Paris during a snowstorm (the Eiffel Tower was frozen), touring Stirling Castle while bracing against a strong wind, or standing at the actual place where Robert the Bruce's heart lies buried.

Thank you, Trizia, for the trip of a lifetime! And thank you, Amanda, for directing me to historical events that have become the backbone of this story.

I'm so very grateful to my publisher, Covenant Communications, Inc. They work very hard to present quality books for their readers. I must thank Michelle Fryer for this book's terrific cover and Stephanie Lacie for promoting my novels, and I especially want to thank my editor, Samantha Millburn. Sam helps me time after time to present the best book I possibly can, and I'm so very lucky to also call her my friend.

As always, I must thank my writers group, who gave me wonderful feedback. I also need to thank those who read the entire novel: Kathleen

Dougherty, Kerri LeRoy, Maureen Mills, and Amanda Sowards. Their wonderful insights helped me fill in the holes.

I need to thank my son, Benjamin. He's always very willing to help me plot and map out fight scenes. And I must also thank my daughter Kris; her husband, Greg; and my grandsons, William and Jonathan. They always support me. Lastly, I must thank my sweetheart, Bruce. He's my rock.

I want to say how very appreciative I am to all those who seek out their ancestors. Their efforts make tracing family history much easier for the rest of us. My mother was a devoted genealogist who had to do research the old-fashioned way, using snail mail and waiting for months on end for answers. If she were alive today, she'd be amazed by our technology and the information at our fingertips. Thanks, Mom, for your labor of love in bringing to life our family history. Your hard work is greatly appreciated.

You may wonder if I'm related to Robert the Bruce. I haven't found the pages . . . yet.

AUTHOR'S NOTE

FOR THE PURPOSE OF MY story, I fabricated that Jeanne d'Évreux sent her daughter Marie with Robert the Bruce to Scotland to marry his son, David. The truth is, Marie actually died at a very young age.

Did Queen Jeanne commission Jean Pucelle to create more pages for her *Book of Hours*? Not that I have found. The Metropolitan Museum of Art in New York currently owns Jeanne d'Évreux's *Book of Hours*.

Are there DNA markers that prove direct lineage to Robert the Bruce? Yes! At the University of Strathclyde, scientists proved a businessman had the distinct genetic markers of Robert the Bruce. However, at this time, I don't believe there has been such a study performed for descendants of Jeanne d'Évreux.

Is there an underground Jacobite cause? No. However, there are people in Scotland today who champion independence. As of this writing, there still may be a vote.

Was there really a man called the Black Prince? Yes. Though the Black Prince in my story is purely fictional, during the Hundred Years' War, Edward, the Black Prince, really did exist. He fought against the French and pillaged and plundered many villages. He was the son of Edward III of England and would have become king if he hadn't died before his father.

Were France and Scotland allies during the Hundred Years' War? Yes, and they still are to this day.

What about the rumor regarding Robert the Bruce hiding in a cave and watching a spider that inspired him? It is a well-known legend. But I don't know how true it is. However, Robert the Bruce did eventually win independence for his country.

ABOUT THE AUTHOR

KATHI ORAM PETERSON LEARNED TO write the hard way, by spending years practicing her craft. Her path to publication took a detour as she raised her three children. During those years, she read all the how-to books on novel writing that she could find. When her last child graduated high school, she returned to college and earned her BA in English. She was fortunate to do an internship for the University of Utah's *Continuum* magazine, where she learned to edit and write articles in the "real world." Shortly after graduation, she was hired by a curriculum publisher to write and edit concept and biography books for children. She worked shoulder to shoulder with artists and computer programmers as she watched her children's stories come to life. But the desire to write full-length novels called to her. Upon leaving the workforce, she focused her attention on writing romantic suspense and YA time-travel novels. The thread she sows in both genres is faith in a higher power.

She currently resides in Salt Lake City. You can contact her through her websites, www.kathiorampeterson.com and www.authorkathiorampeterson. com.